McCutchan, Philip,
1920-

Halfhyde and the
fleet review.

$17.95

DATE			
APR 1 1992			
MAY 1 3 1992			
AUG 14 2007			
OCT 11 2008			

BAKER & TAYLOR BOOKS

HALFHYDE AND THE FLEET REVIEW

HALFHYDE
and the
FLEET REVIEW

Philip McCutchan

St. Martin's Press
New York

HALFHYDE AND THE FLEET REVIEW. Copyright © 1991 by Philip
McCutchan. All rights reserved. Printed in the United States of America.
No part of this book may be used or reproduced in any manner
whatsoever without written permission except in the case of brief
quotations embodied in critical articles or reviews. For information,
address St. Martin's Press, 175 Fifth Avenue, New York, N.Y. 10010.

Library of Congress Cataloging-in-Publication Data

McCutchan, Philip
    Halfhyde and the fleet review / Philip McCutchan.
        p.   cm.
    ISBN 0-312-06991-X
    1. Great Britain—History, Naval—19th century—Fiction.
I. Title.
PR6063.A167H312   1992
823'.914—dc20   91-33835
                                                           CIP

First published in Great Britain by George Weidenfeld and Nicolson
Limited.

First U.S. Edition: January 1992
10   9   8   7   6   5   4   3   2   1

HALFHYDE AND THE FLEET REVIEW

ONE

'Typical,' Victoria said. Naked, she stood glaring across the cabin at Halfhyde, hands on her hips and her colour high. 'Bloody typical of you, this is, mate.'

Halfhyde, his mind already on other matters affecting his ship, sighed. 'Not me. Their Lordships.'

Victoria's voice had become shrill. 'Stuff their bloody lordships, mate! All because of that old geezer!'

'An old geezer with an explosive potential for steam, which is why – '

'Spare me it, mate. Those buggers, they just make rings round you and you bloody know it, too bloody true you bloody do, but you don't seem to bloody mind. What about me, eh? I've a good mind to pack it in and go back to bloody Sydney.'

Halfhyde shrugged, turned to the mirror in his sleeping cabin to finish tying his tie. 'You're a free agent, Victoria. Free to make your own decisions, as you very well know.'

'Too bloody right – '

'But you'll stay. We've sailed too many seas together, my love.' He turned back towards her and took her in his arms. He kissed her; she responded with passion, fiercely. He disengaged himself, lifted her and laid her on the rumpled sheets of the bunk and stood smiling down at her urchin face, the face of a pixie that had never stopped charming him since he had first encountered her many years before in the King's Cross district of Sydney Town as it was known to seamen. Since then, as he had reminded her, they had sailed many of the world's seas together, living aboard his own steamship as man and wife but never to be blessed by Mother Church. St Vincent Halfhyde's estranged wife, Mildred, or her parents at any rate, would see

I

to that. Admirals in Her Majesty's fleet would never permit divorce to sully their families' names. And as for Lady Willard, Mildred's grim-faced mother, she had brought up her daughter very well indeed. Sex had never been on the agenda. Mildred would never transgress that way.

From her position on the bunk Victoria said, 'You're bloody confident, mate, aren't you?'

Halfhyde grinned down at her. 'Shipmasters have to be,' he said.

*

Liverpool again: the everlasting Mersey, the beginning and end of so many voyages for so many seafarers. The scenes were imprinted for all time on so many minds. The busy river, the hustle and bustle of the thirty-six miles of wharves and warehouses, the movement of barges and lighters and cranes, the raucous voices of the stevedores as they grappled the cased cargoes with their wicked steel hooks or adjusted the set of the cargo nets as the ships' davits began to take the strain ready to hoist them into the holds. Liverpool, like Sydney, was a sailors' town. Everywhere in the river were to be seen masts and yards, a forest come to Merseyside, if not quite so thick a forest now that steam was beginning to drive the old windjammers off the seas. Halfhyde himself had deserted sail for steam some years ago; commercially inevitable as the move had been, he had regarded his defection sorrowfully, as in effect leaving the sea.

But Liverpool had not changed, at any rate not visibly: roistering seamen still thronged the public houses, still sang their drunken way along Water Street and Lime Street, still found their women from the sleazier quarters of the town. And there was still the rain. The grey, tearful face of Liverpool, low cloud, lingering mist, wet streets and wharves.

When Halfhyde had climbed to his bridge to prepare for unberthing, Victoria Penn looked through the cabin port at the dreary, depressing day. Often enough she longed to be back in Sydney and its sun, on the splendid beaches of Manly and Bondi with their limitless sands. But she knew that Halfhyde was right: she wouldn't go back; not unless the *Taronga Park* took her, with Captain St Vincent Halfhyde, once of the Royal

Navy but now master of his own ship, in command. In command of her as well as of the *Taronga Park*. Weirdly perhaps for a dyed-in-the-wool Aussie, Miss Victoria Penn was in total thrall to Halfhyde, however bloody tiresome he might be at times. Like now. But she cheered herself up: at least they were bound away from Liverpool. Not all that far it was true; but at least away.

As she dressed Victoria wondered what Portsmouth would be like. A different character of town from Liverpool, filled with the bluejacketed men of Her Majesty's Navy, and the old Queen herself currently, according to Halfhyde, in residence at Osborne in the Isle of Wight just across the water from the Clarence Pier at Southsea, waiting to watch her great battle-ships and cruisers at anchor at their review stations in Spithead as she steamed past in her royal yacht, the *Victoria and Albert*. Victoria reflected on her namesake, the Queen of England: she would probably be critical and a pain in the guts to the poor bloody sailors. In the illustrated magazines that Halfhyde had shown her – the *Illustrated London News*, *Punch* and the *Tatler* – she had looked a right nosey old parker, always scowling.

As for Portsmouth, well. Full to the back teeth with bloody pommie bullshit was Miss Penn's mental picture.

She wished fervently that St Vincent Halfhyde would prise himself loose from those lordships at the Admiralty. He had explained many times but she could never take it in. After leaving the RN as a lieutenant, he had been given a lieutenant's commission in the Royal Naval Reserve and as such he had his duties to Her Majesty as and when required . . . even when temporary recall to the navy meant that he was unable to use his ship for its proper purpose, which was to carry cargoes around the world and provide a living for Victoria and himself. She saw this as unfair and typically bloody pommie.

*

Two days earlier Halfhyde had received a summons to Whitehall by means of a telegram from the Admiralty, a telegram originating from the office of the Second Sea Lord, who fulfilled the functions of Admiral Superintendent of Naval Reserves (Personnel) amongst his other duties. This telegram

3

had been addressed to him in his naval reserve capacity and it had brooked no argument. Feeling in his bones (as did Victoria in hers) that it meant trouble, Halfhyde had taken the train next day from Lime Street station to Euston and from thence had gone by hansom cab to the Admiralty beside Horse Guards' Parade. He had been shown into the office of the secretary to the Second Sea Lord, a bespectacled officer with the rank of Staff Paymaster. White cloth appeared between the gold stripes on his cuffs.

The Staff Paymaster rose to his feet on Halfhyde's entry and extended a hand. 'Shine,' he said.

'I beg your pardon?'

'Shine. It's my name. Do sit down.'

'In that case I beg your pardon again,' Halfhyde said, taking a chair. 'Well, Mr. Shine, what does all this portend?'

Staff Paymaster Shine sat down again behind a large desk. 'Certain difficulties, I fear. Yes, certain difficulties . . . in a diplomatic sense, if you follow me. Rather than a purely . . . er . . . *shipboard* one.'

Halfhyde raised his eyebrows. 'Diplomatic?'

'Yes, precisely. The Admiral will be speaking to you personally in a few minutes. He's currently engaged with the old Duke, you know – the Duke of Cambridge.' Staff Paymaster Shine shuffled papers about on his desk. 'Poor old man, he seems to think he's still Commander-in-Chief of the Army . . . he had to be prised out of the Horse Guards with a shoehorn back in '95 . . . but I'm not to be quoted on that, if you please, Mr Halfhyde.' He went off into what seemed to be a reverie for a few moments and then went on, 'It's all to do with the review of the troops at Aldershot, you know. You, of course, will be concerned only with the review of the fleet at Spithead. And this diplomacy . . . I understand you're well acquainted with a certain Admiral Watkiss, who entered Chilean service as their naval Commander-in-Chief when – er – no longer required by the Admiralty?'

Halfhyde started, his eyes widening. 'Indeed I am, Mr Shine. Very well acquainted from years past. I – '

'I have your record, of course. Your service record.' Staff Paymaster Shine brought a file from a drawer and opened it.

4

'In the Mediterranean Squadron . . . in China, in the Pacific. And then in South America. That was when you were yourself in Her Majesty's service.'

'The old *Meridian*,' Halfhyde said reflectively. 'I well remember.' He could scarcely forget; Captain Watkiss, as that bombastic officer had been when on the active list of the British Navy, had virtually ordered the Portsmouth dockyard seagulls to be fitted with canvas knickers the better to keep his holystoned decks unsullied. 'And since then – '

'Since then you've encountered Admiral Watkiss twice more in South America, in your capacity as master of the *Taronga Park*. Master and owner.'

'Yes. You'll no doubt have it on record that I brought Admiral Watkiss and his sister back from Chile in my ship – '

'Together with a certain Detective Inspector Todhunter from the Metropolitan Police . . . Admiral Watkiss being in certain difficulties with the Chilean government in Santiago. I think I need not go into that. Not into the past, that is. Except in so far as the past impinges upon the present and the future.'

'How so?' Halfhyde asked, easing his long body on a somewhat uncomfortably hard chair. When last encountered, Admiral Watkiss, then disgraced Commander-in-Chief of the Chilean Navy, which he had regarded as a bunch of damned dagoes, seemed to have no future at all. The British Admiralty had not wanted him back; and thanks to Halfhyde he had escaped from his disillusioned Chilean employers by what had been virtually a pierhead jump.

Staff Paymaster Shine said, 'Obviously you have not heard – there is no reason, indeed, why you should. But you probably *have* heard that there was a revolution in Chile, a successful *coup* some months ago. You will recall, no doubt, that Admiral Watkiss was in – er – disfavour with the then current regime on account of his hostility to the increasing influence of the German Emperor in Santiago – '

'He was accused of spying,' Halfhyde interrupted. 'He was much displeased by that.' Admiral Watkiss had in fact fizzed like a fuse, laying about himself in all directions. 'He was accused of disloyalty to his country. That is, to Chile. You can imagine his reaction to that, Mr Shine. His country, he said, was Great Britain, and his loyalty was to Her Majesty Queen Victoria. He was not, he said, a blasted dago.' Halfhyde's tongue was firmly in his cheek. Admiral Watkiss had said very many things inappropriate to his position as C-in-C of the Chilean Navy.

'Quite so,' Shine said, rubbing his hands together. 'Since then, however, there has been the *coup*. The new regime has no love for the German Emperor. To cut a long story short, Halfhyde, an apology was offered to Admiral Watkiss. This he graciously accepted, and he was reappointed some while ago as Commander-in-Chief. He has recently transferred his flag from his shore headquarters to the Chilean battleship *Almirante Smith*. And he is currently on passage from Valparaiso for Spithead, the *Almirante Smith* being the representative Chilean ship to be reviewed by Her Majesty on the occasion of her Diamond Jubilee.'

A pulse began beating in Halfhyde's temple, a warning pulse. He asked, 'How am I to be concerned in all this, Mr Shine?'

Shine leaned forward, fingertips together before his face, and said earnestly, 'With your close acquaintance with Admiral Watkiss, who is not an easy officer to deal with, it is considered that your appointment as liaison officer between Admiral Watkiss and the British naval authorities might be of great value.'

A telephone made a strident noise on Shine's desk and he picked the cumbersome instrument up as though it might bite. After a brief conversation he said, 'The Vice-Admiral will see you now, Mr Halfhyde.'

*

The Second Sea Lord, Vice-Admiral Sir Hartley Waverley, was a bluff seadog of the old school, an officer who had served as flag captain in the sail training squadron under the Earl of Clanwilliam. He was a no-nonsense man of forthright manner.

'Liaison officer's your official title, Halfhyde. But your duties will go beyond that – a long way beyond, I dare say. You're going to have to keep Watkiss on a leash, make certain he doesn't create scenes and upset people, such as, for instance, the Germans, who'll be represented by a battle-cruiser. And the Russians. Also, of course, the Chileans themselves.'

'A tall order, sir.'

'Very tall, knowing Admiral Watkiss. But it's on record that you and he understood one another in a way that few people have ever understood the good Admiral Watkiss. I believe – and will be relying on you to sustain my belief – that Admiral Watkiss will take from you what he wouldn't take from others, myself included. The Admiral Superintendent of Portsmouth Dockyard for one will be in a difficult situation. It has to he remembered that Admiral Watkiss is a full-blown Commander-in-Chief aboard his own flagship, a fairly unassailable position if he should choose to be awkward, which in all conscience is likely enough. Much ingenuity, Halfhyde – that's what will be required of you. Ingenuity, coupled with firmness. You understand?'

Halfhyde nodded. 'I'm well used to Admiral Watkiss, sir.'

'Yes indeed. Now there's something else. Something that is basically sinister and most unpleasant. It is understood in the Foreign Office that certain Chilean elements, persons from the previous administration who managed to avoid being shot after the *coup*, are coming to Britain, indeed that they may be here already. These persons are said to have a score to settle with Admiral Watkiss. In short, it is believed they may mount an attempt at assassination during the period of the jubilee when the crowds in London will be immense and out to enjoy themselves and vigilance will be hard to maintain.'

'Also in Portsmouth, sir.'

'Exactly, Halfhyde – exactly! It's considered that any assassination attempt is in fact more likely to take place in Portsmouth, during the period covering the lead-up to the review, or during the review itself, or afterwards. Which would of course be most unpleasant for Her Majesty.'

'And for Admiral Watkiss,' Halfhyde said innocently.

The Second Sea Lord gave a faint grin. 'A very final end, should it succeed, to a thorn in the Admiralty's flesh over very many years – but of course we must never think in terms of such an attempt succeeding. Admiral Watkiss must and will be preserved at all costs, you understand?'

'Quite so, sir.'

'Good. Now: in all the circumstances you, as liaison officer to the Commander-in-Chief of the Chilean Navy, will be accorded a – er – shall I say, a particular freedom of movement of your own. You'll not be confined to the shore, or to the *Almirante Smith*. You will have the advantage of your own command, indeed of your own ship, the *Taronga Park*. As of now the *Taronga Park* is requisitioned for naval service under the Blue Ensign of the Fleet Auxiliaries, with yourself as a lieutenant of the reserve acting as master. I think that will please you, Halfhyde?'

'Indeed it does, sir. But may I ask if I'm to play an actual role in circumventing any assassination attempt?'

'Not directly. That, principally, will be the responsibility of Foreign Office agents and of both the Metropolitan and local police forces. However, with your independent command, you may be called upon to assist. You will be kept informed and will receive orders as required – *if* required. That will depend upon how matters develop, In the Queen's service, as you're well aware, we are accustomed to improvise as necessary.'

'Yes, sir.'

The Admiral picked up a sheet of Admiralty crested notepaper from his desk. 'Your current orders, then. You will bring your ship from Liverpool on tomorrow's a.m. tide and enter Portsmouth Harbour from Spithead as directed by the Queen's Harbour Master shortly after your arrival in the anchorage.' He paused and gave Halfhyde a direct look. 'It's common knowledge that you have a young woman aboard. That has been entirely your affair – until now. As master of an RFA vessel you will not carry women. I trust that is quite clear. And one more thing: what has been said in this room about the threat to Admiral Watkiss is not to be repeated elsewhere.'

*

'I had no option,' Halfhyde said. Victoria Penn had been a ball of fury, shouting and attacking him with small, clenched fists until he had clamped his hands around both her wrists and held her fast, though still kicking out like an angry horse. 'Orders, Victoria. Orders have to be obeyed.'

'Got no bloody guts, you haven't!' she screamed. Tears ran down her flushed cheeks like a miniature waterfall. 'You should have told that bloody old bastard that I was your woman and he could shove 'is orders up – '

'Now, now, Victoria. You try saying that to a Vice-Admiral in Her Majesty's fleet and see where it gets you. In the meantime you're going to be all right. I shall disobey orders to the extent that I'll take you to Portsmouth . . . we'll see on arrival how best to smuggle you ashore. Once ashore, you'll stay at the Keppel's Head Hotel on the Hard – '

'Keppel's Head, what's that like?'

'First class. All the best people stay there. The management is well used to naval officers and their wives.'

'Wives, eh?'

'And sweethearts,' he amended. 'I shall see you when I can. But there'll be no jiggery pokery. It's a respectable hotel.'

She wailed, 'You know I can't bloody do without it, mate. Jiggery pokery, I mean. Why not find a common sort of lodging?'

He grinned and took her in his arms. The battle was won; she'd do what she was told.

*

Having made his approach from westerly, past the Lizard and Prawle Point, Portland Bill and the Needles, Halfhyde prepared to anchor in Spithead; but even as his cable party mustered on the fo'c'sle, with Halfhyde's Chief Officer in the eyes of the ship and the carpenter standing by the windlass in the fore well-deck, the signal was received from QHM giving permission to enter, though the *Taronga Park* would not be given a berth alongside the wall: already the harbour's dockside berths were filled with the great ironclads of the Channel Fleet, battleships and heavy cruisers, along with a number of ships brought home from the Mediterranean for the great occasion of the fleet review. There were the foreigners also: German, French, Italian, Japanese, Russian, American. No Admiral Watkiss as yet: the *Almirante Smith* was expected at the end of the week; early the following week the great assemblage was to steam out to take up its review positions in Spithead, the planned lines of the anchorage extending back past Fort Gilkicker into the Solent.

Halfhyde proceeded inwards, taking it slow, taking his transit bearings for the turn to port into the buoyed channel. As his ship came past Southsea Castle to head towards the Clarence Pier and the saluting battery he saw the pilot boat making out towards him from the narrows between Fort Blockhouse and the Round Tower.

He turned to his Second Officer. 'Mr Harris, the signal lamp. Make, I do not require a pilot.'

'Aye, aye, sir.'

The signal was clacked out. The pilot boat came on. When it was within hailing distance the response came via a megaphone: 'I have orders to board, Captain.'

Halfhyde was irritated. As a one-time lieutenant in Her Majesty's fleet, Halfhyde had entered and left the port perhaps a hundred times; and officers in command of warships were not required to take a pilot. Masters of RFA ships had the option to take a pilot if they wished; if on the other hand they did their own pilotage, they received extra pay. Halfhyde had no intention of taking a pilot in so familiar a port and this he shouted back through his own megaphone. But the pilot boat still came obstinately on, making its approach to his port side and asking for a jumping ladder to be sent down.

Below the bridge, in Halfhyde's cabin, Victoria Penn was obeying orders by keeping out of sight. She heard the raised tones, heard the anger and frustration in Halfhyde's voice. She saw the pilot boat coming close now to the ship's side. She heard Halfhyde say, 'Will somebody please tell that pilot to bugger off?'

Well – bloody navy and its bullshit! The nobs were not going to treat St Vincent Halfhyde with cavalier disdain, sod them. Australian dander well and truly up, Victoria emerged from the cabin and went to the port side of the master's deck below the bridge.

She saw the pilot boat right beneath her. She called down. 'Hey there, mate! You in the little hut.'

From his wheelhouse the pilot boat's skipper looked up. 'What is it, miss?'

'Keep your bloody ears open, mate, why not?' she shouted down. 'If this was bloody Sydney, they'd think you was a bum from the bloody outback and shove you in the Botanical Gardens along with the nastifellercrawlupyer.' Her voice rose higher. '*Captain says to bugger off!*'

TWO

Several weeks before the Admiralty's orders had been made known to Halfhyde, there had been technical difficulties in Valparaiso and Captain del Campo, Flag Captain to Admiral Watkiss, had been attempting to justify himself – like all dagoes, Watkiss thought angrily, they always tried to slide out from under.

'But *Almirante* . . . it is not my fault if the screws are in the wrong place. It is the engineer officer and the dockyard. Not me, *Almirante*.' Captain del Campo raised his hands palms upwards and looked despairingly at Admiral Watkiss; he also looked hard done by and long-suffering, for the *Almirante* was no easy taskmaster.

Admiral Watkiss brandished his telescope and stamped his foot on the quarterdeck, which was dirtier than normal but this was of course to be expected after the ship had been in dockyard hands for the last three months: an engine-room overhaul in preparation for the voyage to Great Britain for Her Majesty's jubilee review, a voyage of some two months at the old battleship's speed that was scheduled to commence in four days' time. The question of this review had been in the Chilean air for some while past; and now this ridiculous trouble had emerged.

'God give me strength,' Admiral Watkiss said wearily. He gave a hitch to his over-long white shorts, bringing the waistband further up over his stomach. 'Are you or are you not Captain of the *Almirante Smith*, Captain del Campo?'

'*Si, Almirante –* '

'Then you're damn well answerable for all that goes on aboard the blasted ship! When will you blasted dagoes ever learn the basic principles of command? In the British fleet the captain is the ship and the ship is the captain – one and indivisible. And that's fact, I said it. Do you understand, Captain del Campo?'

Del Campo shrugged and looked pathetic. 'I try to, *Almirante*. I do my best.'

'Well, it's not damn well good enough! I refuse to cross the blasted harbour by going round in circles like a blasted duck without a tail.'

The *Almirante Smith* had left the fitting-out basin in the care of four dilapidated tugs with half-naked crews and what looked like a fortnight's washing dangling from the lines rigged across their decks; on the tugs being cast off, the battleship had wavered across the harbour and had then started circling, seemingly unable to answer her helm. Captain del Campo and his executive officer, Commander Latrinez, had panicked, rushing about in circles of their own, like chickens in a farmyard Admiral Watkiss had thought and said. He had himself shouted across the water for the tugs to be buttoned on again and thereafter the battleship had remained static. Admiral Watkiss had ordered an immediate investigation in the engine-room; and when nobody could come up with an explanation, divers had been demanded from the dockyard.

A report had been made to Commander Latrinez, who reported to Captain del Campo. The fault, del Campo had reported to Admiral Watkiss, was a simple one. During the overhaul, both the propeller shafts had been removed from their housings for attention ashore. When they had been replaced there had been confusion.

'What sort of blasted confusion?'

'*Almirante*, the starboard shaft was replaced on the port side. And the port shaft was replaced on the starboard side. So the ship, she go like that.' Captain del Campo demonstrated with his hands. 'She wiggle, then she stop. She cannot help. The adverse pitch, you see, it – '

'You blasted idiot!' Admiral Watkiss shrieked witheringly. 'You've made me look a fool in front of a crowd of blasted foreigners and I won't damn well have it, d'you hear me? I – ' He broke off. There had been a tremor throughout the decks and the *Almirante Smith* had shaken like a wet dog. Then there was a sudden emission of thick, foul-smelling smoke from her after funnel, smoke that, taken by an offshore breeze, came down on the quarterdeck and enveloped Admiral Watkiss in a greasy smokescreen. He marched forward, brandishing his telescope. 'Oh, balls and bang me arse,' he said furiously. 'Why the devil did I ever consent to come back to Chile?'

*

'Washbrook.' Admiral Watkiss waited impatiently near a filthy shoreside market, digging at the air with his impeccably turk's-headed telescope, his squat body bouncing up and down on the balls of his feet as he waited for his steward to appear. The battleship's shafts having been removed once again and replaced in their correct housings, she had been reported ready for sea; but first Admiral Watkiss had some personal shopping to attend to. '*Washbrook!*'

'Coming, sir.' Petty Officer Steward Washbrook, adding *sotto voce*, 'Fast as me perishing legs can carry me,' materialized from behind Watkiss, having emerged from a vegetable-strewn stall. He had acquired some fruit, which lay in a wicker basket hanging from his arm together with some dubious-looking green vegetables. Chile did not produce much that was palatable to the British stomach but in Valparaiso foreign ships had to be provisioned and the stall-holders always had an eye to the main chance. Admiral Watkiss, Commander-in-Chief of the Navy, had a regard for the Britishness of his stomach and was damned if he was going to go to sea in the insalubrious conditions of the *Almirante Smith* without making sure so far as he could of some fresh fruit and vegetables; not that they would last long, but they would help to keep scurvy at bay at least in the early stages of the long voyage round Cape Horn. Later, Watkiss would order a deviation, perhaps into the Falkland Islands, perhaps into Montevideo, so as to replenish his personal larder. The Falkland Islands for preference; at least they were British, with eatable provisions, and of course there was a British naval presence at Port Stanley.

Admiral Watkiss followed Petty Officer Steward Washbrook towards a number of other baskets that stood, clear of the stalls, under guard of two armed seamen and a working party from the battleship. Washbrook, a skinny man with a long lugubrious face, deposited the additional basket and stood back, picking his nose and then wiping it on the cuff of his white uniform jacket.

'Don't do that,' Admiral Watkiss said sharply.

'Sorry I'm sure, sir.'

'Do it again and you'll be a damned sight sorrier. Anybody'd think you were one of the blasted dagoes. Damn it, man, have you no pride in being British?' Not waiting for an answer, Watkiss began prodding at the contents of the baskets with his telescope. 'What a collection of rubbish,' he said, sniffing.

'Did me best, sir.'

'I expect ratings to do better than their best, Washbrook.'

'Yessir.' As the working party, under a leading hand from one of whose pockets dangled an article suspiciously like a pair of female knickers, began humping the baskets on to their backs, Washbrook made coughing sounds preparatory to addressing Admiral Watkiss on a personal matter – not for the first time since the destination of the Chilean flagship had become known.

Watkiss misinterpreted the throaty noises. 'What's the matter with you, Washbrook? If you're sick, report to the Medical Officer aboard, though what he knows about medicine would go on the back of a postage stamp. Well?'

'Begging your pardon, sir. . . .' Washbrook's voice tailed away. Sick, eh? Now why hadn't he thought of that? (As a matter of fact he had; but had known Admiral Watkiss would never permit him to become sick. But now that the old bugger had broached it off his own bat, well!)

But he was to be stymied. Admiral Watkiss screwed his monocle into his eye and glared through it. 'If you use sickness as a means of avoiding passage to England, Washbrook, I'll have your guts for garters and the blasted Chilean leeches will be sure to have the rest.'

'Yessir, but – '

'Oh, God give me strength.' Admiral Watkiss, drenched with sweat brought about not so much by the Chilean climate as by the appalling closeness of the atmosphere around the

15

market, the dust, and the smell of the Chileans, stamped his foot. More dust arose around him, stiflingly. 'I'll hear no more of this, Washbrook, so there. You must make the best of it. It's all your own blasted fault anyway.'

'But begging your pardon, sir – '

'Oh, shut up, Washbrook – '

'If I set foot in Pompey, sir, I'll be arrested and – '

'And if you attempt to desert before sailing, Washbrook, I shall have you arrested in Chile.' Watkiss aimed his telescope at his steward's head. 'I shall have you sentenced to death. Just keep that in mind, Washbrook.'

'Yessir. Sorry, sir. Just as you say, sir.'

'So I should blasted well think.'

The working party set off with its load towards the *Almirante Smith* lying off at anchor in the bay, under the close and watchful eye of their Commander-in-Chief, who had accompanied the party ashore for this very purpose: the C-in-C did not trust Chileans or any other foreigners. They all stole whenever they got the chance; his provisions, destined for the Admiral's galley aboard, could vanish on to the mess decks to be consumed by the not entitled, the unworthy. The ratings didn't need it anyway; they were well accustomed to their own appalling food. A pace behind Admiral Watkiss marched Petty Officer Steward Washbrook, muttering angrily to himself as, in accordance with previous orders, he flicked myriads of flies from the person of Admiral Watkiss. The old bugger was a cruel tyrant. The old bugger knew the facts perfectly well. When the old bugger had originally been appointed to the Chilean Navy, being surplus to requirements, to put it politely (the way Admiral Watkiss himself always put it), in his rank of Captain in the British fleet, he had demanded the services of a British steward; and Washbrook had filled the bill when Watkiss' request had been passed to the Drafting Master-at-Arms at the barrack hulks in Portsmouth. Petty Officer Steward Washbrook had become an embarrassment to the Portsmouth command. Whilst in charge of the wardroom servants aboard the battleship *Lord Rodney* on an occasion when Her Majesty Queen Victoria had been visiting her fleet, and he being drunk, he had grossly insulted Her Majesty, telling her (being angered by the drop in his pay subsequent to the deprivation of a good conduct badge for earlier indulgence in the bottle) that she was as tight as a gnat's arse. Washbrook had later stated that what he had said had been in fact of a patriotic nature, a bosom bursting with loyal thoughts saying that she was the light of a nation's hearts. This not being believed, and Washbrook having other charges pending, including the selling of wardroom stores for his own financial gain, he had been faced with a court martial. But the insult to Her Majesty had been of a very personal nature and the naval authorities, having no wish to cause Her Majesty pain, had seen a way out when Admiral Watkiss' requirements had become known. At the Admiralty it was seen as the killing of two birds with one stone. Each, they said, deserved the other. Naturally, now, Washbrook had no desire for an enforced return to England and the Portsmouth command, for he was still on the active list of the Royal Navy and the charges against him, except perhaps that involving Her Majesty, could be resuscitated.

In the meantime Petty Officer Steward Washbrook had made a bob or two on his own account and had done so again today. Old Watkiss had always obstinately refused to comprehend Chilean currency; and cash had changed hands in the market. It was really surprising how you could diddle the old bugger with a bit of astuteness.

*

Within half an hour of the *Taronga Park* having taken up her anchorage in the higher reaches of the harbour, a steam picquet-boat had come alongside and a senior lieutenant, an officer wearing two and a half gold rings on his cuffs, had boarded to represent the Queen's Harbour Master. A report had been received from the pilot boat, whose skipper had been outraged at having been told to bugger off by what he had termed a harlot.

Coldly rejecting the particular term, Halfhyde had pacified his visitor. Very unfortunate, he had said, and asked for his humble apologies to be conveyed to the skipper.

'Humble be – blowed,' Victoria had burst out. 'I reckon he – '

'That'll do, Victoria – '

'There's no need to bloody humble yourself, mate! Master aboard your own ship, you are.'

'I sometimes wonder,' Halfhyde said acidly. 'However, there is no need to smuggle you ashore now, Victoria. This officer insists on your removal – '

'Bloody likely, I don't think – '

'Orders, Victoria. We're in the navy now. You'll be perfectly all right. Lieutenant Seaton will see to your accommodation in the Keppel's Head. And I shall be ashore as soon as possible tomorrow morning.'

'Now just you bloody listen, mate – '

'You are under orders, Victoria. There will be no further argument.' St Vincent Halfhyde's long jaw was thrust out and steel came into his eyes. She knew what it meant when he looked like that. She capitulated.

'All bloody right, then! Only I got me gear to pack.' She turned on the embarrassed Lieutenant Seaton. 'And *you* can sod off while I do it, mate.' She flounced into their shared sleeping cabin and started banging about in drawers and wardrobe, flinging her garments topsy-turvy into a hump-backed trunk that someone was going to have to put over the side for her. She was in a temper and was intending to make it obvious. In the day cabin Halfhyde took no notice. Ringing for his steward he had whisky brought, and healths were drunk with Lieutenant Seaton. Halfhyde refrained from asking about Admiral Watkiss and the forthcoming arrival of the *Almirante Smith*. In the circumstances it was prudent to keep well away from the subject of Admiral Watkiss, who would be the first to make his own presence known before he had been in the port five minutes. But Halfhyde's mind wandered as he drank, moved back across time and ocean to Chile as he pondered on who Watkiss' enemies in Chilean ex-governmental circles might be.

The answer was: almost anyone. Watkiss had a way of upsetting even the most unlikely people, and the Chileans had not been particularly unlikely, Halfhyde reflected. Concerned in the hunt for Admiral Watkiss, and concerned in his ultimate arrest, had been not only the Chilean Minister of Marine but also Colonel Opago the Chief of Police in Santiago, and General Puga the Commander-in-Chief of the army, to say nothing of the German Ambassador Count von Gelsenkirchen. With his customary extraordinary bounciness and his perennial refusal ever to admit that he was wrong, Admiral Watkiss had almost succeeded in getting General Puga and Colonel Opago to arrest each other instead of himself.

There would be any number of people from that Chilean administration who might seek revenge. Even to the point of assassination; South Americans were undeniably a bloodthirsty lot, and hot-headed with it.

*

She had been crying but as dusk came down she went over the side dry-eyed and shaking a fist at Halfhyde. Two seamen carried the trunk down the accommodation ladder. Lieutenant Seaton, going over the ship's side ahead of her, turned at the lower platform to assist her into the sternsheets of the picquet-boat.

'Don't need that, mate.' She glared at him. 'Know something, do you? I reckon I got more bloody sea-time in than you have. Sitting on your bum in an office most of the bloody time, I reckon, right?'

'Not – '

'Me, I've been round Cape bloody Horn and – and all over with Captain Halfhyde. He and me, we've been good mates a long while now.' Her face was beginning to crumple as she stepped with agility into the picquet-boat and the bowman and sternsheetsman lifted their boathooks ready for bearing off when the order came. 'And sod the bloody navy,' she added viciously.

'I'm sure you have no need to worry, Miss Penn. Captain Halfhyde is simply following orders and he'll be – '

'And sod you too,' Miss Penn said. 'Down under, they'd bloody soon wipe that daft soulful expression off your phiz.' She sat down with a thump as the picquet-boat gave a sudden lurch in the wash from a destroyer moving up the harbour. 'Bugger,' she said. 'If you'll pardon me.' She added that because the lieutenant looked as though he was about to fall overboard with shock. He'd probably never heard a lady say bugger before, she thought. Pommies were like that, didn't know they'd been born, half of them. She looked back at the decks of the *Taronga Park* as the picquet-boat moved away and turned to head down the harbour towards the South Railway jetty where the flagship of the Channel Fleet was berthed. She looked for St Vincent Halfhyde; she looked in vain. He had gone back to his cabin, hadn't even waited to wave her off.

Well! She hoped he'd be bloody lonely when night came. Come to that, she knew she'd be bloody lonely herself. But need she be? A wicked grin began to twist her lips. Make him jealous, why not? Pay him back, that would. She gave a genteel cough, lifted a hand to her mouth and wished she'd been wearing gloves like pommie ladies did. She kept silent thereafter, not trusting herself to forgo the normal Australian adjective if she opened her mouth. As the picquet-boat moved on down harbour, the dark increased. Lights came on aboard the great grey ironclads and weird calls were heard across the water, voices demanding to know what ship the boat came from. Each time this happened the picquet-boat's bowman answered, 'Passing,' which Victoria thought rude really, not answering the question properly. As they came to some stone steps not far from the flagship's berth, and the boat stopped, Lieutenant Seaton once again offered his arm for disembarkation. Accepting it gracefully this time, Victoria asked, 'This Keppel's Head. You going to take me there, are you, eh?'

'Of course, Miss Penn.'

'Right you are, then,' she said cheerfully. 'You married, are you?'

Seaton smiled. 'No, I'm not. Few officers can afford marriage when they live on their pay alone. No private means,' he added.

'Oh. On your beam ends, are you, no sponduliks?'

'Well – not exactly – '

'But you don't get married, any of you?'

'Well – as I explained – '

'Oh, well, never mind. All poufters, are you? Sorry,' she added quickly, noting his reaction to what had been intended as a joke. 'It's just me, it's in me nature. So if you're not married, how about taking me out for some tucker tonight, eh?'

'Well – er – '

'At least you're honest about being bloody strapped for the ready,' she said, still determinedly cheerful. 'And don't bloody worry about money. I got enough so I'll pay. How about that, eh? Fair offer?'

Lieutenant Seaton, as it happened, had an uncle who many years before had been sent out to Australia as a remittance man with a strong taste for drink and women. Now and again he wrote letters home asking for increased funding. Lieutenant Seaton had picked up an Australian expression or two. And he didn't mind taking Miss Penn out for some tucker, though it wouldn't be dinner at the Keppel's Head. 'Fair dinkum,' he said.

Miss Penn gave a giggle and dug him in the ribs with an elbow. 'Good on yer, mate,' she said. 'Human after all.'

*

The train from Waterloo pulled smoothly into Portsmouth Town station, alongside the high-level platform from which the main line continued to the harbour station and a branch line ran into the dockyard near the Neptune Gate. From the train window a pale face peered from beneath a bowler hat secured to its owner's lapel with a length of black silk cord made fast with a toggle. The suiting was neat blue serge, the starched collar and cuffs of purest white. The man, heavily moustached, signalled from the window for a porter and having caught the eye of one reached down a Gladstone bag from the luggage rack above his head. Wishing to observe the Portsmouth scene, he had decided to disembark here rather than go on to the harbour station.

Bag in hand, he opened the door and stepped down. 'A cab, if you please,' he said to the porter.

'Yessir.' The man touched his cap. 'There'll be other luggage, sir?'

'Yes, a trunk in the guard's van.'

'Right you are then, sir.'

Detective Inspector Todhunter watched while his trunk was retrieved from the guard's van. His stay in Portsmouth might be a lengthy one for all he could tell, and the trunk contained his long pants among other items, and the sea, if he had to venture upon it, might well be cold. This he knew from past experience. He did not like the sea; but was able to comfort himself with the parting words of his Chief Superintendent at the Yard. 'You're the very man for the job, Todhunter. The best. Admiral Watkiss knows you and trusts you. I have every confidence in you myself, and I know you'll succeed.'

It had been most gratifying to hear that, and to have his hand warmly shaken by his Chief Super as the oration came to an end.

Following behind the porter and his trunk, and carrying the Gladstone bag, Detective Inspector Todhunter hired his cab. 'The Keppel's Head Hotel,' he said. The horse roused itself from what looked like a stupor and, urged on by the cabbie, ambled out of the station yard and turned past the Town Hall in the general direction of the Hard.

There were a number of rough-looking sailormen about, some of them drunk already. They staggered and lurched and sang songs with doubtful words to them. They sobered up remarkably when a warrant officer, a hard-looking person with a single thin gold stripe on his cuffs, loomed up ahead wearing black patent leather gaiters and a sword. They saluted punctiliously. Some distance behind the warrant officer came a naval patrol, the town patrol of four gaitered seamen with side arms under the orders of a bearded petty officer, one of their functions being to charge any rating who neglected to salute the wo. Detective Inspector Todhunter stared sleuth-like from the recesses of the cab and gave a sigh. There were so many sailormen in Portsmouth and so much inebriation, also so many whores. During his past experiences in connection with Admiral Watkiss, Todhunter had been largely confined aboard a ship at sea where the sailors were under firm control. To be in a naval port where many thousands of bluejackets were at liberty was a very different kettle of fish.

*

'I shall call for you with a cab, Miss Penn, in one hour's time,' Lieutenant Seaton said.

'Right you are, mate. Where do we go for tucker?'

22

'I know a place,' Seaton assured her. He went off; Victoria, having checked in at the hotel, went upstairs to her room where her trunk had already been taken. It was a nice room but it was at the back of the building and had no outlook. Never mind that, though: what to wear tonight? After a good deal of thought and a lot of trying on she settled for a low-cut dress that she'd run up from a length of scarlet silk that she had bought in Santiago during a shopping spree while St Vincent Halfhyde was attending the court of inquiry into that Admiral Watkiss' alleged spying activities. St Vincent Halfhyde hadn't liked it; he had consistently refused to be seen with her when she was wearing it. Now was her chance. She reckoned she looked a right stunner in it. She twisted and turned before a long mirror, admiring herself. She completed the effect with a black lace shawl, draped carelessly over head and shoulders. Spanish, the effect was, like one of those Spanish dancers. Flamingoes, she believed.

When dressed, she went down to the lounge to await Lieutenant Seaton. She attracted the attention of an elderly waiter. 'Hey,' she said. 'You in the soup-and-fish.'

The waiter raised his eyebrows a little but came over politely. 'Yes, madam?'

'I c'd do with a drink, my oath! Got any Swan beer? Comes from Fremantle.'

'I'm sorry, madam – '

'Vickers gin, Old Soldier rum? Oh, never bloody mind, old timer. Get me a port and lemon, right?'

'Right,' the waiter said between his teeth. He wondered how many more Australians this fleet review was going to dredge up. Possibly the colonials were sending a representative ship in honour of their distant but much-loved monarch. He moved away slowly, hobbling on a number of corns. Victoria giggled; his tail coat gave him the appearance of a black beetle on its last legs.

After two port and lemons Lieutenant Seaton arrived in plain clothes, apologizing for his lateness: there had been difficulty in securing a cab. Portsmouth was filling up. Lieutenant Seaton looked different out of uniform. Not quite so good-looking, sort of ordinary in a Norfolk jacket and breeches with thick woollen socks, not, Victoria thought, what the pommies would wear in the evening in a high-class joint like the Keppel's Head. She began to feel a little overdressed in her scarlet and black, but what the hell, the port and lemon was making her feel more devilish than usual.

'Like the look of me, mate?'

'Oh – yes, splendid, simply splendid, Miss Penn.'

'Where we going, then?'

'Somewhere cosy,' he said, offering his arm. The sooner he could get her out of the Keppel's Head the better: there were sure to be people he knew before long. They left the hotel and he handed her into the waiting cab. As they left another person was booking in at the reception desk. This was an elderly woman, short, thick and square. As Victoria passed by, not paying any attention, the woman turned her head and stared in amazement. For a moment she was speechless; then she addressed the man behind the desk.

'That person. In the scarlet dress. Do you know who she is, and is she staying here?'

'She is, madam. Her name is. . . .' The clerk scanned a list of arrivals. 'A Miss Penn, madam.'

'I thought so. God bless my soul, that woman!'

'Madam?'

'Oh, nothing, nothing. There should be a letter for me. Is there?'

'Mrs Weder-Ublick . . . yes, I believe there is, madam.'

A letter was handed over. 'Thank you. Now, it may be that you will be asked for another room at some time next week. For my brother, don't you know. Admiral Watkiss. He is the Commander-in-Chief of the Chilean Navy and is arriving for Her Majesty's review . . . he may wish for some nights ashore where the sheets are clean, I dare say. I shall be obliged if you'll be sure to let me know if this proves to be the case.'

Mrs Weder-Ublick, following in the wake of a hall porter bearing the first instalment of her luggage, marched upstairs. Her brother would be immensely surprised to see her in Portsmouth. It was not in fact her brother who had drawn her to Portsmouth. Had it not been for someone else, she would have avoided Portsmouth like the very plague until her brother had gone back to Chile; and if he should book into the Keppel's Head she would at once move to another hotel. There had never been any love lost between Admiral Watkiss and his sister, whom Watkiss had never forgiven for marrying a German, or, as he put it himself, a blasted Hun.

*

Naturally enough, Victoria knew nothing of the geography of Portsmouth Town. It had been easy for Lieutenant Seaton to have a quiet preliminary word with the cabbie, and for a golden half-sovereign to change hands and be made quickly to disappear. The cabbie was well acquainted with the whims and fancies of the young and not-so-young naval gentlemen. The horse took the long way round, turning left instead of right, then passing beneath the railway arch that carried the line from the town station to the harbour station, down to Cambridge Barracks and along the High Street of Old Portsmouth. Lieutenant Seaton pointed out the historic George Hotel where Vice-Admiral Lord Nelson had breakfasted for the last time on English soil before leaving from Southsea beach by the King's Bastion to embark aboard the *Victory* and sail to a glorious death at Trafalgar.

'Think a lot of that bloke, you poms.'

'Indeed we do – '

'My friend Captain Halfhyde, he's always on about him. Thinks the sun shines out of his backside. Me, I don't reckon so much to him. All that bloodshed, and that Emma Whatsit.'

'Lady Hamilton, yes.'

'Had a wife of his own, didn't he?'

'Well, yes. But all great leaders have had their – er – '

'Something on the side, eh? Me, I'll take bloody good care Captain Halfhyde bloody doesn't,' Victoria said with asperity, disregarding the fact that, like Lord Nelson, Halfhyde also had a wife and that she, Victoria Penn, might well be looked upon as his 'something on the side'. Lieutenant Seaton offered no further comment; his own aims currently ran somewhat similar to those of Lord Nelson and there was no point in arguing with his quarry. The cab turned left along Penny Street and then right towards the Clarence Pier outside the bars of which the

25

sailors from the assembled fleets were roistering and seeking women. Many of them had women already, sluttish women with drooping breasts and predatory looks, hanging like leeches on to the stout arms of seamen and marines, determined not to let their sixpennyworths get away before services had been rendered and payment made.

Victoria giggled. 'Just like the bloody Cross, this is, mate.'

'Cross?'

'King's Cross, Sydney. Red light district.' Victoria, to whom the Cross had once been home, had a mental dichotomy when it came to women, one law for the poor who couldn't be blamed, another for the rich who ought to know better. Victoria was perennially on the side of the underdog.

The cab turned down eventually past the Ladies' Mile and from there headed along Palmerston Road towards the Town Hall and Edinburgh Road for Queen Street, which, had Victoria but known it, lay just a stone's throw behind the Keppel's Head Hotel. Lieutenant Seaton, no fool, knew that a long outward journey provided the perfect reason for an equally long run home after dinner, or tucker.

Handing Victoria down from the cab to a littered, greasy pavement, and shielding her from the jostling mob of libertymen from the barrack hulks and the fleet – for Queen Street was the sailors' Portsmouth paradise, like Grant Road in Bombay, the Gut in Malta, and the Street of the Prostitutes in Shanghai – Lieutenant Seaton once again offered his arm and led her into the side door of a hostelry known as the Live and Let Live. Inside a sleazy passageway he was met by the publican.

'Upstairs room, sir.' The man hesitated, appearing a little distrait. 'Begging your pardon, sir. If I might 'ave a word.'

'Very well, Bates.' They moved away.

Bates spoke from the corner of his mouth, shielding his lips with a dirty hand. 'What with the review an' all, sir. Them bleeding patrols, they're shoving their noses into everybody's business. Even the gennelmen aren't left alone. I need to be whiter than bleeding white just now, sir, so if I may make so bold, sir, no funny business, not on the premises like.'

'Don't worry, Bates,' Lieutenant Seaton said briskly. 'There'll be no funny business. Not on the premises.'

'Thank you, sir.' Bates gave a sigh of relief. 'That's a load orf of me mind, sir.' His manner changed, becoming brisk, and he said, 'Now you'll be wanting a drink, sir, likely, you and the lady, before the meal.'

In a small, low-ceilinged room with an overpowering stench of spilt beer and cat, the drinks were brought to Lieutenant Seaton's order. Victoria chose port and lemon again, Lieutenant Seaton was brought John Haig whisky. Victoria said, 'Bottoms up,' swilled the glass clean, and asked for another. She looked around the room. 'Cosy right enough,' she said. 'And private. This one of the high-class places, is it?'

'Yes,' Lieutenant Seaton said mendaciously. 'Expensive. . . .'

'Said I'd pay, din't I?'

'I wouldn't dream of allowing you to, Miss Penn,' Lieutenant Seaton said gallantly.

'A bargain's a bargain, mate. I reckon I stick to mine.' She changed the subject abruptly. 'That bloke, the one who let us in. Shifty-looking bugger and smelt of fish. If this joint's high class . . . what I mean is, just because it's private don't mean you c'n get your flippers up me skirt, right?'

Lieutenant Seaton laughed it off; such, he said, had never been in his thoughts. Victoria looked sardonic. The meal was brought: brown Windsor soup and a bread roll, stale, with a small pat of butter; two sausages each, with a thickish gravy, mashed potatoes and peas, followed by suet pudding with demerara sugar, then coffee. Victoria had four more port and lemons, Lieutenant Seaton, with an eye to the remainder of the evening, held back on the whisky. At ten-fifteen the cab returned for its fares and the overlong journey back to the Keppel's Head was begun. In the cab Lieutenant Seaton proved that whatever else he might be, he was no poufter. Victoria had a full-scale fight on her hands. She fought like a tigress protecting its young; making St Vincent Halfhyde jealous was one thing, potential rape was another. Also, she had in the end honoured her bargain by paying for the meal. And all the drinks. This result simply was not fair though it might be normal pom behaviour. She managed to get the cab stopped at the fringe of Southsea Common by yelling blue murder and threatening a report to the cops if she wasn't let go. In a flat fury Lieutenant Seaton ejected her, the cabbie looking quite philosophical about the whole thing. The naval gentlemen had their foibles, like all the gentry. The cabbie's father had been coachman to a lord and that had been quite revealing.

Weeping tears of sheer rage, Miss Penn started walking back to the Hard. The black silk shawl hung like a strip of mourning from one scratched shoulder and the scarlet dress had been torn, ripped right away to reveal one breast that no amount of ingenuity could hope to cover fully until the sanctuary of her bedroom had been reached.

THREE

At breakfast next morning in the dining-room of the Keppel's Head Hotel, Detective Inspector Todhunter, who had finished his porridge and was waiting for a kipper to be brought by the elderly retainer, looked in some puzzlement at a stout woman dressed in black bombazine who had just entered the room and was marching towards a table for one set discreetly in a corner.

The stout figure was familiar but was not immediately placed. Detective Inspector Todhunter was a busy man who had encountered very many people of very many different sorts, from peers of the realm to down-and-outs dwelling beneath newspapers or in cardboard boxes in various parts of the Metropolitan Police Force's area, or patch. Naturally, as was expected of him by his Chief Super, he never entirely forgot a face; but these days recognition was sometimes not as immediate as it had been when he was a younger man.

Then, with a start of self-criticism, memory returned. Of course! How *could* he have forgotten . . . but really she was the last person he would have expected to see in Portsmouth . . . Todhunter got to his feet, politely. 'Well, I never did! Mrs Weder-Ublick I do declare!'

Mrs Weder-Ublick looked disdainful. 'That is my name, yes.' Then she, too, remembered the shiny blue serge suit and the high starched collar and the Gladstone bag now resting upon an unoccupied chair. 'Goodness gracious me,' she said. 'Are you not the policeman from the *Taronga Park*?'

'Detective, madam – '

'The same thing, surely? What on earth is someone of your . . . what on earth are you doing in the Keppel's Head, may one ask?' At that moment the elderly waiter shuffled up with Todhunter's kipper. 'Apart from having breakfast, that is?'

Detective Inspector Todhunter knew the answer to that one: he had been carefully instructed by his Chief Super – Chilean spies might lurk anywhere, the old waiter could not be held entirely above suspicion and even Admiral Watkiss' sister could not be informed of the facts, since such were secret. He answered the lady's question. 'You'll be aware, madam, that the Metropolitan Police have the honour of guarding the gates into the dockyard – '

'No, I didn't know. Your name's Todhunter, isn't it?'

'Detective Inspector Todhunter, yes. I have been sent down to Portsmouth, madam, in charge of the uniformed men. Because of the review, you understand. And the presence of Her Majesty at Osborne House just across the water.'

'I see. I'm sure Her Majesty is much relieved. Now tell me something.' Mrs Weder-Ublick lowered her voice. There were other persons in the dining-room: a purple-faced Rear-Admiral in uniform, half concealed by a wide spread of the pages of the *Morning Post*, and a timid-looking wife on the far side of the newspaper; an officer of commander's rank with a pert young woman whom Mrs Weder-Ublick did not believe to be his wife; two gentlemen in morning dress who had the bluff aspect of naval officers in plain clothes – these gentlemen had loud voices and louder laughs and Mrs Weder-Ublick heard a reference to something or somebody who had an extraordinarily large stern and draught enought to need a battleship's anchorage. Mrs Weder-Ublick leaned closer to Mr Todhunter. 'I wish to know if Captain Halfhyde and his ship are in the harbour.'

Detective Inspector Todhunter saw no harm in releasing this information; his Chief Super had made no secret of the presence in Portsmouth of the *Taronga Park*; vessels of all kinds had converged and were still converging upon Spithead and the Solent and Portsmouth Harbour. 'I understand that is so, madam,' he said.

Mrs Weder-Ublick snapped, 'I thought as much. Thank you, Mr Todhunter.' She turned away towards her own table, sitting down with a thump. Like the Rear-Admiral, she spread the *Morning Post* in front of her as a screen against the likely appearance of Captain Halfhyde's appalling woman. Victoria Penn, the Christian name an insult to the dear Queen, a woman of the most impeccable chastity and uprightness. Miss Penn would no doubt be down for her breakfast at any moment; Mrs Weder-Ublick remembered she had had a most vulgar appetite and dreadful table manners, stuffing food into her mouth as though it were an oven. But she need not have worried; too much port and lemon had produced the father and mother of all headaches and Miss Penn was lying inert upon her bed with a mouth like the bottom of a parrot's cage that had not been cleaned out for a month.

*

The *Almirante Smith* was now two days' steaming from the British Isles, after an arduous voyage during the course of which the Chilean ship's company had demonstrated their total lack, in the eyes of Admiral Watkiss, of any seamanship abilities whatsoever. A hash, referred to loudly by Admiral Watkiss as a balls-up, had been made of the entry to Port Stanley in the Falkland Islands for the purpose of topping up Admiral Watkiss' personal commissariat. When Captain del Campo had put his engines ahead instead of astern, a British picquet-boat had almost been run down; and when the old (British) battleship *Canopus*, stationed off the port as guardship, had done the proper thing and, in honour of the approach of the Commander-in-Chief of the Chilean Navy, dipped her ensign, sounded the Still on the bugles and saluted him with the bosun's pipes, the Chilean officers and ratings had appeared to panic. Led by Commander Latrinez they had run around in circles as if about to vanish up their own backsides as Watkiss had put it. The Chilean bugler had been found asleep – in the officers' wardroom of all places; the piping party had not been mustered in time and when they were their bosun's pipes had sounded like the squawks of chickens upset by a fox. When the Chilean ensign had been lowered in response to the civilities from the British battleship, the signalman on watch on the flag deck had let the halliard run away from his grip. The ensign had flown off in a strong wind and had lain drooping down into the water, fouling the screws while the halliard had wrapped itself round the barrels of the after guns.

The entry to the River Plate for fresh fruit and vegetables for the Admiral's table had been if anything worse. Washing lines, to Watkiss' fury, had appeared on deck, and in attempting to remove them to the Admiral's screeched order, a seaman had fallen overboard. And since they were entering the territory of fellow dagoes, the ship's company went entirely to pieces, deserting their stations for entering harbour and yelling and shouting down to the bumboats as the flagship turned off the port of Montevideo. One man was seen to be relieving himself over the side, putting a bumboat's crew at some risk though they didn't appear to mind, being no doubt used to it, Admiral Watkiss thought. Attending upon him was Petty Officer Steward Washbrook, dressed in a fairly clean white uniform preparatory to going ashore to seek food bargains and if possible make some money on his own account; Admiral Watkiss would be even less familiar with Argentinian currency than he was with Chilean. Now, the old bugger was seeking his sympathy.

'You're the only blasted rating aboard who speaks a civilized language, Washbrook.'

'Very kind of you to say so I'm sure, sir.'

'It's not intended as a compliment particularly, you fool. I'd not expect you to speak anything else. What I'm asking is this –I don't speak their blasted language, why should I, and so I'm out of touch with what the buggers are thinking, if they can think – I'd like to know what blasted well *motivates* them to behave as they do. Why, for instance, do they appear to have gone blasted well mad here in Montevideo?'

Washbrook scratched his head, lifting his cap to do so.

'Put that damn cap back on your head, Washbrook. Anybody'd think you were a Chilean.'

'Yessir, sorry, sir. I don't know, sir. Hard to say like, sir.'

Watkiss sighed. There was some sort of commotion aft now, Commander Latrinez exchanging undignified shouts with the tugs standing by in case the Admiral should decide, which he would not, to order the flagship into the port. 'Have you *no* idea, Washbrook? Surely you've picked up a word or two of their wretched lingo, speaking to them man to man, as I cannot?'

'Well, sir. Maybe I 'ave, sir, yes. In a manner of speaking. I reckon they feel sort of . . . easier like, in an Argentine port. Not so much bullshit, sir.'

Watkiss glared. 'Bullshit?'

'All the routines, sir. Piping, sir, and bugles – '

'Oh, balls and bang me arse, Washbrook, that's our British way as you blasted well know! Standard practice – *proper* practice as required by Her Majesty's regulations – it's not bullshit!'

'No, sir, course not, sir,' Washbrook said quickly. 'But them Chileans, sir, they do seem to think it is, see.' He added, tongue in cheek, 'I done me best to tell 'em, sir, to make 'em understand that it's not bullshit, sir.'

'You did, did you, Washbrook?' Watkiss was obviously pleased.

'Oh yes, sir, I did.'

'What did you say?'

Petty Officer Steward Washbrook racked his brains. 'Well, sir, I told 'em the truth, sir. I said it was a simple act of respect, sir, to 'Er Majesty the Queen.'

'Yes, quite. Her Majesty – whom I have the honour to represent. No doubt you explained that.'

Washbrook gave a discreet cough. 'With respect like, sir. Not as a Chilean like.'

'Don't be blasted well impertinent, Washbrook.'

'No, sir. Very sorry, sir. I just – '

'Oh, never mind.' Admiral Watkiss paused. 'Did you tell them that any self-respecting seaman would damn well *wish* to pay the proper honours and would wish to appear smart and – and seamanlike at all times?'

'Oh yes, sir, I told 'em that, sir,' Washbrook said unctuously and without truth.

'Well done, Washbrook. We of the Royal Navy,' Admiral Watkiss added in forgetfulness of his current loyalties, 'must stand together against this – this damned crowd of cut-throats.' Suddenly his eyes narrowed as he stared suspiciously at Washbrook's white tunic. 'What's that stain?'

'Coffee, sir. Very sorry, sir – '

'Go and ship a clean tunic, Washbrook, this instant.'

Admiral Watkiss lifted his telescope and trained it on one of the bumboats. Just as he did so an Argentinian was seen to lower his trousers and drop down on the boat's gunwale with an expression of concentration visible on his face. Admiral Watkiss glowered and closed his telescope with a snap. As he turned away in disgust, one of the only other two Britons aboard apart from Washbrook was seen proceeding towards him: a clergyman of the Church of England wearing an immense black cape that, as it streamed in the wind away from his bulky body, gave him the appearance of a bat. Canon Rampling, once a chaplain in Her Majesty's ships of war, then rector of a windswept Pennine parish in the North Riding of Yorkshire, and more recently resident in Chile, was a man who appreciated God's good fresh air.

Canon Rampling beamed. 'Good morning, Admiral.'

'Good morning,' Watkiss said abruptly, and pointed with his telescope. 'Don't look down there, Canon.'

'Really? May one ask why not?'

'Because I say so, that's why not. Filthy dagoes!'

'What have they – '

'Never mind that, they're just filthy, and that's fact, I said it.'

'Well . . . we can't all be British, Admiral.'

'What a pity.'

Canon Rampling nodded but offered no further comment. Admiral Watkiss, under whom he had sailed in the past when the then Captain Watkiss, RN, had commanded the old battleship *Meridian*, was a somewhat bigoted man with whom it was unwise to argue. Besides, he owed an immense debt to Admiral Watkiss, who had been personally responsible for his presence aboard the *Almirante Smith*. Bidden at the last minute (for a certain dignitary of the Church had unfortunately died suddenly) to proceed to England to resume temporarily his naval chaplaincy and to attend upon Her Majesty for the period of the fleet review at Spithead, Canon Rampling had been unable to obtain a passage home in any of the liners of the Pacific Steam Navigation Company. He had appealed to Admiral Watkiss for passages on what amounted to royal duty for himself and his one-time churchwarden, Mr Tidy, who had accompanied him into retirement in Chile where Canon

Rampling had taken up residence with an elderly and ailing cousin who had been in need of companionship. Canon Rampling was an earnest man who took his responsibilities very seriously indeed. He had been relieved of them only by the recent death of the cousin.

Admiral Watkiss had had no wish to be much bothered by what he by naval custom called a Holy Joe; but he had been too well aware of his Englishness to refuse a request from a fellow Briton marooned in a country like Chile. He would do his best; and to do it he had written at once to the Minister of Marine in Santiago. When the Minister had very curtly refused the request, Admiral Watkiss had felt his hackles rise at dago churlishness and had at once gone himself to Santiago and an audience of the Minister.

He had plugged religion: the Chileans were at least very religious. 'Canon Rampling, Minister, is a clergyman of the Church of England.'

'Of England, yes.'

The tone was derogatory. Temper rose within the Commander-in-Chief. 'Any decent navy appoints chaplains of *both* religions in the case of a capital ship such as the *Almirante Smith*, Minister. I am not asking for free passages. I ask for Canon Rampling to be appointed to serve for the voyage as Church of England padre.'

'Aboard a ship where all are Catholics, Admiral?'

'I'm not,' Watkiss pointed out. 'I'm Church of England.'

'And you need personally the services of a clergyman?'

'Well – yes. Suppose,' Watkiss added with sudden inspiration, 'suppose I was to die at sea. Who'd take the service, I'd like to know? Not a blasted Catholic priest, let me tell you that!' Seeing from the Minister's face that he had gone too far this time, he made an attempt at retraction. 'Not, of course, that I have anything against Catholic priests. A fine body of men who do an immense amount of good. We even have them in England, you know.'

'Yes?'

'It's just that I happen to be Church of England.'

'And likely to die at sea?'

'That,' Admiral Watkiss said stiffly, 'is in the hands of God.'

'Quite so. God is God of Chile as well as of England, Admiral. He makes no distinctions. Your body would be as well committed to the deep, should God call you on passage, by a priest of the Faith as by a heretic.'

That was when Admiral Watkiss' temper got the better of him. 'Heretic my backside,' he said loudly. 'The Church of England is not composed of heretics and I'm damned if I'll sit here and have them called that. And if you do not permit me to embark Canon Rampling and his man Tidy, then you can find someone else to take your blasted ship to Portsmouth – something that will certainly not please Her Majesty or the British government.'

Watkiss had known he was on a winner. Captain del Campo would never find the English Channel on his own and would be likely enough to end up at the South Pole. The Minister of Marine knew this as well as did Admiral Watkiss. And there were no other admirals in Chile. And the government in Santiago would wish neither to lose face with Her Majesty nor lose the British trade that was to be the mainstay of the new regime.

Canon Rampling and Churchwarden Tidy had embarked aboard the *Almirante Smith* in Valparaiso the day before sailing, having spent the previous night in the Valparaiso citadel of the Salvation Army.

*

Whilst awaiting her breakfast in the Keppel's Head Hotel, Mrs Weder-Ublick reread the letter that had been delivered to her upon her arrival the evening before.

The letter was from Canon Rampling. It ran:

Dear Mrs Weder-Ublick, You may possibly have heard through ecclesiastical channels or from your brother Admiral Watkiss that I have been honoured to be appointed to Her Majesty's personal retinue for the period of the fleet review upon the occasion of HM's Diamond Jubilee. It is a matter of personal sadness and great regret that I am able to accept this honour only on account of my dear Cousin Alfred having been called to Higher Service to be with Our Lord in Heaven. Such a dear man and to be greatly missed.

Mrs Weder-Ublick rustled the page irritably; all this, she knew already. She read on, hoping to approach the nub, which she shortly did.

For the period of this honourable duty, when, that is, I am not required by Her Majesty, I shall be staying as a guest of the incumbent of the parish of St Thomas in the High Street, Old Portsmouth. The Revd William Scale is a friend of long standing. Dear lady, I write merely in order to fulfil the promise I gave you when we parted in Valparaiso so long ago, the promise to advise you should I ever return to England. I regret very deeply that my duties to Her Majesty must preclude any meeting. This I am quite certain you will understand and forgive. Your Humble Servant, Osterley Rampling.

Well, fancy that. Until her first reading of the letter the evening before, Mrs Weder-Ublick had had no idea Canon Rampling's Christian name was Osterley. She had always addressed him as Canon during that voyage in the *Taronga Park* to Chile with Captain Halfhyde. She didn't at all like the name Osterley; but no matter, there were more important things to be faced now. It was clear from the tone of the Canon's letter that she was being cold-shouldered. Well, she would see about that: Mrs Weder-Ublick's already firm jaw set even more firmly, becoming like the ram of an ironclad. She would not be put off: she had endured widowhood for far too long, and as the widow of a minister of the Lutheran Church in Germany she regarded herself as eminently suitable as wife to a canon of the Church of England, if only he could be made to see . . .

Meanwhile Mrs Weder-Ublick had her other avenues, one of them being the sub-dean of the Chapels Royal, an old friend of both her and Canon Rampling who had apprised her of the forthcoming return to England of the latter. The ecclesiast, acting as go-between, had corresponded with Canon Rampling and the letter which Mrs Weder-Ublick now held in her hand had been forwarded from his residence in Windsor Castle. Or to put it another way, Canon Rampling did not know she was staying at the Keppel's Head Hotel but a stone's throw from the church of St Thomas.

He was due for a surprise. Mrs Weder-Ublick put away the letter and concentrated on her breakfast. She had chosen a poached egg on toast and it was a little runny. She complained about this.

*

At 10 a.m. Halfhyde arrived at the Keppel's Head and sent his name up to Miss Penn's bedroom. Away from the *Taronga Park* the conventions had to be observed and gentlemen did not go to the bedrooms of single ladies. A message came down that Miss Penn would receive Captain Halfhyde shortly in the hotel's drawing-room.

He waited, pacing up and down the hall impatiently: he had work to do aboard and that afternoon there would be a meeting with the Admiral Superintendent of the Yard and a representative of the Metropolitan Police Force to discuss the forthcoming role of the *Taronga Park* vis-à-vis the Chilean threat to the safety of Admiral Watkiss.

Victoria appeared after a wait of half an hour. Halfhyde, meaningfully, drew his watch from his waistcoat pocket and flourished it in her face.

'All right, mate, all right – '

'It's not all right.' Halfhyde peered closer. 'What's the matter with you, Victoria?'

'Hangover,' she said briefly. 'Feel bloody awful, I do.'

It's not that. You're bruised – your neck – '

'Fell out of me bloody bed.'

'Did you indeed. Tell me – did Seaton look after you properly?'

She giggled; she had recovered her spirits. 'Not in bed, he didn't. He behaved as a proper naval gentleman. It was in the cab, see. Didn't get far and that's dinkum, honest – '

'So that bruise – '

'Look, mate, I said he didn't get far. Let's bloody leave it, eh?' She looked around the hall, currently deserted. She slid her arm through Halfhyde's. 'Let's get out of here, mate. Place gives me the willies.' She giggled again. 'What Lieutenant Seaton bloody didn't, so there.'

*

38

Aboard the *Almirante Smith* there had been an error of navigation, as Admiral Watkiss had expected there might be: Captain del Campo and his navigating officer had, Watkiss suspected, applied the deviation of the compass, and the variation, the wrong way round. Either that, or they didn't know east from west. The result was that Admiral Watkiss had the astonishment when coming on deck after breakfast in his quarters of seeing the white cliffs of Dover when he should have been seeing either Portland Bill or the Needles rocks at the western extremity of the Isle of Wight.

In a temper he sent for Captain del Campo, who arrived looking harassed and upset.

'You've entered the Channel the wrong blasted way, you fool!'

'*Si, Almirante* – I am so sorry – '

'Sorry, are you, Captain del Campo?' Admiral Watkiss thrust himself close to the Chilean and looked upwards into the moustachioed face. He prodded his telescope into the unhappy captain's stomach. 'God give me strength to endure blasted idiots like you! Tell me something: were you not surprised when your blasted lookouts didn't report raising the Fastnet – and then the Bishop Rock – and then the blasted Lizard – and then Start Point – and then Portland Bill?' Each landfall was stressed by a further prod from the telescope. 'Well, Captain?'

'But *Almirante* – the lookouts they do not see everything, you – '

'Then they blasted well should – if there was anything to be blasted well seen! Thanks to your tomfool ideas of navigation, there wasn't.' Watkiss, purple in the face, seethed. 'Balls and bang me arse, man, if this was a British ship I'd have had you damn well keel-hauled in front of your own ship's company – and that's fact, I said it. As it is, you've made me look a fool in front of Her Majesty – '

'*Almirante*, Her Majesty, she is not here – '

'Oh, hold your tongue, you fool, and don't split hairs. We shall now enter Portsmouth late – and Her Majesty will know all about *that* – a damned bad start to her Diamond Jubilee celebrations! All I can do now is to order you to send a signal to – '

'*Almirante*,' Captain del Campo interrupted desperately, 'do you wish, perhaps, that I turn round and approach England from another way? If – '

Admiral Watkiss danced with rage. He ground his teeth, and his monocle flew from his eye to the end of its mooring. 'Don't be more of a blasted nincompoop than you are already. And don't damn well interrupt me when I'm talking to you. Now: make a signal when we come within distance . . . if your blasted signalmen are awake they can make it to Dover Castle for onward transmission by the telephone apparatus to the Queen's Harbour Master at Portsmouth. Indicate your apologies – yours, not mine – for a late arrival owing to your utter incompetence leading to a balls-up – and stop wriggling about like some blasted ordinary seaman. What's the matter with you?'

'*Almirante*, when you called for me, I was about to go below to relieve myself, and – '

'Oh, you were, were you? With the ship coming into pilotage waters?'

'Nature, *Almirante* – '

'Oh, bugger nature, duty comes first. Now get out of my sight.' As Captain del Campo turned away, pale faced and shaking, Admiral Watkiss roared after him, 'And send that signal before going to the heads, do you understand?'

Watkiss glared frustratedly towards the white cliffs as his flagship lumbered through the Channel on her wrong course. His murderous thoughts were interrupted by a cough from behind him and he swung round.

'A beautiful morning, Admiral,' Canon Rampling said. 'Very refreshing. And such a splendid sight.'

Watkiss grunted. 'One we should not be seeing.' He explained what had happened. 'I'll be a blasted laughing-stock, all the way from Dover to Portsmouth! Her Majesty will be much displeased and I'm not surprised.'

Rampling poured oil, as he thought, on troubled waters. 'I doubt very much if Her Majesty will know, Admiral.'

'Oh, don't be an ass, padre,' Watkiss said irritably. 'There's nothing Her Majesty doesn't know, nothing.'

'Well – a most remarkable woman to be sure, of course.'

40

'Very.' Making the best of it, Watkiss turned his attention to what shouldn't be there: the white cliffs. He pointed them out with his telescope. 'Impressive, are they not? A reminder of Empire, of England's greatness. It inspires one just to think of all those victories over those damn scoundrels.'

Canon Rampling was a little hazy: Admiral Watkiss was a man of varied and quickly changeable moods and on occasions there were *non sequiturs* in his speech. 'The Chileans, Admiral?'

'Oh, no, no, no, you fool,' Watkiss said testily. 'The blasted French! All those frogs they eat – despicable people, don't you know. One wonders why God created them at all, does one not?'

'Ah. I wouldn't go so far . . . I think we should live and let live – '

'Oh, what rubbish, and you know very well what I mean.' Watkiss paused, a frown starting to crease his forehead beneath the gold-encrusted uniform cap. 'Talking of God, padre. On the night before you embarked aboard my flagship, you lodged, did you not, at the Salvation Army citadel?'

Canon Rampling nodded solemnly, his bull-like face registering something like respect. 'Yes, indeed, and most comfortably. Major and Mrs Barnsley are most estimable people, upright and sincere – and most hospitable.'

'Yes. Common, of course. But well-meaning. I have put up there myself when there's been nowhere else available apart from the fleapits the dagoes call hotels. Mrs Barnsley makes the most dreadful tea, very strong. Of course, she comes from Yorkshire, and as well as strong tea is addicted to very thick ham. But that was not what I intended to speak about, padre.'

'Ah?' Canon Rampling bent his head solicitously, as if about to hear a confession.

'It was the fact of the Salvation Army, don't you know.'

'Ah.'

'The Salvation *Army*. I'm not an especially religious man, padre. I am not a regular churchgoer. Yet for many reasons I have a strong belief in the Almighty.'

'Because you are a seaman, Admiral? Because you've spent your life upon great waters?'

'Well – '

'And you've seen God's majesty in the great storms, and in the winds of heaven, and in the peaceful calms sent by God as recompense for the stormy times . . . and in His sunrise and sunset, the splendid colours of the sky at – '

Admiral Watkiss was growing restive. 'No, no, no, not exactly. Oh, I grant your point – very spectacular, all that. And impressive, of course. But there is a meteorological explanation none the less. My point is that I see the Almighty as very necessary to discipline. More especially, of course, *naval* discipline. In the – er – shadow of the Almighty people damn well come to recognize their proper station in life. Under the good providence of God and all that, don't you know. God figures a very great deal in the Articles of War, and in Queen's Regulations and Admiralty Instructions – excellent guidelines which it's a confounded pity these blasted dagoes haven't got.'

'But – '

'Anyway, be that as it may. What I say is, why should the blasted *army* have it all their own way?'

'I don't think I follow, Admiral.'

Admiral Watkiss looked impatient at stupidity. 'Salvation *Army*. Damn it, I see no reason why there should not be a Salvation *Navy*. Do you?'

Canon Rampling was perplexed. 'A difficult question, I fear.'

'Oh, rubbish, parsons are used to answering difficult questions.'

'Oh, quite. But perhaps of a different sort . . . the Salvation Army sees itself as being at war with evil, as fighting a war to the glory of God, hence the military – '

'Yes, yes, yes,' Admiral Watkiss said, stamping a foot on the deck, 'I know all that! But why the devil shouldn't one *sail* to the glory of God? Can you answer me that?'

'Well,' Canon Rampling said cautiously, 'I must say I see no reason why one shouldn't do that. One can indeed, within oneself – in the heart, you see – '

'Oh, balls and bang me arse, padre, I'm not talking about within anything – I'm visualizing a properly disciplined organization. Akin to the Salvation Army – there's nothing "within" about them, is there? All those uniforms and bands, banging drums and so forth, and trumpets. That's what I see. A bluejacket band, marching smartly, well disciplined, parading through Portsmouth or Devonport or Chatham.' He added, 'To the glory of God, you see.'

'Er – '

'I thought you'd probably agree. I understand you happen to know the sub-dean of the Chapels Royal?'

'Yes, indeed, an old friend – '

'Quite a senior job, is it not? Influential. More or less ranks with an admiral. With but after, of course.'

'Yes, I – '

'Speak to him about it if ever Captain del Campo manages to bring us into Portsmouth. He'll probably be in some sort of attendance upon Her Majesty at Osborne, I imagine.' Admiral Watkiss drew a turnip-shaped watch from the pocket of his uniform waistcoat. Captain del Campo, the watch told him, had better get a move on. 'Well, then, that's settled,' he said. 'And remember, it's all *my* idea.' Going off at one of his tangents he spoke again. 'That sister of mine. You'll remember her – you went to Chile with her in Halfhyde's ship.'

'Yes – '

'If ever you come into contact with her again, and of course as you know she's back in England now, came back willy-nilly in Halfhyde's ship with me after that blasted fracas with Santiago – the Chileans didn't want her and her damned missionary work, upsetting the natives and so on and I can't say I blame 'em . . . if you ever meet her again, not a blasted *word* about what I've been saying. As you know, she married a damn Hun parson, a Lutheran – I was thankful to hear of his death – and she's completely gone on religion, says it keeps the natives in their place. Of course I agree with that, but given half a chance she'll go and claim the idea as hers, just to – er – annoy me, really.'

'Ah. Do you happen to know where Mrs Weder-Ublick is currently, Admiral?'

Something like a chuckle came from Admiral Watkiss. 'Remember her name, do you? More than I did for a number of years. These damn Hun names – tongue-twisters, not at all British. No, I don't know her whereabouts and thank God for that, I say, can't stand the woman.'

43

At that moment a hail came from the navigating bridge. Captain del Campo was making a report. '*Almirante*, the signal, it has been sent.'

Admiral Watkiss seemed to quiver all over his short body. 'Reports are *made*, Captain, not damn well shouted along the decks at flag officers. Kindly come down here at once and make it in the proper fashion. Or if you can't leave the bridge for navigational reasons, send your blasted Executive Officer.'

*

As the *Almirante Smith* began to draw westwards and Worthing Pier was sighted distantly to starboard, Captain del Campo drew Commander Latrinez aside, away from the ears of the Officer of the Watch and the seamen lookouts and a lugubrious midshipman engaged in stubbing out a cheap cigar on the binnacle, and spoke in low tones.

'The *almirante* is not for much longer to be endured, my friend. I have reached the pitch of my tether, I shall suffer a breakdown of my health. The *almirante*, he is so abominably rude, so domineering, and makes no allowances for the long voyage and the fact that we have not been to sea for so far ever.' Captain del Campo was shaking all over and his lips were trembling as though he were on the verge of tears. 'What do you think is the matter with the *almirante*?'

Commander Latrinez lifted a hand, extended a finger and touched it against his forehead. When he saw that Admiral Watkiss was staring at him through his telescope, he quickly changed the gesture to a salute, which irritated Watkiss for even he did not expect to be saluted every time he was spotted at a distance and certainly not through the end of a telescope. Commander Latrinez turned his back for safety's sake and said, 'Captain, I believe the *almirante* to be taking leave of his senses. I suggest an interview with Dr Baeza.'

'The *almirante* has already expressed several opinions on Dr Baeza as well as the other way round.' Admiral Watkiss had; the flagship's medical officer was a disgrace to his profession, a buffoon who had refused point-blank in Valparaiso to embark leeches for use during the voyage to England. 'The *almirante* would refuse to be examined. I think I have a better way. If you

44

and I are both agreed that the *almirante* is becoming mad, then I shall have a private word with Dr Baeza . . . and when we reach Portsmouth a report will be confidentially made to the British naval command and the opinion sought of an *almirante* doctor, one that I believe is known as the Medical Inspector-General of the Navy, the only one who is senior enough to cope sufficiently with the *Almirante* Watkiss. . . .'

FOUR

'You may come aboard for the day,' Halfhyde said as he and Victoria walked towards the main gate of the dockyard. They had crossed the road towards an expanse of tidal mud over which a bridge ran to the harbour station and the trains to Waterloo. 'That is agreeable to the Admiralty. You must go ashore again by sunset.'

'I reckon those lordships of yours are a set of bloody old maids.'

'They have a navy to run,' Halfhyde said irritably, 'and women don't come into the scheme of things.'

'Oh, well sod 'em,' Victoria said. She wrinkled her nose. 'What about the Queen, eh? Her navy, isn't it?' She added, 'She's a woman, right?'

'She's the Lord High Admiral – '

'That's what I mean – '

'Which in itself leads to a point of naval protocol.'

'Point of what?'

Haldhyde sighed. 'As Lord High Admiral, Her Majesty is technically in command of her fleet. The fleet that is assembling to be reviewed by her. But she can't be in two places at once, if you follow. So, in accordance with naval practice, she's obliged to make a signal to the Admiral who's actually in command, asking him to continue to administer the fleet.'

'Which lets the old lady off the hook, eh?'

'It's a way of putting it, I suppose.'

'Thank God I'm an Aussie,' Victoria said. She seemed to lose interest and pulled at Halfhyde's arm, drawing him towards the guardrail above the mud flat. A number of urchins were standing knee-deep in the mud, looking upwards expectantly and calling out in an accent that Miss Penn didn't understand. 'What do they want, eh?'

'Pennies,' Halfhyde answered. 'You fling them down, and they burrow in the mud for them. Mudlarks, they're called. Part of the Portsmouth scene.' He reached into a pocket and threw down three pennies. All the mudlarks converged on where they had fallen, and virtually vanished into the mud. Squabbling took place when one of the urchins emerged triumphant, clutching a penny.

'Poor little buggers,' Victoria said. 'They depend on that for a living, do they? Does the Queen know?'

'I really couldn't say. Probably, yes.'

'Then I reckon she ought to do something about it,' Victoria said indignantly. 'Eh?'

'You can't interfere with tradition, Victoria. No one would be more upset than the mudlarks themselves.'

'Want their heads read, then.' Victoria opened her purse and brought out a florin which she cast down before Halfhyde could stop her. That, he said, would start a riot and there could be blood shed from the juvenile noses. For a florin, you could buy enough food to last a week.

They walked on towards the main gate as the expected fighting began. Behind them, Mrs Weder-Ublick left the Keppel's Head and turned along the Hard towards the High Street of Old Portsmouth. She was attracted across the road by the shouts of the mudlarks. She stared down in disbelief. Then she asserted herself. 'You boys,' she called down loudly. 'Stop that fighting this instant, d'you hear me?'

In sheer astonishment, the fighting stopped and a number of small faces looked up, the eyes bright in the overall body-covering of mud.

'What are you doing down there? Do your fathers know?'

'Course they do, lady,' one of the urchins called up. 'Chuck us a penny, lady?'

Mrs Weder-Ublick was scandalized. 'Most certainly not! Begging is a crime, and if you don't come up *this instant* I shall fetch a constable.'

'Garn, silly old bitch! Best bugger off before my old man comes along and plants one on yer!'

Mrs Weder-Ublick, scarlet-faced, turned away before she could be subjected to more bad language. As ever, there wasn't a constable in sight. Even the Metropolitan Police who were supposed to be guarding the main gate seemed to have withdrawn into their guardroom . . . she would speak to the man Todhunter and report the whole affair. What a place England had become! Mrs Weder-Ublick continued on her way to the vicarage of St Thomas.

*

Halfhyde's Chief Officer reported a visitor just disembarked from a boat at the accommodation ladder. 'Detective Inspector Todhunter, sir.'

From behind the Chief Officer the familiar blue serge suit emerged, as did the toggled bowler hat and the Gladstone bag. Mr Todhunter's black boots squeaked as he entered the cabin at Halfhyde's invitation. 'Well, well, Captain Halfhyde, sir, we meet again – '

'So it seems, Mr Todhunter.'

'And Miss Penn I do declare.' Todhunter's tone was cautious; as a Christian the Detective Inspector did not approve the curious status aboard of Miss Penn – the liaison he was forced to see it as. His old mother, now dead, would have been scandalized had she known of such carryings on and so would his Chief Super be. However, it was really none of his business and he made a point of being civil to the woman, unprincipled though she might be and was. Holding his bowler hat, now removed from his head, across his body like a shield against sin, he observed that it was a fine morning. 'Sun over the harbour, Miss Penn. It no doubt reminds you of Sydney?'

Victoria stared and then laughed. 'This bloody place? Like Sydney? Want your head read, you do, mate. Why, you c'd get ten bloody Portsmouths into Sydney Harbour between Onion Point and bloody Cockatoo alone.' Feeling sorry for his crestfallen look, she gave him a smile. 'What you after this time, eh, mate? Queen's bloody enemies?'

'Her Majesty has no enemies, Miss Penn. She is much loved by all her subjects – '

'Maybe, but soon bloody Portsmouth's going to be full of

foreigners. Germans, Japs, Chinks likely enough. Frogs and Russkies. Thank God we've got you, mate, to protect us all.' She giggled suddenly, and Mr Todhunter knew why: he was scarcely a heroic figure, however highly his Chief Super at the Yard rated his skills as a detective. He fiddled with his bowler hat and caught Halfhyde's eye. 'With respect, Captain Halfhyde. There are urgent matters to discuss, and I – '

'Of course, Mr Todhunter, and I'm at your service.' Halfhyde gave Victoria a hard look. 'Victoria?'

'I know the tone, mate.'

'If you would be so kind.'

'All right. all bloody *right*, I'll make meself scarce.' Huffily, she turned away and left the cabin, walked out on to the Master's deck and from there went down the after ladder to the well-deck where the ship's bosun, who was overhauling some of the gear, wished her a polite good morning.

'G'day, bose. Though I don't know what's so bloody good about it come to think of it. Sometimes, some people, they get right on me bloody tits, my oath they do.' She paused. 'What do you reckon to the bloody Royal Navy, eh, bose?' She was still chagrined at not being permitted, by Admiralty regulations, to remain aboard Halfhyde's own ship after sunset.

By way of answer the bosun gathered saliva in his mouth and spat skilfully over the side, a long stream that only just missed Detective Inspector Todhunter's waiting boat. 'Tarted up, they are, if you'll pardon the expression, miss. All gas and gaiters, spit and polish . . . I've 'eard yarns that some of them battleships, they can't go far out to sea because the skippers 'ave ordered the watertight doors to be burnished so they're not watertight any more. And they don't fire their guns cos the paintwork'd get damaged.' He drew a hand across his forehead, dislodging sweat. 'Thank Gawd we've got an army, I say.'

Victoria nodded, and moved disconsolately to the ship's side, where she draped herself over the guardrail. A series of whistles came across the water from a boatload of dockyard mateys crossing the harbour from Whale Island to Fort Blockhouse on the Gosport side. Victoria did a little flounce and waved. The whistles increased and she waved again. The day wasn't so bad after all. She was still appreciated by somebody.

*

'So you're here not on account of the Queen, but wholly of Admiral Watkiss?'

'That is so, Captain Halfhyde, sir. That is so.'

'A task of much importance.' Halfhyde's tongue was in his cheek. Todhunter was susceptible to flattery.

'Yes, indeed,' Todhunter said. 'As my Chief Super made a point of – of pointing out to me back at the Yard. Desperate men, Captain Halfhyde, who must not be allowed to harm a visiting Commander-in-Chief.'

'Quite. I had, of course, been told of your appointment, but I fancied you might also be involved with Her Majesty's safety – '

'No, Captain Halfhyde, Admiral Watkiss is to have my whole and undivided attention.' Todhunter paused and fingered his moustache. 'I, for my part, have been informed of your own particular appointment in regard to Admiral Watkiss, and I am very happy to liaise with you. Which, if I may say so, sir, is why I am here this morning.'

'Yes. Have you anything particular in mind, Mr Todhunter?'

'A plan of campaign, sir.'

'I see. I think you'd better expound.'

'Very good, sir.' Detective Inspector Todhunter bent and unlocked his Gladstone bag. From it, after some fishing about, he brought a chart of the Spithead and Solent areas, a chart that included the nearer approaches to the port. He brought out also a plan of the harbour itself, showing the berths alongside the various dockyard walls and the anchorages and mooring buoys that would be used by some of the ships prior to their proceeding outwards to anchor in Spithead when the time of the great assemblage grew closer. The plan included the lay-out of the dockyard installations: the many warehouses, the basins, the graving docks, the signal tower by the South Railway jetty. With the plan of the harbour came a small package wrapped in greaseproof paper, which fell to the deck of the cabin and was at once pounced upon by Todhunter and restored to the Gladstone bag.

'Beg pardon, sir. That's my luncheon sandwiches, prepared by the canteen at the Yard. Scotland Yard, that is. On subsequent days I shall approach the management of the Keppel's Head for something similar.'

Halfhyde stared in concern. 'Good heavens, man, you'd have been welcome enough to lunch aboard my ship.'

'I thank you very much, sir, but unfortunately I'm unable to stay that long. I have much to do, and my Chief Super is of the view that if a man has his sustenance with him, it gives him greater flexibility in the pursuit of crime. Besides which, my Chief Super is always of careful eye when it comes to the expense sheet.'

'I see. Well – very right and proper, I suppose.'

'The nation's resources, sir. According to my Chief Super, they are not to be squandered. I understand Her Majesty is of similar view.'

'I am sure she is, Mr Todhunter. Now – what's your plan of campaign to be?'

'For now, Captain Halfhyde, a watching brief. Admiral Watkiss is not expected until Saturday, as I understand. Thus my immediate duties will not commence at this moment. I propose to occupy my time, however, to full advantage. What I shall do is to make myself familiar with the town and the dockyard and the various departments of the latter which may be visited by Admiral Watkiss in his official capacity as Commander-in-Chief of the Chilean Navy . . . or indeed in what one might call his private capacity as an interested officer once of the British Navy. Revisiting once familiar scenes, like, sir, if you follow me. Reliving the past.' Todhunter gave a polite cough into his palm. 'If perhaps you would be so kind, Captain Halfhyde, as to give me some guidance as to official and other places likely to be visited by Admiral Watkiss?'

'By all means. I suggest the signal tower for a start. Possibly a tour of the whole yard – he's likely to be interested in the cruisers and battleships under construction at the slipways. Possibly even the barrack bulks for all I know. And of course the office of the Admiral Superintendent of the dock-yard.'

'Yes, sir, I see.' Todhunter was busily making notes with an indelible pencil upon a pad of paper. This done, he craned his neck through one of the ports of the cabin. 'And the glorious past, sir?'

Halfhyde gave a short laugh. 'Admiral Watkiss, as I recall, carries his own glorious past. It is with him night and day.'

Mr. Todhunter looked puzzled. 'I was referring to the old wooden walls, sir. Them that those Frenchies spoke of . . . those far-distant, storm-tossed British ships that they said stood between that Napoleon Bonaparte and the dominion of the world. The blockade of the French ports, like, sir.'

'Yes, I know.' Halfhyde raised an eyebrow. 'I didn't know you were a student of naval history, Mr Todhunter?'

'It was my old mother, sir. Despite illness upon embarking aboard the paddle-steamer to Ryde from the Clarence Pier whilst on an outing from London, sir, my old mother had a very great regard for the British tar. Jolly Jack, she called them. Lord Nelson was her hero . . . even after all those years since.'

'Since Trafalgar, Mr Todhunter?'

'Not exactly, sir, no. Since my great-grandfather, my old mother's grandfather, you see – since he had the great honour of being brought from under a horse to look through the dining-room windows of the George Hotel in the High Street of this very town, sir, to watch his lordship, a man of humble origins who had made good, having his last breakfast, as it turned out to be, in England. My great-grandfather was an ostler, sir,' Todhunter added, 'thus the horse.'

'I see. A family connection with greatness.'

'As I like to think of it, sir, yes. And out there,' Todhunter waved an arm comprehensively towards the port-hole, 'lies the *Victory*, and the *Foudroyant*, and the *Implacable*. Reminders of days past, sir, days of glory and valour, full charged, if I may quote a poem, sir, with England's thunder – '

'That was the *Royal George*, Mr Todhunter, which lies beneath the waves. Perhaps Admiral Watkiss would care to visit her, charging her with his own thunder.'

Detective Inspector Todhunter looked quite shocked at
levity, his expression calling it *lèse-majesté*, no less. Coughing
again, he intimated that he had believed Admiral Watkiss
might decide upon a voyage into history. 'If only as a lesson
to those Chilean gentlemen, Captain Halfhyde.' He paused.
'Now, sir. There are other matters to be gone into, if I may
make so bold . . . '

*

'Did that dick,' Victoria asked after Todhunter's departure
ashore, 'say anything about the old bag?'

'I assume you mean Mrs Weder-Ublick.' Earlier, Victoria
had lost no time in telling Halfhyde that Mrs Weder-Ublick
was also staying at the Keppel's Head – she had observed
her making for the bathroom clad in the modesty of an immense dressing-gown and carrying a sponge-bag.

'He did,' Halfhyde answered.

'And?'

Halfhyde lifted an eyebrow, quizzically. 'Is there something else, Victoria?'

'No, I reckon not.' Victoria was much relieved. For all she
knew, the searching eye of Mrs Weder-Ublick might have
spotted her torn clothing, and Mrs Weder-Ublick would
certainly not have been above spreading slander about Miss
Penn. However, that hadn't happened – yet. But a moment
later it transpired that Todhunter had had certain anxieties
about the unexpected presence of Mrs Weder-Ublick. Halfhyde, pacing his cabin, turned to Victoria.

He said, 'A word in your ear, Victoria. Strictly between
the two of us, d'you understand?'

'To do with the old bag?'

'Yes – '

'And the dick?'

'Yes,' Halfhyde said again. 'Now, just listen for a moment.
You'll remember that when we were all together aboard this
ship – '

'Going to Chile?'

'Yes. Mrs Weder-Ublick came under suspicion of being a
spy – '

'Only because of that stuck-up bloke from whatsit, the Foreign Office, and she being the widow of a German, and the bloody Germans being involved in – '

'Yes. I said, just listen – '

'Not that she's not the bloody sort to snoop and spy.'

'*Victoria*!'

She sighed and tried to look penitent. 'Sorry, mate, I'll keep me trap shut. Try to, anyway.'

'Good. Todhunter is still not entirely happy about Mrs Weder-Ublick – '

'No more am I, mate.'

'For different reasons,' Halfhyde said irritably, 'from Todhunter's. Kindly listen. Todhunter believes it strange that Mrs Weder-Ublick should turn up in Portsmouth at this particular time – a time when her brother's expected in the port. You'll remember she had no time for her brother at all, although it was certainly she who got him free of the last Chilean administration – '

'Because the German Ambassador had been up to some jiggery pokery in the past, buggery it was, and she knew – '

'Well, we'll not go into that now, Victoria. Todhunter seems to see something sinister in her being in Portsmouth, even that she might be in league with the people who wish to assassinate him. That, I myself consider total rubbish – '

'Not when it comes to old Watkiss, mate. Reckon she could be a sort of . . . sort of whatsit . . .'

'Trojan horse?'

'Eh? Come again?' She wrinkled her nose, urchin-like as ever.

'Never mind, Victoria. Let's call her a decoy – in your view. Also in Todhunter's.'

'First time I ever bin in agreement with a dick, I reckon.'

'No doubt. Anyway, Todhunter seems to think she could lure Admiral Watkiss somewhere – deliver him into the hands of these desperadoes as he calls them. Or even, since she could be expected to have a kind of easy access to a brother, that she might do the deed herself.'

'Bump him off, eh?' Victoria giggled. 'Reckon I c'n see the old bag doing that.'

'I think it's nonsense. Mrs Weder-Ublick is a religious woman for a start. Even apart from that, I don't see her as an accomplice to villainy. Todhunter disagrees. He postulated that she might be under some kind of duress. Under,' he added as he saw the girl's uncomprehending look, 'some sort of threat from the Chileans.'

'Do her in unless she does him in first?'

'Possibly.'

'So why tell me all this, mate? Nothing I can do about it.' Victoria looked up at Halfhyde suspiciously. 'Or is there, eh? You got something in mind, have you?'

He smiled. 'Yes. You and Mrs Weder-Ublick are both accommodated in the Keppel's Head Hotel. Todhunter can't be everywhere at once. I want you to keep an eye on Mrs Weder-Ublick and report anything suspicious. Be friendly with her, get her to talk. Be . . . *companionable.* Accompany her on walks, for instance – '

'You must be stark, staring mad, mate! The old bag hates me guts – you know that! Besides, if it's going to be dangerous – '

'It won't be,' Halfhyde assured her. 'I've already said, in my view Todhunter's barking up a very wrong tree. But your appearing to co-operate will set his mind at rest to some extent. Remember, too, that I also am here to help protect Admiral Watkiss, so you'll be helping me as well – for what it's worth.'

*

Detective Inspector Todhunter had been insistent that Mrs Weder-Ublick must be considered as suspect. What better person than a sister to suborn, a person presumed to be beyond suspicion? Todhunter knew very well that passions lurked deep between siblings, even between parents and children. The East End of London, where Detective Inspector Todhunter had sent many a murderer to his just deserts, had long since ceased surprising him by the many facets of human nature to be found there. Terrible things lurked, and not only in the East End. They manifested also amongst the aristocracy and the gentry. Also in the Church: Mrs Weder-Ublick's connection with the Lutheran Church through her late husband was no guarantee of saintly thoughts and actions. Often enough religion was a cloak, a surface thing only, and could cover the most unholy and uncharitable things, the worms that ate the mind. Why, he, Detective Inspector Todhunter as ever was, had dealt with a canon of St Paul's Cathedral who had one night forced rat poison down his wife's throat as she lay innocently in bed, for the sole reason that she had refused him his desires on so many occasions that he had bedded a young female assistant to the head verger and now wished to marry her. Todhunter's Chief Super had never allowed close relationships to weigh too heavily towards any presumption of innocence. As in the case of Admiral Watkiss and Mrs Weder-Ublick, siblings very frequently detested each other more than anyone else in the world. Todhunter's Chief Super was in the habit of recounting very often a story from his days as a detective sergeant in which a sister, a regular churchgoer and member of her choir, a young lady who had taught in Sunday School, had slit her younger brother's throat with a curved dagger brought back from North Africa by an elder brother, a soldier, and had concealed the body in the hollow bole of a long dead tree on her father's farm, where it had lain until fatherly suspicions had been aroused by the preponderance of carrion crows visiting the tree. Such, Todhunter's Chief Super always said, was certainly unusual; but the fact of murder within families was by no means to be discounted.

Leaving Halfhyde to ponder this, Todhunter had gone ashore to begin his peregrinations round the town and dockyard. For her part Victoria had refused point-blank to leave Halfhyde before sunset that day. There were, she said, certain urgent matters that called strongly for attention in the meantime. Grinning wickedly she had said that there was always Lieutenant Seaton. Halfhyde, noting all the signs of an almighty scene building up, and expecting a visit at noon from an officer on the staff of the Admiral Superintendent, gave in more or less gracefully; and Victoria remained aboard until the booming of the Evening Gun from the eastern fortifications, and the bugles blown from the ships in the port as the White Ensigns were lowered, unequivocally announced sunset.

FIVE

During the forenoon Mrs Weder-Ublick had arrived at the vicarage of St Thomas in Old Portsmouth and had pulled at the bell which had presumably rung, unheard from the front door, in the back regions of the house. A housemaid appeared, immaculate in mauve-striped dress with starched collar, cuffs and belt; the white cap was also starched. Mrs Weder-Ublick was surveyed somewhat haughtily; visitors calling without notice and cabless were likely to be for the back door, not the front. Yet Mrs Weder-Ublick, to whom a cab was an unnecessary expense what with the charge at the Keppel's Head being a monstrous seven shillings and sixpence a day, didn't quite look like the back door, though her clothing was unfashionable. She had the appearance of a headmistress or the matron of a large hospital. But you couldn't go by appearances and the vicar was a snob. So was his wife.

'Yes?' the housemaid said.

Mrs Weder-Ublick boomed at the servant. 'Kindly do not look at me like that, girl, I don't like it and that's fact, I said it.'

The voice was that of a lady

'Sorry I'm sure'm,' the housemaid said in some agitation. 'I –'

'I wish to see the vicar.'

'Yes'm – '

'Is he free?'

'I can't say'm – '

'Then don't just stand there, go and *find out*.'

'Yes'm.' The girl hesitated, looking upset and embarrassed. 'Have you an appointment'm?'

58

'No,' Mrs Weder-Ublick answered categorically. 'I should scarcely need one. I am Mrs Weder-Ublick. Kindly go and tell the vicar that.'

'Yes'm. But – '

'There are no buts about it, my girl. I have said, have I not, that I am Mrs Weder-Ublick? Go at once to the vicar. And in the meantime, have the common politeness to ask me in.' Not waiting for the maid's response, Mrs Weder-Ublick lifted her skirts and marched into the hall.

*

Detective Inspector Todhunter had a few words, after leaving the *Taronga Park*, with a sergeant of the Metropolitan Police at the main gate of the dockyard. Todhunter did not personally know the man, who was called Sergeant Sadley. Todhunter had already identified himself on his way into the yard earlier, and now, to be on the safe side and also to give Sergeant Sadley a lesson in security and never taking anything for granted, he did so again.

'You can never be too sure, Sergeant, that's what my Chief Super always says.'

'No, sir.'

'Eyes wide and ears a-flap, my Chief Super says. And so do I.' Mr Todhunter adjusted the set of his bowler hat, which had come a little awry as he had dodged one of the many workmanlike steam engines that chugged and chuffed along the railway lines inside the yard, pulling truckloads of naval stores and armaments. In dodging, Todhunter had bumped inadvertently into an officer wearing the uniform of a commander in the Royal Navy. This person had snapped at him, unnecessarily rudely in Todhunter's view, telling him to watch his step and muttering about damned landlubbers as he had ostentatiously flicked dust from the three gold-laced stripes on his cuff. Recalling the incident with some annoyance, Mr Todhunter addressed Sergeant Sadley again. 'I understand you've been here just under a year, Sergeant. No doubt you've come to know Portsmouth well?'

'Born and bred 'ere, sir, a Pompey man. And glad enough of the posting to the dockyard, sir.' Sadley added helpfully, 'Me dad, sir, was a fishmonger. Shop in Southsea . . . me brother runs it now.'

'Southsea. . . .'

'Yes, sir. The posh part o' Pompey, sir. Where the officers live.'

'I see. No doubt you're fully aware of the trust being placed in you by Her Majesty, Sergeant, at a time like the present.'

Sadley said unctuously, 'Oh, yes, sir. Very aware, sir. No evil-doers, sir, will get past me and the lads.'

'I'm relieved to hear that.' No mention of Admiral Watkiss: that was secret. Detective Inspector Todhunter had heard that in the Royal Navy there existed documents so secret that they were placed in sealed envelopes marked TO BE BURNED BEFORE BEING READ and even though he was inclined to believe this to be a mere leg-pull, he was acutely conscious that secrecy at this time was of the utmost importance. He nodded, checked once again that the lock of his Gladstone bag was secure, and said by way of farewell and dismissal, 'Maximum alertness, Sergeant Sadley, never fails to pay dividends. That's what my Chief Super always says. Good-day to you.'

'Good-day, sir.' Sergeant Sadley, hitching at his leather belt and inserting a finger between his neck and the band of his tunic, for his neck bulged redly over the top and he was a man who sweated profusely, looked sardonically at the retreating back of the Detective Inspector. The little bloke seemed to think the sun shone out of his Chief Super's backside; probably it paid dividends to think that . . . and all that guff about Her Majesty! Her Majesty had more than a detachment of the Metropolitan Police in the port to keep her safe and happy; foot guards and horse guards, the artillerymen manning all the forts surrounding Pompey and Gosport, to say nothing of the three big sea-forts guarding Spithead . . . plus almost every British warship that floated, and thousands of sailors and marines from the fleet and the barrack hulks, and two battalions of infantry of the line in the military barracks. She was all right. Sergeant Sadley wasn't; he was thirsty, and Brickwood's excellent beer called strongly to a thirsty copper.

Mr Todhunter, reflecting that the uniformed branch were the thick end of the Force and that all the thinking had to be done by the plain-clothes men, feared for Admiral Watkiss' safety if it lay in the hands of such as Sergeant Sadley's constables. There were a number of red noses among them, good testimony to the strength of the local beer if he, Todhunter, was any judge of men. Teetotalism was the proper thing for a conscientious policeman. His Chief Super was a total abstainer; but it had been not the Chief Super but Todhunter's old mother who had made him sign the pledge shortly after he had joined the Force as a rookie on the beat. Piously thanking God for his old mother's life upon earth, and uttering a silent prayer for her well-being in her present abode, Mr Todhunter went back to the Keppel's Head where, in the security of his bedroom, he once again opened his Gladstone bag and pored over his charts and plans.

*

The Reverend William Scale, incumbent of the parish of St Thomas, was somewhat at a loss when Mrs Weder-Ublick was shown into his study. She looked a formidable woman, the equal of any pushing female parishioner that he had ever come across during a lifetime of serving God.

He hummed and ha-ed. 'A parishioner?' he enquired.

'No. One would have thought that you would know your own parishioners, Mr Scale.'

'Ah – yes, indeed. I thought perhaps a new one, recently arrived in – '

'Well, I'm not. I said, my name is Weder-Ublick. *Mrs* Weder-Ublick. My late husband was a minister of the Lutheran Church. In Germany. My late husband was an *Old* Lutheran. *Not* of the Reformed Church. The distinction is of course important, as you'll know.'

Mr Scale, who didn't know, nodded knowledgeably. 'Of course, dear lady. Mrs Weder-Ublick,' he said to himself with a far-away look on his face. 'Well, well.'

Mrs Weder-Ublick made a sound like a snort. 'You seem not to have heard of me. You may as well be honest and say so. I'm a woman who appreciates *directness*, don't you know.'

'Ah, yes, yes. No, I have to admit . . . may one enquire precisely what you have come to me for?'

Mrs Weder-Ublick had opened her mouth to reply when the servant came in. Mr Scale said, 'Yes, Hawkins, what is it?'

'Begging your pardon, sir, I was wondering if the lady would like some coffee?' This speech was preceded by a curtsy, not, Mrs Weder-Ublick thought, very well executed: the girl had not been well trained, evidently, had perhaps been in some tradesman's employ previously, where the wife would not have known how things were done in polite society, being in a sense (although of course white) not so far above the Hottentots to whom Mrs Weder-Ublick had once mounted a mission in Africa. Not waiting for Mr Scale to transmit the message, Mrs Weder-Ublick answered for herself.

'Yes, I would like some coffee, not strong, with milk and sugar. *One* spoonful, demerara. And biscuits.'

'Yes'm. Sweet or plain'm?'

'Plain.' Mrs Weder-Ublick settled her thick body more comfortably in her chair, adjusted her hat and widow's veil, and gripped her handbag on her lap as though it were some missile waiting to be thrown. Then, waiting for the coffee and biscuits to be brought, she began. 'Mr Scale, I am an old friend of Canon Rampling. I understand you are also.'

The vicar's face brightened as light dawned. 'Oh yes, indeed I am! Osterley Rampling, such a dear man.'

'Yes – '

'Charming, absolutely charming, would you not agree, Mrs Weder-Ublick?'

'Yes – '

'A life dedicated to God, and to good works among the unfortunate – '

'Oh?'

'And conscious of his duty towards his relatives, don't you know – an elderly cousin in Chile – '

'Yes – '

'So self-sacrificial, dear lady. The elderly cousin – '

It was time to boom: no notice was being taken of ner attempts to gain a hearing. Mrs Weder-Ublick boomed. 'I know all about the elderly cousin, Mr Scale. I also know that he has died.'

'Yes, yes. So sad – so sad.'

'Rubbish. I expect it was a happy release. The cousin was very old indeed.'

'Oh, quite.' The vicar answered somewhat sharply: the deceased were to be spoken of with reverence, in hushed tones, not with an implied sense of criticism for having lived too long. Besides, he had not liked being cut out of the ordering of his own coffee and biscuits. He uttered a rebuke. 'We all grow old, Mrs Weder-Ublick. God's will – and God disposes – '

'Kindly do not lecture me upon God, Mr Scale. I am very well acquainted with God. Through my late husband, don't you know.'

'Of course – I'm so sorry. I – '

'Canon Rampling,' Mrs Weder-Ublick interrupted remorse-lessly 'is, as I understand it, to stay in your vicarage during the period of Her Majesty's review of her fleet.'

Mr Scale nodded over the tips of his fingers, which were interlaced in front of his face. 'That is so, yes. Old friends . . . we shall have much to talk about.'

'That's the point,' Mrs Weder-Ublick stated. 'That is why I am here now.'

'Ah?'

'Canon Rampling will be informing you, if he hasn't already, that the Commander-in-Chief of the Chilean Navy, Admiral Watkiss, formerly a British naval officer, will be entering the port with his flagship the *Admiral Smith*, or the *Almirante Smith* as the Chileans call her.' Mrs Weder-Ublick paused. 'Admiral Watkiss is my brother.' She paused again and eyed the cleric closely. 'Were you aware of that, Mr Scale?'

'Er – no, I was not, dear lady. Nor indeed was I aware . . . I'm afraid Rampling didn't mention you when he wrote – '

'I see. I confess I scarcely expected him to do so.' All at once Mrs Weder-Ublick seemed to undergo a transformation, almost miraculously in the vicar's view. She appeared to melt, to grow slighter in build, less forceful in character, and from somewhere close to her bosom she produced a frilly handker-chief, an affair of lace, with which she dabbed at her eyes. She looked almost feminine and even defenceless, a woman in much pain and sorrow. Mr Scale was half inclined to ring the bell for his wife to be summoned. Before he could do so Mrs Weder-

Ublick squeezed a tear from her eye and said, 'Oh, Mr Scale, I am so sorry. I do hope and pray that you'll bear with me for a moment.'

'Of course, of course.'

'Alone.' Mrs Weder-Ublick had interpreted correctly the wife-seeking look in the vicar's eye. 'I shall not keep you long.'

'Very well,' the vicar said cautiously, not committing himself by asking questions.

Mrs Weder-Ublick heaved a convincing sigh and dabbed again at her eyes. She allowed her voice to tremble a little as she went into her spiel. She was interrupted by the arrival of coffee, quite nicely served but Mrs Weder-Ublick had upset herself too much to eat the biscuits. She and Osterley Rampling, she said, had been close when travelling out together in the *Taronga Park* to Valparaiso; she had nursed him back to health when he had fallen overboard in bad weather in the South Atlantic; for his part he had attended upon her in a religious sense when she had sustained injuries in falling out of her bunk, also in bad weather. He had brought his travelling communion set and had administered the sacraments. He and she had spent much time together subsequently, and there had been what Mrs Weder-Ublick now called an understanding between them.

The vicar coughed delicately. 'You mean – ?'

'Yes,' Mrs Weder-Ublick said. 'A widow, and a lonely bachelor. I'm sure you understand, Mr Scale . . . as a man of God.'

'Oh, indeed, yes. Very natural in the circumstances, and you the widow of a – a clergyman. Yes, quite proper I would say. Though I scarcely see Rampling as a marrying man . . . however. May one ask – what happened, dear lady?'

Again the handkerchief, skilfully used. 'We – we – became separated in Valparaiso. Largely because of my brother, but that is a different story. Basically it was because of the elderly cousin – Cousin Alfred. Canon Rampling's sense of duty intervened is, I think, the best way of putting it.' Mrs Weder-Ublick naturally did not intend to mention the indecent haste with which Canon Rampling had departed up-country. 'Such a dedicated man, as I believe you yourself said, Mr Scale.'

'Yes. Duty weighs with Rampling.'

64

'Yes.'

'Self-sacrifice was always his watchword.'

'So I believe. But there surely comes a time – '

A small smile of understanding had creased the vicar's lips. 'With the death of Cousin Alfred dear lady?'

Mrs Weder-Ublick almost started: this was easier than she had allowed herself to believe it might be. Mr Scale was playing into her hands, smoothing her path beautifully towards her goal. 'Yes,' she said simply. 'I trust you'll not call such thoughts wicked, Mr Scale. There was never any sin in my mind, never.'

'Oh, indeed not – '

'My thoughts, my hopes, were all for – Osterley.' Such a pity about that name. 'Such a dear man and so lonely and rather sad – also shy with ladies. And much in need of a woman's touch in his more senior years. I can only hope you'll agree, Mr Scale.'

'Well, of course, it's really not my concern and as I've already mentioned, Rampling and marriage ... yet it's perfectly true,' the vicar said, beginning now to intone, 'that God moves in a mysterious way and it's not the province of us who are as yet unadmitted to the splendour of His wondrous light to question His dispensations – '

'That's very beautifully put,' Mrs Weder-Ublick lied, seizing what she saw as her advantage. 'All along, I've been so very much aware of the hand of God.'

'In your – er. In what way precisely, Mrs Weder-Ublick?'

'Why, urging us together,' she said with a touch of sharpness, instantly regretted – but no matter, Mr Scale hadn't noticed.

'And Rampling?' he asked disconcertingly.

'Osterley has *always* placed his trust in God, Mr Scale.' It was as good an answer as any other and Mrs Weder-Ublick felt that God Himself had thrust it into her mind since it seemed to work.

'Yes, yes, of course. Yes, he always has. Well now, Mrs Weder-Ublick.' Mr Scale glanced across towards the clock on his chimneypiece: in fifteen minutes' time sundry ladies of the parish were due to congregate in his study to discuss the final arrangements for showing the parishioners' loyalty to and affection for Her Majesty when she was brought across Spithead and the Solent from Osborne House to visit the poor of Portsmouth, of whom it had to be admitted there were many. 'Is there, perhaps, some way in which I can be of help, dear lady?'

'How very kind of you, Mr Scale. Yes.' Mrs Weder-Ublick was making a recovery now and was becoming businesslike. 'I shall attend matins in your church on Sunday. No doubt Canon Rampling will also, if Her Majesty permits. If not, then evensong. I would be *immensely* grateful if you would catch my eye upon leaving . . . or perhaps you'll be shaking hands at the west door . . . and ask me back to the vicarage for coffee. If matins, that is. If evensong, a glass of sherry. My brother, you see, will provide the link, if unknowingly. The fact that he is coming here to Portsmouth, don't you know, and that in the past he has sailed with Canon Rampling.'

*

It was a very hot day. Shortly after Mr Todhunter had left the Keppel's Head upon his self-imposed tour of Portsmouth Town, his high starched white collar had become damp with sweat and so had his neat cravat. He rather wished he had taken his Chief Super's advice to wear a celluloid collar, but Chief Super or no Chief Super he had not done so, for his old mother had always insisted that starched linen was superior, the mark of a gentleman. Thus he suffered. He walked beneath the railway arch whilst the train from London thundered and rattled over his head, no doubt carrying more dignitaries in connection with the great review – admirals, field marshals, even Princes of the Blood perhaps; Mr Todhunter, a loyal man, gave a small, tight bow in salutation, just in case. There might also be Ministers of the Crown – there might be Her Majesty's Principal Secretary of State for Home Affairs, the boss. Another loyal bow, which caused an approaching able-seaman, a stout man wearing three gold good conduct chevrons on his left upper arm, to utter a coarse laugh.

'Wotcher, mate! Trousers too tight for yer arse, eh?'

Mr Todhunter flushed deeply, forbearing to answer, for there really was no answer to such rudery, and walked on. The sailor was drunk, obviously, and at such an hour of the morning! The rough voice pursued him. 'Stuck-up old bugger.'

66

Well, of course, sailors and soldiers were like that and one had to be philosophical and understanding; they led rough and dangerous lives, the soldiers facing rifle fire in the field such as on the dreadful North-West Frontier of India full of shrieking, angry natives bearing spears and long-barrelled guns, the sailors facing the awful thunder of the batteries and broadsides of foreign battleships to say nothing of the ferocious sea itself, the great waves that washed over the decks and smashed themselves against the gun turrets, the terrible force of the winds that shrieked through the rigging and with plucking fingers tore men from masts and yards to lie broken and helpless upon the decks far below, or sent them overboard to drown in boiling seas of foam and strange fish, the horrible denizens of the deep. Yes, one had to make allowances. When at sea, no doubt coarse language was used fairly frequently as indeed it was in the Metropolitan Police Force – but a policeman returned when off duty to the civilizing influence of a home with women in it. Those who served Her Majesty the Queen at sea or on the land in the far corners of the earth had no such influences to calm them and Mr Todhunter had heard many a tale of the unfettered oaths of such persons as bosuns and gunners' mates and sergeants of dragoons.

He walked on towards the Town Hall, the splendid building opened only seven years before by Their Royal Highnesses the Prince and Princess of Wales who were still, even now, waiting to become King and Queen. Outside this great building stood, or crouched, stone lions. Before setting out from Scotland Yard on his present assignment, Mr Todhunter had been told a doubtful story by the uniformed inspector: these lions were reputed to roar whenever a virgin passed by. They had never been known to roar yet.

Mr Todhunter passed on into Commercial Road, the centre of the town's business enterprise that included many public houses. He passed a store called the Landport Drapery Bazaar, the sort of place he would once have gone into to buy a present for his old mother. He passed the Royal Sailors' Rest, a place of cheap lodging and refreshment for the sailors of the fleet when ashore, a place known to all as Aggie Weston's. Bluejackets were going in and coming out, in some cases rolling out to lurch with unsteady steps along Edinburgh Road towards Queen Street or the Neptune Gate into the dockyard, where stood more constables of the Metropolitan Police Force, guarding in the name of Her Majesty. Some of the sailors wore foreign uniforms, men from such of the ships from overseas that had already arrived in the port.

Mr Todhunter became sharp-eyed, seeking Chileans. So far as he could tell, there were none. Of course, Admiral Watkiss had not yet arrived . . . but even so. Unprincipled scoundrels masquerading as seamen, Chileans intent upon the nefarious business that he, Detective Inspector Todhunter, had come to nip in the bud, could already be infiltrating.

Mr Todhunter, nose metaphorically to the trail, followed behind a party of seamen making for the dockyard. Two of them were plain British tars, one with a gold anchor above the two good conduct chevrons on his left arm; two more wore caps bearing ribbons with gold lettering saying HMAS *Kurumba*. Men of the Royal Australian Navy. But the one who had caught the keen eye of Mr Todhunter had a South American aspect. His uniform was tawdry, and a tarnished tassel hung from the crown of his cap. The face was swarthy and not well shaved; he could be a Chilean.

Mr Todhunter kept a discreet distance. Nevertheless, when he crossed the road in the wake of the roistering party, and then went on following them down the road towards the dockyard gate, suspicions were aroused ahead and the party came to a stop. One of the Australians walked back.

'Follering us, are you?'

'Most certainly not!'

'Oh, no! Course not. Bloody likely. I know your sort, mate. Bloody pom poufter, think seamen are after any port in a bloody storm.' A large fist with the luridly tattooed statement I LOVE KATIE visible upon its back was waved close to Mr Todhunter's nose. 'If you don't bugger off fast, mate, I'll do you and then hand you over to them flatfeet on the bloody gate.'

Mr Todhunter turned and scuttled away. In his agitation he dropped his Gladstone bag. Turning to retrieve it, he was in time to see it whistle past his ears. His face flaming with mortification he picked it out from a pile of horse manure in the road. Oh dear, oh dear . . . what a narrow thing it had been! He couldn't possibly risk being handed over to his own Force – naturally, it would have been quickly smoothed out but his cover would have been blown in front of a possible Chilean and his Chief Super would have been livid, very disappointed in him. But what a thing for anyone to think, quite shocking. Even the Chilean had looked shocked.

All at once Mr Todhunter was brought face to face with the appalling difficulties of his assignment.

*

Next morning brought an unwelcome deterioration in the weather, such that augured badly for the great review. There was a lash of rain made worse by a strong wind from the south-west. Fishing boats made for shelter; storm cones were hoisted at the signal tower alongside the South Railway jetty, where the flagship of the Channel Fleet rigged extra headropes and sternropes and springs. Aboard the *Taronga Park* Halfhyde ordered steam on his main engine as a standby precaution in case his anchor should drag, and set an anchor watch on his bridge. Until there was an improvement, Victoria Penn would not be permitted to come aboard. As to that, Halfhyde was philosophical: she would have more time in which to keep an eye on Mrs Weder-Ublick, acting as Todhunter's unpaid and unofficial detective constable.

And still making his approach from the wrong direction, and a little late on his ETA, Captain del Campo, muttering to Commander Latrinez about the so terrible *Almirante* Watkiss, brought the flagship of the Chilean Navy inwards towards the old sea-forts built to the order of the then British Prime Minister, Lord Palmerston, to keep out the wicked French if they should decide, which they did not, to invade England.

*

The report was made from the signal tower to the Queen's Harbour Master and transmitted onward to the Admiral Superintendent of the dockyard: the arrival of Admiral Watkiss was imminent.

'God damn! That's all we need,' Admiral Fitzgibbon said. 'We still haven't got everything worked out, have we, Peters?'

'As regards protocol, sir, no.' Fleet Paymaster Peters, secretary to the Admiral Superintendent, looked worried. He was a thin, clerkly officer wearing gold pince-nez and a stain of blue ink on his right-hand forefinger. Nervously he shuffled through a sheaf of papers and selected a thick folder marked ADMIRAL/CAPTAIN WATKISS, ROYAL/CHILEAN NAVY. He said, 'It must depend upon Admiral Watkiss himself, I fancy, sir. He has the option. If you remember, after the fracas with the last Chilean administration, it was admitted by the Admiralty that he still had, and has, the rank of captain on the retired list of the British Navy as well as admiral in the Chilean Navy – '

'Yes, yes, yes,' the Admiral Superintendent snapped. 'That's why I asked you the blasted question in the first place – '

'I beg your pardon, sir. I apologize . . . but felt it wise to recapitulate so that you – '

'Oh, get on with it, Peters.'

'Yes, sir.' The Watkiss file was examined again. 'As I see it, he must enter the port as a Commander-in-Chief. That is to say, full honours as such. Gun salute from the saluting battery. All our ships in the port to sound the General Salute, ensigns at the dip. Piping parties in ships not carrying marines – '

'Agreed. That's to be the drill.'

'But when Admiral Watkiss wishes to appear as a Captain RN, then he is so entitled, sir.'

The Admiral Superintendent sighed. 'Why the devil should he wish to demote himself, Peters? It's not like him.'

'With respect, sir. From the record, it appears that Admiral Watkiss is unpredictable – '

'Good God, man, I know that! I've served with him, years ago – *under* him what's more – as a midshipman in the old *Thunderer* when he was sub of the gunroom. In my view, not to be repeated, the man's as mad as a hatter. But *why* should he wish to appear other than as an admiral?'

'It's a question of his back pay, sir. His back retired pay in his British rank. This has been withheld while his case was studied by the Board of Admiralty. While his rank, as you know, was agreed, his back pay has not yet been credited to him. I've no doubt he'll wish to make his claim in person now that he has the opportunity and he may feel it appropriate to make it whilst wearing British uniform.'

'I see. Well, I don't propose to embroil myself in Watkiss' payment claims.' The Admiral Superintendent got to his feet, rising from before his roll-top desk and walking over to a big window from which he had a view of the entry to the harbour. 'Now, about this blasted threat to Watkiss. From now on, there's to be the fullest possible alertness – and see to it that the detective, Todhunter isn't it, is informed that his man's about to enter.'

'Yes, sir. Also Captain Halfhyde – '

'Yes, of course.'

Fleet Paymaster Peters once again shuffled papers. 'If I may ask, sir – do you believe there's anything behind this threat – do you think we should take it really seriously?'

The Admiral Superintendent gave a grim laugh. 'I don't know, Peters. But I have to confess, I hope there is and I hope they get him! He's a confounded liability wherever he goes. But because if the threat should materialize and succeed I would have to account to the Admiralty for allowing it to happen, my hope must not be fulfilled. I trust you understand? Watkiss must be protected at all costs. I repeat, *at all costs* – blast it!'

SIX

As his flagship neared the harbour entry, Admiral Watkiss strode his quarterdeck in his full-dress uniform, with cocked hat and sword, his telescope constantly picking out well-remembered landmarks from the past, from his long service with Her Majesty's fleet. His uniform was something of a mixture: the insignia were those of the Chilean Navy: the sword was of British pattern and so was the cocked hat; the Chilean version of a cocked hat was in Watkiss' view an abortion, fit only for use in a comic opera.

By Watkiss' side was Canon Rampling together with his one-time churchwarden from his parish in the Yorkshire Dales, Mr Tidy. 'A reet filthy day,' Mr Tidy observed as rain ran down the inside of his collar.

'Yes, Mr Tidy, indeed it is.'

'What about a coop o' tea?' Tidy asked. 'I'll bring it oop like – '

'Well – '

'Not on the quarterdeck,' Admiral Watkiss snapped, lowering his telescope from a sight of Southsea Common behind the castle erected by order of His Majesty King Henry VIII.

'Why, but look 'ere – '

'Hold your tongue, Tidy.'

Churchwarden Tidy seemed about to expostulate; Yorkshiremen were never put down by what he had learned to call t'brass. He was, however, cautioned by the pressure of Canon Rampling's fingers on his shoulder: Admiral Watkiss was getting himself into a state and the moment was far from propitious for argument. Admiral Watkiss had now begun to jump up and down and was brandishing his telescope. Suddenly he gave tongue.

'The stupid bugger should be altering course to port by now! He's going to miss the blasted buoyed channel, can't read a blasted port-hand buoy from a starboard, God help us – '

'God will – '

'Oh, balls and bang me arse, padre, this isn't a case for God, it's a case for good seamanship.' Admiral Watkiss began moving at a corpulent trot towards the many ladders leading to the navigating bridge, shouting at the top of his voice as he ran, his monocle streaming out behind at the end of its cord, 'Put your blasted helm over to starboard so as to come round to port, you blasted idiot, or you'll damn well put my ship aground and block the blasted fairway for all ships entering! Oh, God give me strength. . . .' He vanished into the battleship's superstructure but his bellowing voice could still be heard. There was a good deal of extra blasphemy and a few moments later the Admiral reappeared and was seen gesticulating at Captain del Campo, who was gesticulating back and appeared once again to be on the verge of tears. Churchwarden Tidy shook his head and pursed his lips in disapproval.

'Language, Reverend,' he said.

'Yes, Mr Tidy, I fear so. We must simply hope the Chileans don't understand fully.' At that moment his gaze lit upon something that had fortunately been missed by Admiral Watkiss: a banana skin hanging down across the tampion of one of the great after guns. Canon Rampling removed it and cast it overboard and it took the water at the same moment as there was a tremendous gush of refuse from the vent from the main galley. The *Almirante Smith* moved on, her after end passing through a turgid mass of potato peelings, gravy, plum duff, pastry, currants and sultanas and corpses of rats and cockroaches scoured out by the half-yearly cleaning of the massive vessels in which cocoa was always on the boil for the sustenance of the watchkeepers. Canon Rampling shook his head, recalling his own years as a chaplain with the British fleet. To be sure, one could scarcely, at times, blame Admiral Watkiss for his reactions. If, say, the flagship of the Mediterranean Fleet had entered Portsmouth Harbour with the previous

73

weeks' plate-scrapings swirling around her stern and banana skins drooping from her guns, any admiral or captain would have exhibited signs of paranoia and not a few persons would have been clapped in cells below.

Churchwarden Tidy was about to speak again when there was a loud clang from for'ard, then a sort of scraping sound, followed by a lurch of the ship's head and a demented yell from Admiral Watkiss.

*

The report was made to the Queen's Harbour Master. It was made by Lieutenant Seaton. 'The *Almirante Smith*, sir, Captain del Campo in command – '

'Plus Admiral Watkiss. Yes, Seaton?'

'She's fouled the port-hand buoy, sir, carried it away – '

'Good God!'

'She's lying across the dredged channel, sir, and is about to foul the starboard-hand buoy as well. There's more than a chance she'll ground ahead and astern.'

QHM reacted fast. 'Tugs, Seaton. And divers. I'll go out myself in one of the tugs.' He seized his uniform cap and made for the door of his office. 'And see to it the Admiral Superintendent is informed – repairs may be called for.'

'Yes, sir.' Lieutenant Seaton kept a straight face when he added, 'And a medical officer, sir?'

'Why an MO? No injuries, surely?'

'No, sir, but Admiral Watkiss has a certain reputation . . . he may be about to have an apopletic fit.'

*

As if by a miracle, the *Almirante Smith* managed not to go aground, but by this time Captain del Campo was a total nervous wreck. Admiral Watkiss had been very forthright as he took over the bridge himself, extricated the flagship from her predicament and settled her with engines stopped in the centre of the dredged channel. 'You are a blasted incompetent nincompoop, Captain del Campo, and so is your blasted navigator, and that's fact, I said it. You – '

'But *Almirante* – '

74

'Don't blasted well interrupt your Admiral when he's speaking to you, you – you useless apology for a blasted seaman!' Admiral Watkiss flourished his telescope furiously. 'I'm relieving you of your command as of *this instant*, d'you hear me? *This instant!* Go below to your quarters.'

'*Almirante*, I beg of you – the indignity aboard my ship – '

'It's not your blasted ship any more,' Admiral Watkiss said energetically, poking Captain del Campo with his telescope, 'It's mine. If you think I'm going to be made a laughing-stock before the entire British fleet – and Her Majesty the Queen who is no doubt observing all this carry-on through a telescope from Osborne House – then all I can say is, you must think I'm mad. Obey orders and get below out of my sight. Remain there until I say you can come out.'

Shaking like a leaf, and with tears of rage and humiliation streaming down his cheeks, Captain del Campo turned away and fled. It was so unfair: in the Chilean Navy one was not expected to take a ship actually to sea very often: he had heard the same thing said of the much-vaunted British Navy as well. One swung round buoys and anchors or remained safe alongside a dockyard wall with strong hawsers out; as for going continually to sea, that was the lot of sailors in the merchant ships. Warriors, and Captain del Campo was accustomed to think of himself as a warrior, had other things to do: the exercising and cleaning of the guns (he had not been informed of the banana skin), also the social duties required of naval officers, the tea parties given by the various wives of the senior officers, the great receptions given by the civic leaders in Valparaiso and other ports, together with a certain amount of dalliance with other men's wives when bidden on duty to naval headquarters in Santiago. All this took time, and was of more moment than the impossible study of the entries to every port in the wretched English-speaking world. And of a certainty the Admiral Watkiss really was mad.

Under the personal direction of Admiral Watkiss the *Almirante Smith*, having regained the channel, moved on again, drawing with her a good deal of the filth from the galley discharge and with a stoker relieving himself through a porthole low in the ship. As she came past the saluting battery, the shore guns, with blank charges, boomed out in honour of the Commander-in-Chief of the Chilean Navy, who turned and stood pompously in answering salute, keenly aware that the dislodged buoys marking the dredged channel had somehow managed to catch their parted moorings on the foremost booms on either side of the flagship, and that he was entering a British port, the first time for many years, with an integral part of that port's requirements for safe navigation being borne willy-nilly back to where they had come from, and dangling from either bow for all Portsmouth to see.

*

'Most unfortunate,' the small, swarthy man said. He was from the Chilean Embassy in London, and had been sent to welcome his country's naval pride. 'Most unfortunate, Captain.'

Captain del Campo, to whom the diplomat had been brought soon after entry without reference to Admiral Watkiss, who was closeted in his cabin with the Queen's Harbour Master and a representative of the Engineer Captain responsible for dockyard management, began to justify himself. 'It is a difficult task, Señor Rodriguez, to bring a big ship into a narrow channel. Such would tax the abilities of – of Vasco da Gama himself.'

'You refer to the odd-shaped buoys, the can and the conical, of different colours?'

'Yes –

'But it is not the buoys that are unfortunate. What is a buoy or two? They are so easy to replace, and my Embassy will naturally pay for the replacement.' The swarthy man gave a nonchalant wave of his hand. 'That is as nothing. It is of the Admiral Watkiss I speak. It is unfortunate for the Admiral Watkiss, who has no right to relieve a Chilean national of his command.'

Captain del Campo sat forward at the edge of his chair, eagerly. 'Ah?'

'Such a high-handed act, Captain, is not to be tolerated. It will of course be reported to my Ambassador.'

'Yes?' Captain del Campo broke out into a sweat of relief and hope. Revenge would be sweet.

76

'My Ambassador will, I believe, be much disturbed that his country is to be represented by such a person. Such a very unreasonable person. Tell me, Captain del Campo. . . .' The swarthy man lowered his voice discreetly, as though the unreasonable Admiral Watkiss might lurk behind del Campo's settee which was in current use as a sleeping place for a large and somewhat unkempt cat of indeterminate colour. 'Tell me, have you found the Admiral Watkiss to be always unreasonable?'

'Yes,' Captain del Campo answered, exhibiting anguish.

'You have suffered?'

'Yes, I have suffered.' Captain del Campo spoke with rage. 'He is rude. He uses bad language and he speaks to me as though I were a fool. He has called me a useless nincompoop.'

The diplomat nodded. 'I have always found that the British, they believe everyone but themselves to be fools. It is a national characteristic of the British people . . . not that this is any consolation to your feelings, Captain del Campo.'

'No, it is not. Señor Rodriguez. The indignity before my officers and men! Why, at this moment I am not permitted to leave my quarters, not until the Admiral Watkiss says I may emerge, like a monkey from a cage. I tell you, Señor Rodriguez, I believe and so does Commander Latrinez that the Admiral Watkiss is truly mad and should be examined by a doctor. Dr Baeza agrees also.'

'Ah.' Señor Rodriguez stroked his obvious chin-bristles thoughtfully. 'Be so good, Captain, as to send for Commander Latrinez and Dr Baeza and we shall consider the matter very carefully.'

*

'Detective Inspector Todhunter of Scotland Yard,' Todhunter said at the main gate, and produced his card.

'That's all right, sir,' Sergeant Sadley said reassuringly. 'I know 'oo you are – '

'Security, Sergeant Sadley!' Mr Todhunter lifted an admonitory finger. 'I could be – er – masquerading as myself for all you could tell until I had shown you an authority. I've spoken to you before of the need for alertness.' Mr Todhunter paused and wiped raindrops from his moustache: the weather was simply appalling. 'Another thing. I am not to be saluted when I approach. Why, who knows who may be looking? It is vital that my anonymity is preserved, Sergeant.'

'Yessir. Sorry, sir.'

'Well, so long as you bear it in mind. Now, for your private ear, I am about to go aboard the Chilean ship, the *Almirante Smith*, for a word in the ear of Admiral Watkiss himself.'

Sergeant Sadley looked properly impressed at being on speaking terms with someone who talked with admirals. 'I see, sir. The gentleman himself, who's being – '

'That is not to be spoken of, Sergeant Sadley.' Mr Todhunter spoke sharply, raking the sergeant with a stern eye. 'Goodness gracious me, whatever next! What my Chief Super would say I don't know, I really don't! I say again, be very, very careful. Why, even Her Majesty is not aware of – what may happen.' Mr Todhunter turned away, his bowler hat looking hairy with the rain despite his umbrella. Clutching his Gladstone bag tightly he made his way through the dockyard, past the boatyard, dodging the many chuffing engines. Sergeant Sadley, brought up in the Force to salute his senior officers upon every occasion, had nearly saluted again as the Detective Inspector left the gate bound inwards. He was relieved that he had overcome his natural impulse; already he had heard quite enough of what Mr Todhunter's Chief Super had said, did say, and might go on for ever saying.

Watched sardonically by Sergeant Sadley, Mr Todhunter passed by parties of seamen, looking gloomy in their shiny, rain-drenched oilskins, under the charge of raucous-voiced leading hands and petty officers marching them to their places of work in the different parts of the dockyard, in stores and warehouses, engine shops, armouries and other places. As he walked among these horny-handed toilers, the sons of the sea, Mr Todhunter felt his heart swell to bursting point with pride that he was walking the cobbles of Portsmouth dockyard, the hub of the British Empire and principal home of the glorious British Navy that in the name of Her Majesty the Queen-Empress ruled the seas of all the world and kept the Pax Britannica in the unruly lands contiguous to them. The thought that he had a part to play, however small it might be in relation to the admirals and generals and princes that surrounded Her Majesty, in regard to the safety of the forthcoming review, was a matter for considerable satisfaction. Why, any attempt on the life of Admiral Watkiss would have the most serious repercussions, possibly – it was no exaggeration to say – for the very peace of the world itself. The hand of a Chilean assassin could without doubt send the British fleet to its war stations, and the great battle squadrons would steam out from Spithead, bound down through the South Atlantic, round the terrible rigours of Cape Horn, and up the coast of Chile to bombard Valparaiso and show the uppity natives who was master. And there was another worry for a detective inspector: the assassins might go and make an unholy cock-up – Mr Todhunter blenched at the word that had come unbidden into his thoughts (where from, for goodness sake?) – they might make a very serious mistake and even blow up the royal yacht with Her Majesty herself embarked, and then his, Mr Todhunter's, name would be mud and his Chief Super would be angrier than he had ever been before . . .

By now very wet indeed, Mr Todhunter approached the *Almirante Smith*, which was lying at a berth alongside the outer wall a very great distance from the South Railway jetty. With his cover story firmly in his mind and a small volume of Spanish phrases written for the benefit of English gentlemen touring in Spain, Mr Todhunter approached the gangway, the foot of which was guarded by a Chilean seaman who was chewing what appeared to be a nut and spitting in many directions. This seaman carried a rifle with a long, rusty bayonet and round his body was wrapped what Mr Todhunter understood was called a bandillero – anyway, it was a sort of belt stuffed with cartridges.

Mr Todhunter smiled propitiatingly: the man had scowled at him and pointed his rifle. '*Adios, señor*,' he said. He had rehearsed this.

'You want? You tell.'

So the seaman had already summed him up as an Englishman. Also, he had seemed to have a word or two of English, which meant that the phrase book might not be necessary, which was a relief really. Mr Todhunter smiled again; more Chileans, had now appeared, hanging over the guardrails at the head of the gangway and accepting small cigars from a person who seemed to be an officer: there was a lot of gold braid and while the seamen were mostly barefoot this man wore sandals from which very large toes peeped. Mr Todhunter took the plunge.

'I wish Admiral Watkiss. To speak to him, that is. If you please.'

The seaman grinned, turned and called up to the watchers on deck, a longish conversation conducted, not unnaturally Mr Todhunter thought, in Spanish. Then the sandalled officer took over, calling down to the wall to ask, if Mr Todhunter understood his English correctly, what he wished to talk to the Admiral Watkiss about. Mr Todhunter trotted it out. He had come, he said, with various documents to do with life assurance (this he had thought a rather clever ploy) for the benefit of seafarers. He had the documents, he said, to prove his words. He had. All vital papers to do with the Foreign Office and Scotland Yard and nasty threats had been placed in a sealed envelope and locked away in the safe of the manager of the Keppel's Head Hotel, and the Gladstone bag contained quotations from the London, Liverpool and Globe Assurance Company. Still smiling his ingratiating smile, Mr Todhunter produced a document or two and waved them.

'The Admiral Watkiss, he is busy.'

'He will see me, señor, I know he will. He – he asked for me to attend upon him on his arrival.'

'*Si?*'

'*Si,*' Mr Todhunter called back.

There was a conference; then the officer intimated that the Admiral Watkiss would be informed of his presence.

'*Grassy arse,*' Mr Todhunter called up in response. 'Mind, be sure to mention that my name is Todhunter. *Todhunter*, got it? And also mention Captain Halfhyde. That's very important. All right?'

*

'I don't believe a blasted word of it,' Admiral Watkiss stated firmly. 'Good God, man, do you really think any blasted dago would damn well *dare* to lift a hand against me? He'd know blasted well he could never succeed, and then the British government would have his guts for garters and his balls for breakfast. I've never heard such blasted rubbish, Todhunter – '

Todhunter was sweating. 'Oh, sir, I really must disagree. There is ample – '

'You're a blasted fool, Todhunter, always were as I remember, and what, may I ask, has Mr Halfhyde got to do with all this?'

'Captain Halfhyde, sir, is under orders from the Admiralty to join me, in a seaborne sense if you get my meaning, sir, for the purpose of – er – dealing with this dastardly threat – '

Watkiss stared. 'Did you say the Admiralty, Todhunter?'

'That I did, sir. Also the Foreign Office.'

'Foreign Office?'

'Yes, sir. Mr Mayhew, sir. You'll recall the gentleman – '

'Oh, that pimp. Well, that feller's totally mad, so – '

'With respect, sir. The threat is real, sir. There's great concern that – that Her Majesty herself may be discommoded and upset.'

'Well, yes,' Admiral Watkiss said reasonably, 'I imagine she would be if I were to be assassinated, it would be perfectly natural. But I shall not be, and you're a blasted nuisance, Todhunter. I've got enough to worry about . . . what with a nincompoop in command of my flagship, or was until I booted the bugger off the navigating bridge and confined him to his cabin. . . .' Watkiss' voice trailed away and his eyes widened. 'Good God, Todhunter! That slimy little bugger would stick a knife into me if he got half a chance, that I *will* say!'

'Yes, sir. I do assure you, sir – '

'Oh, balls and bang me arse, Todhunter, you blasted detectives are all the same, never come out with things straight as a seaman would. Why the devil didn't you *say* how serious it was?' Admiral Watkiss stamped his foot on the deck of his day cabin. 'Typical, to wrap it up in meaningless twaddle!'

I did try, you daft old idiot, Mr Todhunter thought but didn't say. Instead, he said, 'I do think, sir, you should take great care from now on. I am sure Her Majesty would wish that. I – '

'Oh, very well,' Admiral Watkiss said ungraciously. 'Tell me the whole thing and then I shall decide what I propose to do about it – once I've had that bugger del Campo keel-hauled and then flogged round the fleet, six lashes at each blasted gangway!'

Mr Todhunter looked staggered. 'Oh, sir, a foreign national, he can scarcely – '

'Hold your tongue, Todhunter, I'm thinking, can't you see?'

*

Commander Latrinez came out on deck from the Captain's quarters together with Señor Rodriguez, Captain del Campo remaining below in case he should encounter his Commander-in-Chief. This was just as well, since Admiral Watkiss and Detective Inspector Todhunter moved out from the Admiral's palatial suite at the same moment. They were in fact concealed behind the after gun mounting but the voice of Admiral Watkiss was very clearly to be heard addressing the salesman of the London, Liverpool and Globe Assurance Company.

'That's all very well, Todhunter, but the point is, they're *all* damn well disloyal aboard this ship, can't trust any one of the buggers, but what, I ask you, can you expect of a bunch of blasted dagoes who are probably at this very moment busily eavesdropping?'

Commander Latrinez was shushed at by Señor Rodriguez, and the two Chileans withdrew silently to a place of greater anonymity. Admiral Watkiss accompanied the insurance salesman to the gangway but nothing further appeared to be said. A few minutes later Commander Latrinez saluted Señor Rodriguez over the side, pushing past the sandalled Officer of the Watch in order to do so: the Officer of the Watch had had his foot up on a stanchion of the guardrail and had been examining a verruca on his big toe with an air of preoccupation, leaving his backside blocking the gangway until thrust aside. As the diplomat walked away to where a boat provided by the Queen's Harbour Master was waiting to take him direct to the harbour station and the train for Waterloo, he reflected with a scowling face on the words he had overheard. All disloyal – disloyal to whom, pray? Buggers who couldn't be trusted. Blasted dagoes. Persons who would sneakily overhear.

Well – they had overheard, all right! Señor Rodriguez sat in a corner seat of a first-class compartment, biting his nails in great impatience to reach his Embassy and have words with his Ambassador.

SEVEN

'A gennelman to see you, sir.'

'Oh, God damn!' Admiral Watkiss was counting money, Chilean money to be exchanged as soon as possible for real money: he couldn't wait to see golden sovereigns again, bearing the likeness of Her Majesty. 'Who is it, Washbrook? Not a blasted dago, I gather.'

'No, sir. It's Captain Halfhyde, sir. You remember – '

'Yes, of course I do, you fool, I'm not damn well senile.'

Admiral Watkiss reflected upon Halfhyde, formerly Lieutenant Halfhyde RN and latterly master of his own merchant ship, master and owner both. A good man, Halfhyde, with a sense of loyalty even though they had had many disagreements in the past and even though Halfhyde had an acid tongue when he chose and had never been overawed by brass, which of course was a pity but still. At least he was honest and straightforward, which was something you couldn't say of everybody in today's world. Yes, Halfhyde had served under him in many ships of war and indeed Halfhyde had brought him back from Valparaiso aboard the *Taronga Park* along with his blasted sister after his fracas with the Chilean Minister of Marine, a blasted dago of course, one of the fallen regime who according to that detective were behind the dastardly plot to assassinate him. Yes, he would be pleased to see Halfhyde again and no doubt have his support. . . . Coming out of his reverie of old times he rounded on Washbrook. 'Well, send Captain Halfhyde in, you blasted dimwit, what the devil are you waiting for?'

'Yessir.' Petty Officer Steward Washbrook scuttled out into the lobby of the Admiral's quarters and Halfhyde was ushered in.

'Ah – Halfhyde. Glad to see you I must say, I'm sick and tired of sallow faces and too much hair. I observed that the *Taronga Park* was in port. What are you doing here?'

'Acting as a fleet auxiliary, sir.'

'Oh, really? Why is that, my dear fellow?'

'For your protection, sir.'

'Oh? I don't see how. That fellow Todhunter did mention you in passing but he didn't go into details. He's like that, of course.'

'He's been aboard already, sir?'

Watkiss looked irritated. 'Yes, this morning, I've already said that, haven't I?'

'No, sir.'

'What? Oh, don't start off by arguing with me, Mr Halfhyde, I don't like it, and it's just like you, and I've had enough to put up with, what with that disgraceful exhibition upon entering. Damn channel buoys draped along the side! No doubt you've heard.'

'I have, sir. I'm sorry . . . the Admiral Superintendent's staff have boarded me – '

'Admiral Superintendent . . . Fitzgibbon, isn't it?'

'Yes, sir – '

'Good God, a real old fogey who should be in his grave. In fact he's younger than I but he hasn't worn as well, or hadn't the last time I saw him. Worse now, no doubt.' Suddenly Admiral Watkiss gave a loud laugh. 'First encountered him when he was a wart in the old *Thunderer* and I was the sub-lieutenant of the gunroom. Cut half way through his hammock lashing one night and it parted when his weight came on it. Dropped like a stone . . . broke a leg as I recall. Midshipman's chest flat was awash with blood from a dent in his skull. Little bugger never forgave me. He was put ashore to Haslar Hospital for six months. Still, no harm done in the end. He learned never to be impertinent to his seniors again and that stood him in good stead, you know. I rather congratulate myself really.' He raised his voice. '*Washbrook!*'

Petty Officer Steward Washbrook, listening at the door of his pantry, ears a-cockbill (for you never knew what you might pick up that would come in useful at a later date and he had not been able to listen during Todhunter's visit since he had been checking stocks in the Admiral's food store) appeared after a propagandic half minute with a drying-up cloth over his arm.

'Yessir. You sh – called, sir?'

'Oh, balls and bang me arse, Washbrook, what did you think I did, whistled in my bath? Whisky, and at once.' Admiral Watkiss glanced at Halfhyde. 'You still prefer whisky to gin, as I do, of course.'

This was a statement, not a question. Washbrook went away; Halfhyde was bidden to sit. Washbrook returned with the whisky. Admiral Watkiss uttered a perfunctory toast and then spoke again to his steward.

'Washbrook, leave the whisky decanter. Carry on checking my food store, and don't come back.'

'*Don't* come back, sir, did you say, sir?'

'You heard very well, Washbrook. You're not deaf, far from it. It hasn't escaped my notice that you have blasted ears like sails rigged on deck in the Doldrums to catch rainwater.' Admiral Watkiss extended an arm and waved a fist at the steward; the movement pulled back his starched cuff to reveal the tail end of the tattooed snake that wound up his forearm. 'If I come out and catch you at the pantry door, Petty Officer Steward Washbrook, I shall lose no time in sending for a British naval patrol and having you escorted to the barracks hulks *en route* for detention quarters to await court martial for offences hereinbefore committed – as you know only too blasted well, don't you, Washbrook?'

Washbrook had gone pale, those past offences coming back with terrible clarity, his insult to Her Majesty and all. 'Yessir. I'm very sorry, sir, there won't be any listening, sir, not that I ever did – '

'Oh, for God's sake, don't add perjury to all the rest, Washbrook, just hold your tongue and – and go away!'

Washbrook went off quaking. Watkiss said, 'Now then, Mr Halfhyde. I gather you know about this rubbish – this hypothetical threat?'

'Yes, sir – '

'Then you know more than I do. Todhunter wasn't able to

offer anything concrete, just a welter of confused verbiage really. Well?'

'I know no more than Todhunter, sir.'

'Oh, dammit, Todhunter spoke of the Admiralty – '

'Who have also spoken to me,' Halfhyde said. 'They, too, were vague as to how the threat would be likely to materialize and who would be behind it. Also as to the timing. But I was left in no doubt at all that it was being taken with extreme seriousness.' Halfhyde gave a cough. 'It was suggested that . . . you were not popular with certain persons in Santiago and Valparaiso, that you had upset Chilean susceptibilities from time to time – '

'Oh, what rubbish, Mr Halfhyde, that's the most utter balderdash and a very subversive thing to say. The blasted Chileans like having me there to put some discipline into their rotten ships. They *respect* the British, don't you know. They respect *me*. I may have been outspoken from time to time – I don't deny that – but they would never even consider threatening my life.' Admiral Watkiss' face went purple suddenly and he brandished his telescope across the day cabin. As though to reassure himself he repeated some of what he'd said to Detective Inspector Todhunter. 'The buggers wouldn't dare! They've too much regard for their own skins. The one possibility is that bugger del Campo – '

Halfhyde put a point. 'The Admiralty's reference was to the members of the previous administration, sir. Not, as I understood, to the present government, your present superiors – '

'Oh, balls and bang me arse, Mr Halfhyde, *they are not my superiors* – I am British and am by right a post captain in the British fleet, or anyway on the retired list. Kindly refrain from using the word *superiors* in any context regarding myself, is that clear, Mr Halfhyde?'

'It is, sir, and I apologize. But to return to my point about the previous administration. They are the people to watch.'

'Yes. Well, I'm not really worried, Mr Halfhyde, they were a very puny lot and all out for their own ends as is usual with dagoes as I'm sure you know. I really can't see them coming all the blasted way to Portsmouth to assassinate me when they could more easily have made an attempt upon me in Chile itself. The whole thing is ridiculous in my opinion, and that's fact, I said it.'

Halfhyde said, 'Have you considered the possibility that the assassins might already be in the United Kingdom, sir?'

'No, I damn well haven't,' Admiral Watkiss said irritably. 'The same thing applies – they'd have to have got here in the first place and it's a very long way to come when – I repeat – they could have attacked in Chile.'

Halfhyde nodded, but put another point. 'The previous administration, remember. *Persona non grata* in Chile – they could have left Chile for voluntary exile in the UK. Even if they were unwelcome over here, they could quite easily have found ways of entering.'

'True, true. Stowaways, that sort of thing. They're all such a slippery bunch, and low enough to crawl beneath a snake's belly with a tall hat on – I wouldn't trust any of 'em an inch, my dear Halfhyde.' Admiral Watkiss bounced his portly body up and down the day cabin for a few turns; Halfhyde believed he was now becoming just a little anxious about threats. After a while Watkiss halted and faced Halfhyde. 'I suppose one should perhaps be on one's guard.'

'Just in case, sir, yes. The Admiralty doesn't usually issue warnings unless there's some basis for – '

'Hah! I wouldn't be so sure about that, Halfhyde. Set of damn pasty-faced clerks plus a few land-bound officers who've forgotten all they ever knew about actual seagoing. Put 'em aboard a ship, my dear fellow, and they'd not sort out their arses from their elbows. No, I put no faith in the Admiralty . . . which reminds me: I have to visit the Admiralty before the review takes place. I have urgent business, you know, Half-hyde.' Watkiss frowned and drew out his gold-rimmed monocle from a recess of his uniform frock-coat. Screwing it into his eye he regarded Halfhyde thoughtfully. 'My dear fellow, I must ask a favour of you.'

'Of course, sir.'

'I'm not speaking to that nincompoop del Campo, or his blasted Executive Officer. And I have to remain aboard this afternoon to receive a courtesy visit by the Commander-in-Chief of the Portsmouth Port Command. I'd be obliged if you'd be kind enough to send a telegram to the Second Sea Lord's office - or perhaps make use of the telephone system. The Second Sea Lord is to be informed that I shall attend upon him at eleven o'clock on Monday morning.'

'Very good, sir. But suppose he's otherwise engaged at this time of Her Majesty's review?'

Admiral Watkiss shifted irritably. 'Oh, nonsense, he won't be! You'll quote me as what I am - the Commander-in-Chief of the Chilean Navy. He'll not take the risk of upsetting Santiago, what with all our trading agreements and so on, all the goodwill that I've been largely responsible myself for engendering.'

'Indeed yes, sir,' Halfhyde said, tongue in cheek. 'But just supposing the First Lord – or Her Majesty herself even – '

'Oh, very well, very well, you must always try to put a spoke in people's wheels, Halfhyde. Let it be put as the Second Sea Lord or his blasted representative.'

'Yes, sir. Er – may I enquire what your business is, in case they should ask if I use the telephone?'

'You may indeed. It's the question of my back pay, my back *retired* pay as a post captain of Her Majesty's fleet – the buggers are shilly-shallying about it, possibly hoping I haven't noticed, it's just like them, cheese-paring down to the last damn farthing, and for all I know pocketing it all themselves. And,' Admiral Watkiss added somewhat mysteriously, 'there's something else. It's something I've been discussing with Canon Rampling.'

'Yes, sir?'

'Rampling apparently knows the sub-dean of the Chapels Royal, who is likely to be in attendance on Her Majesty over the period of the review . . . but I believe it to be important to obtain the backing of the Admiralty before broaching the matter to an ecclesiastic.'

'The matter, sir? May I – '

'I intend to propose the formation of a Salvation Navy, Halfhyde, along the lines of the Salvation Army. That man Booth, you know, calls himself a general which is poppycock, of course, but still. He's done a great deal of good. I'm thinking of the lower deck ratings, you see.'

'The Chileans, sir?'

'Oh, don't be ridiculous, Halfhyde, they're heathens. No, our own British seamen. Why should they not have a Salvation Navy might one ask? If I can do some good,' Admiral Watkiss went on in what was nearly a maudlin tone, 'before I die, then I should like to do so. A memorial to me, in a sense. I trust you understand, Halfhyde.'

*

During the afternoon Mrs Weder-Ublick, her thoughts centring on the possibility of next day encountering Osterley Rampling in the church of St Thomas, and then again later, if God was willing, in the vicarage, once again left the Keppel's Head Hotel and started on the long walk into Southsea which she understood to be the more salubrious and civilized part of Portsmouth. In Southsea there would be not rough bluejackets but ladies and gentlemen. On enquiring she had been told that on Saturday afternoons the shops of Palmerston Road and Osborne Road would be shut, but no matter: Mrs Weder-Ublick was not intending to shop. Things were very expensive and she had nothing in mind to buy in any case. She wished simply for exercise and fresh air now that the rain had stopped and the wind had subsided, which she was much relieved about for the dear Queen would not like to be assailed by the weather whilst she was steaming aboard the royal yacht between the lines of her warships.

Exercise. And another thing: a visit to St Jude's Church at the corner of Kent Road and Palmerston Road. In St Jude's Church a number of years ago her late husband, on a visit to England as part of an exchange of views between the established Church of England and the Lutheran Church, the *old* Lutheran Church, had been permitted to preach, an honour that he had much appreciated. Mrs Weder-Ublick, on account of a sharp attack of lumbago, had been unable to accompany him. Now she looked forward to sitting in a pew close to the pulpit and to hearing in her imagination her late husband's strong words echoing round the church and its silent, attentive congregation. With her she had a transcript of the actual sermon he had preached on that very auspicious occasion.

Behind her as she left the Hard came Victoria Penn, obedient to St Vincent Halfhyde's wishes. Or orders: captains of ships were like that.

The wind had not entirely gone away; a gust of it, when Miss Penn was passing beneath the railway arch, caught at her hat, which was a large one with flowers and fruit and red berries. She snatched at it and in so doing impaled her hand on the hatpin. 'Bugger,' she said crossly, and sucked at a bleeding finger.

Sergeant Sadley of the dockyard gate guard, having just come off duty, was passing by on his bicycle and was witness to the young lady's distress.

Throwing a leg backwards over his machine, he dismounted.

'What's the trouble, miss?' he enquired, touching his helmet politely.

'Me bleeding finger, mate, that's what.'

Sergeant Sadley clicked his tongue at such language and Victoria giggled. 'It really is me bleeding finger, mate. Look.' She held up the finger for inspection. This time Sergeant Sadley's tongue clicked with a different emphasis and he drew a clean handkerchief from his trousers pocket. 'Have it right in a jiffy, miss,' he said, and bound the finger neatly, securing the makeshift bandage in place with a safety pin. 'There you are, miss, no 'arm done.'

'Reckon you'd make a good nurse, mate,' she said. 'Thanks. What about the hanky, eh? Returning it.'

'It's of no consequence, miss – '

'Hey, look,' she said, recognizing the beefy face and its heavy walrus moustache. 'You one of the coppers on the dockyard gate, aren't you?'

One of the coppers, eh. 'In a manner o' speaking, yes,' Sergeant Sadley said a little coldly. 'I'm – '

'Give it back when I see you. Wash it, I will.' She added, 'Me mate's Captain Halfhyde. *Taronga Park.*'

'Oh, ah.' Disbelief in the air?

'I'll be in and out. Thanks for yer help, mate. Married, are you?'

Sergeant Sadley looked startled, as if believing himself about to be propositioned. 'Yes, miss, as a matter o' fact I am.'

Victoria grinned. 'Thought so. Domestic, trained proper. Me mate Captain Halfhyde, he'd never put himself out for a bleeding finger.' Suddenly she remembered her mission: Mrs Weder-Ublick, who had vanished somewhere ahead. Which way? The road led ahead but further along there was a bend, and closer at hand another road that turned off to the right. 'Lost the old bag,' she said in a tone of annoyance.

'Beg pardon, miss? Your handbag do you mean?'

'No, I don't,' she said. 'But never mind, mate, it's all me own fault.'

'Oh, ah,' Sergeant Sadley said for the second time. 'Anything else I can do, is there, miss?'

She gave him a coy look. 'No, thank you very much. I'm bespoke, see.'

Sergeant Sadley bridled. 'I'm sure I meant no such thing, madam. I only – '

'Think nothing of it, mate, it's just me, can't bloody help it. Don't let it spoil your day, eh?'

Nonplussed, Sergeant Sadley remounted and bicycled away, reflecting that it took all sorts and it was a lucky thing that the skinny plain-clothes inspector from the Yard wasn't hanging about.

*

Victoria having made the right blind choice of route, Mrs Weder-Ublick was brought within view at the western end of Kings Road where she had stopped to ask the way of an old lady, who turned out to be almost stone deaf so that the information took a while to be passed. This had helped. Victoria remained a safe distance behind Mrs Weder-Ublick, who set off at a smart pace along Kings Road. Victoria wondered just what the hell she was supposed to do if Mrs Weder-Ublick should act suspiciously. Even the old lady with the ear-trumpet could have been a Chilean spy for all she knew, gleaning information, intent upon doing away with that old Watkiss. Unlikely, really: Victoria giggled at her own thought. Mrs Weder-Ublick did not, however, act suspiciously again but moved steadily on like a battleship pushing through a calm sea. There were a fair number of people about but they gave way to Mrs Weder-Ublick without rancour. She was clearly a lady; the denizens of Kings Road and Elm Grove into which Kings Road led were not quite ladies and gentlemen. There was a distinction between Kings Road and Palmerston Road, not much but a little and it was important. The presence of passers-by helped Victoria, who was unaware of the social niceties of Portsmouth and Southsea, to retain her anonymity vis-à-vis Mrs Weder-Ublick.

Mrs Weder-Ublick hesitated at a street corner, looked around, up and down, saw the name of the road – Grove Road it was – and turned along it to the right. Victoria followed: Mrs Weder-Ublick seemed to have a definite objective, a target, and *that* could perhaps be suspicious. At any rate, that dick Todhunter might think it was. A contact in Southsea, someone she had to meet? A man friend? Victoria giggled at the thought as she had giggled at Sergeant Sadley. It was ludicrous, really. Even though, as Victoria remembered, she had seemed gone on that Canon bloke, Rampling, aboard the *Taronga Park* en route for Valparaiso many months earlier. Old Rampling had had quite a job, getting out from under.

At the point where Grove Road met Marmion Road, Palmerston Road and Kent Road, Mrs Weder-Ublick turned right again and went into a church.

So that was it. A wasted walk and a long one. The old bag was going for a pray, that was all. Or was it? Victoria knew what the dick would say and Halfhyde would probably agree with him. Churches could give good cover for people to meet; you didn't suspect people who sat in pews and prayed. Not unless you were a dick you didn't. Victoria was now acting as dick's mate and she might as well, she thought, do the job proper. In a way, it was turning out to be fun, not a bad way of spending the time waiting to be readmitted to the captain's cabin aboard the *Taronga Park*. Giggling again at the thought of what the old bag would think if she could read her thoughts, Victoria entered St Jude's Church.

EIGHT

Shortly after the *Almirante Smith* had berthed in the harbour Canon Rampling had left the ship with Churchwarden Tidy and had embarked aboard a cab, booked for him ahead by the Winchester diocesan representative in Portsmouth as a result of a signal made to the shore once the battleship had been set on a straight course in the entry channel together with the marker buoys. This cab took Rampling and Tidy with their gear, including the canon's travelling communion set (not in use during the voyage from Valparaiso since the Chileans regarded him as a heretic) to the Clarence Pier where the cab was despatched with the luggage to St Thomas' vicarage, and the pair took the paddle-steamer to Ryde pier on the Isle of Wight. From there, another cab to Osborne House where Canon Rampling was to pay his respects to Her Majesty upon introduction by the sub-dean of the Chapels Royal.

'You'd think,' Churchwarden Tidy grumbled, 'that she'd have like sent a brake to pick us oop.'

'She, Mr Tidy?'

'You know who I mean, Reverend.'

'Yes, I think I do,' Canon Rampling said in a tone of disapproval. 'Her Majesty, Mr Tidy, has other things to think about, you know. The review – affairs of state – '

'Aye, but she has people paid to think for her. Lord Chamberlains and such. Major domos, like.'

Canon Rampling clicked his tongue. 'We mustn't criticize, Mr Tidy. The royal expenses are enormous and Her Majesty is known to dislike extravagance. Besides, it's a great honour for me to be invited to attend upon the Court – '

'Ordered more like, Reverend.'

'Yes, well, it comes to the same thing. It's still an honour.'

The cab proceeded out of Ryde, up a very steep hill. The horse seemed reluctant; Canon Rampling was of very great size, reminiscent of a bull bodily as well as facially. The journey was to be a long one; Osborne House was quite close to Cowes. To the occupants of the cab, it seemed even longer as the horse meandered through country lanes redolent with the scent of English flowers – that was certainly pleasant enough to nostrils so recently accustomed to salty air and before that to the terrible dust of Valparaiso and Santiago – dust and open sewers and garbage of all kinds overflowing from the hovels of the town dwellers. That was all very well, but the cab was most uncomfortable as to its upholstery and its sagging springs, and this discomfort was not helped by the continuous grumbling of Churchwarden Tidy.

'Oh, do please stop, Mr Tidy. It won't be far now.'

'You said that some while back, Reverend.'

'Oh, well. It really won't be far now.' It was like reassuring a child. Canon Rampling tried to close his ears and at long last the cab entered the great gates of Osborne House, moved on and pulled up at a flight of steps leading to a splendid front door. A number of liveried servants emerged, led by what appeared to be a butler. Canon Rampling, to his dismay, failed to see among them his friend the sub-dean of the Chapels Royal. But from a path leading between two superbly kept lawns of emerald green emerged a bath chair with a basketwork body, three wheels, two enormous and one quite small, with a steering device attached to the latter. In the bath chair sat a frail-looking old woman dressed overall in black and with very white hair pulled back into a tight bun. As this bath chair, propelled by a man who seemed to be little stronger than the occupant, drew near, Canon Rampling stiffened to attention and then, bowing from the waist, removed his clerical headgear, hissing at Churchwarden Tidy to do the same. Tidy obeyed but, as a Yorkshireman, did so with obvious reluctance.

'Your Majesty,' Canon Rampling said in a hushed voice.

An ear-trumpet was produced. 'What was that?'

'Your Majesty, I – '

95

There was a shrill cackle of laughter. 'Caught again! You're not the only gentleman that's been caught these last few days. I'm not Her Majesty . . . I was nurse to His Royal Highness the Prince of Wales, then His Royal Highness the Duke of York, till the rheumatics caught up with me. Sorry you've bin 'ad, sir.' There was another cackle and the bath chair was propelled away round the back. Canon Rampling, his face scarlet, muttered something to the effect that the pensioned-off old nanny-goat should not have been permitted to look like Her Majesty. Churchwarden Tidy suggested *sotto voce* that perhaps she was used us a decoy for the crowds to cheer and save the Queen having to bow in return.

'What nonsense, Mr Tidy.'

A moment later salvation came. As the servants descended upon him *en masse*, a familiar figure came down the steps: the sub-dean of the Chapels Royal.

This man was hearty and cheerful. 'Rampling, my dear fellow! So delighted to see you. You look well, old friend, in spite of your sojourn in South America. All those flies, you know, and the lack of sanitation.' He paused. 'Her Majesty is expecting you, of course. There will be an audience, and then we'll have a word ourselves as to your duties during the review. As an ex-naval chaplain you'll be invaluable. I'll try to see that you're aboard the steamer for the Clarence Pier before nightfall. It's not far from there to St Thomas' vicarage.'

Canon Rampling, reflecting that much as he liked his friend the incumbent of St Thomas', room really might have been found for himself and Tidy in Osborne House. It seemed quite big.

*

Mrs Weder-Ublick apart, the church was empty. There was a silence, total except for the slight shuffling of paper by Mrs Weder-Ublick as she sat in the front row of pews near the pulpit. She was oblivious of the entry of Miss Penn, who came in on tiptoe, awed by the atmosphere of religion and by church architecture and fitments. All those marble slabs, memorials, she read, to departed persons all of whom without exception, so far as her range of vision took her, had led beautiful and blameless lives and were much missed by those whom they had left behind, which Miss Penn considered a load of rubbish, everyone couldn't be that good, it stood to reason, but perhaps a number of indiscretions had never come to light. What the eye didn't see . . . Miss Penn, not accustomed to churches, crept into a pew and concealed herself behind a large pillar that supported a balcony. Like a theatre really, or the music halls where the sailors used to roister when ashore in Sydney, though the atmosphere was certainly very different. She crouched down, not in fact to pray but to observe Mrs Weder-Ublick without being observed herself. After a while there was a sound: Mrs Weder-Ublick, she believed, was talking to herself. Or something. A Chilean spy, concealed in the next pew back? But the old bag was talking as it were ahead, towards where a short flight of steps led into what looked like a marble barrel without a top, and a shelf on which maybe someone could put a Bible or something, probably to read from.

Mrs Weder-Ublick's voice droned sonorously on. Something about God, and dissent, whatever dissent might be, between two Protesant religions. Victoria had more than a suspicion that Mrs Weder-Ublick had gone crazy. After a while there was silence, quite a long silence, and then Mrs Weder-Ublick's voice came across louder, an incomprehensible utterance strongly, almost defiantly made.

'He would have expected it of me I feel certain. Therefore I shall do it.' A pause. 'It's for your sake, Joachim.'

Joachim? Who was Joachim? At first Victoria had thought the 'He' must refer to God, but this was evidently not so, unless Joachim was another of God's names, of course. Back in Sydney, years ago, before St Vincent Halfhyde had come on the scene, Victoria had lodged in the King's Cross district, a somewhat insalubrious area with many red lights, many drunks and many shady deals. She had worked, until rescued by St Vincent Halfhyde, for one Porteous Higgins, the shadiest dealer of them all. Porteous Higgins, a man of many parts and as sharp as a hatpin, had for a while, a short while, taken up with a group of earnest persons who had called themselves Jehovah's Witnesses. They believed very strongly in heaven and hell and that any sin committed whilst on earth would lead inevitably to the latter place. Porteous Higgins had sensed that money was to be made out of these somewhat simple people and had contracted to deliver to them certain persons, seamen mostly, who had repented of their ways and were ripe for conversion. Porteous Higgins ran among other ventures one of the notorious boarding-houses whence drunken men were shanghaied aboard outward-bound ships that were short of crews on account of desertion, drunken men who woke up to find themselves not only at sea but committed to it for a very long time. Porteous Higgins, used to dealing in drunken men, delivered drunken seamen to the Jehovah's Witnesses. His contract had expired after the first delivery had created such a scene that the whole Cross area had been in a turmoil of fists and knives and broken beer bottles, but Porteous Higgins, accompanied by men as strong as himself, had nevertheless extracted payment as per contract for deliveries made. Miss Penn, on the fringe of all this, had learned that Jehovah was the personal name of the Lord God of Israel. But Jehovah wasn't Joachim . . .

While Victoria was mentally recapitulating, Mrs Weder-Ublick had mounted the steps to the topless barrel and had rested a sheaf of papers on the shelf arrangement.

Clearing her throat, she started to declaim. Although Victoria had no means of knowing this, the words were those once in this very church uttered by the late pastor of the Old Lutheran faith. They were weighty words, words of much wisdom; they had traced the early history of the Lutheran Church for the benefit of the uncaring residents of Southsea, dimly hearing the pastor's Germanic tones while looking furtively at their watches, anxious to get home to their roast sirloins of beef being prepared by cook. And, like her late husband, Mrs Weder-Ublick went on and on while Victoria crouched uncomfortably in her dusty pew behind the balcony-supporting pillar. Mrs Weder-Ublick first extolled Martin Luther, who had lived from 1483 to 1546 and had led the Protestant reformation in Germany.

'Such a great man, brothers and sisters. A man of humble origins, son of a peasant living in Mohra near Eisenach in Saxony . . . in the year 1501 he took residence at the University of Erfurt as a student of law . . . Later he entered the convent of the Augustinian monks at Erfurt, where he submitted himself to the most stringent discipline . . . but in spite of fasts and vigils and unremitting industry in his religious studies he failed to gain the peace of mind for which his soul craved and he fell, poor man, into a state of morbid melancholy . . .'

'Not bloody surprising,' Victoria muttered to herself. She wriggled her hips and legs: stiffness was setting in and her nose was being assailed by disturbed dust. When Mrs Weder-Ublick had reached the bit about Martin Luther refusing to absolve the customers of a monk named Titzel, or was it Tetzel, Victoria was uncertain of Mrs Weder-Ublick's pronunciation, who sold pardons and what sounded like tickets of leave from purgatory, and Martin Luther had nailed his ninety-five theses, whatever these might be, all in Latin, to the church door in Wittenberg as a protest against Popery . . . at this point of drama Victoria was racked by the most enormous sneeze, such that echoed around the shattered silence of St Jude's Church.

In mid sentence, Mrs Weder-Ublick stopped, a hand going to the region of her heart. In a rather fluttery voice, for she had been immensely startled even to the point of wondering for an instant if the spirit of her late husband had manifested to revisit the scene of his glory, she said, 'Have I an audience? Yes, I see someone,' she went on, craning her neck over her notes, 'I see someone in that pew at the rear. Do please stay.'

Caught red-handed, Victoria got to her feet. 'Like bloody heck I'll stay. Know what? I reckon you need yer head read, mate. Nutty as a fruit cake, you are. Heard all I can bloody take, I have – '

'That word,' Mrs Weder-Ublick almost screamed. 'Not in God's House, you *vile* woman – '

'Bloody? Oh, sorry, didn't bl – didn't think.' Victoria turned about, intending to make fast for the door: like an offended battleship Mrs Weder-Ublick was under way already. In her haste to be gone, Miss Penn tripped and fell headlong into the pew. She lay like a trapped rabbit, scared as hell.

Mrs Weder-Ublick advanced inexorably, her fury visible in every step.

*

Canon Rampling found it almost uncanny: Her Majesty was the very image of the crone in the bath chair, although it might have been more tactful to have thought the thought the other way round. The sub-dean of the Chapels Royal preceded Canon Rampling along an immense and thick red carpet that seemed to stretch for a hundred yards into a great chamber where Her Majesty the Queen-Empress sat, oddly as it seemed, in a perfectly ordinary armchair of a rich brocade. Sub-dean and canon, as they approached more closely, bowed stiffly from the waist. Her Majesty fiddled with a pair of gold-rimmed eye-glasses suspended from a button affixed to her *décolletage*. A jerk of her wrist brought out a long, sprung cord that extended as the eye-glasses were perched upon a thin, beaklike nose.

'The dear dean,' she said, as if surprised.

'Your Majesty . . . my humble duty, ma'am.'

The Queen nodded and gazed through the eye-glasses at the sub-dean's companion. 'Who is this?'

'Canon Rampling, ma'am, to be attached to your Court for the duration of the – '

'The review of our fleet, yes.' The Queen surveyed Canon Rampling as though he were a dead butterfly stuck on a pin. 'Yes, I remember Lord Salisbury saying . . . I am given to understand that Canon Rampling has served in our fleet as a chaplain?'

The sub-dean bowed again. 'That is so, ma'am.' He paused as the close scrutiny continued and Canon Rampling gave a loyal beam towards Her Majesty, at which she seemed to frown a little, for it was perhaps a shade too familiar. Canon Rampling extinguished the beam. The sub-dean went on, 'Canon Rampling is very cognizant of the great honour you have done him, ma'am, in commanding him – '

'Is he? *We* didn't command him, dean. We were *told* by Lord Salisbury that he would be attached to our Court. *That* is why he is here.'

'Of course, ma'am. He understands that.' Canon Rampling didn't, and was conscious of a sudden deep disappointment and disillusion.

'Now he's here, dean, what precisely is he going to do?'

Canon Rampling was quite glad at this point that he was

being discussed as though he were not present, since he had no need to answer Her Majesty's question. He had not the faintest idea of what he was there for, not yet having had this explained to him by his friend. It was the friend who now supplied the answer.

'Canon Rampling, ma'am, will be in attendance upon Your Majesty at the time of the review of your fleet, ready to point out matters of . . . er, ecclesiastic interest in so far as waterborne religion is concerned – '

'Hmph.' The Queen seemed to understand that the dean was tending to flounder. 'Kindly be more precise.'

'Your Majesty.' Another bow. 'Also to attend upon you on your forthcoming visit to the poor of Portsmouth, many of whom will be the dependants of sailors in your fleet – the kind of men whom Canon Rampling came to know during his service afloat. That is to say, he became aware of their mode of life, their various problems and so on, and he will be able to answer with authority should there be matters into which Your Majesty may wish to probe.'

'Very well. No doubt we shall be glad of that. Now, where is Pitzie?'

'Beneath Your Majesty's chair, ma'am' The sub-dean bent and ferreted about beneath the chair. This was unwise; yapping broke out and the pink-eyed face of a white Sealyham dog peered out suddenly and made snapping motions at the sub-dean, who backed and straightened.

'Pitzie hasn't had his dinner,' the Queen said in a tone of rebuke, 'and he dislikes being *poked* at, as we would have expected you to know.'

'My apologies, ma'am. I agree I should have known.' The eye-glass cord was given a jerk and the mechanism operated to withdraw the spectacles back to their button. The audience was at an end. Sub-dean and canon backed away from Her Majesty, bowing as they went, an extremely awkward progress along the red carpet to the door. It was a great relief to be outside, and Canon Rampling wiped at his large face with a handkerchief.

'A charming woman,' he said. 'And such a great honour.'

'Yes, indeed, most charming. Mind you, she can be a hard taskmistress, and upon occasions has a sharp tongue.' The sub-dean rubbed his hands together and smiled jovially, to indicate that his words had been nothing more than a joke, with disloyalty never to be read into them. He underlined this conscientiously. 'One doesn't mind Her Majesty's occasional tartness, of course. The other times so much more than make up for it, don't you know, and of course she has the loyalty of her whole Court, though I do find that my loyalty doesn't extend to that confounded dog.'

*

Next morning the weather had much improved and seemed set to continue fair for the review. Victoria Penn was permitted once again to board the *Taronga Park*. In a fury about Mrs Weder-Ublick, and consumed with impatience to have words with Halfhyde, she swept past Sergeant Sadley and his constables at the gate, calling an apology for having forgotten to bring back the handkerchief. Sergeant Sadley indicated that that was quite all right.

'Good-oh. Hope you've got another one, mate, so you can get acquainted with other ladies.' She gave him a wave and left him to face the quickly removed grins of his constables. She moved on through the Sunday peace of the dockyard, past the silent workshops, the battened-down warehouses, the chuffing engines taking their rest. A message had reached her from the office of the Queen's Harbour Master advising her that the *Taronga Park* had now been moved alongside the dockyard wall from her anchorage. No need now to wait about for boats. Reaching the ship's side she climbed the gangway fast. She was met by a deckhand coiling down a rope in the after well-deck.

'Morning, miss – '

'G'day to you, mate. Captain aboard, is he?'

'Yes, miss, in 'is cabin – '

'Well, good on him! He's going to get a real bloody ear-bashing, mate, and I don't care a fish's tit who knows it.' She made rapidly for the ladder to the master's deck, her flowery hat a little cockeyed and her skirts clasped in her hand so far up as to show a fair length of thigh. The deckhand dropped his coil of rope and stared open-mouthed. An elderly man, he hadn't seen such for quite a while. Sucking his teeth, he reflected that the sea life was all right for some.

Victoria reached the cabin and yanked the door open. Halfhyde was sitting at his desk, writing. He looked up with a frown. 'It's you, Victoria – '

'It bloody is an' all and don't look too bloody welcoming, will you? I've had – '

'I'm sorry, Victoria. Of course I'm glad to see you. But I have reports to make and I have to see the – '

She interrupted him. 'You can bloody see this first, mate.' She turned her back on him and with a swift movement she gathered up her skirts and a number of underlying garments. Her knickers came down as though lead-weighted and she bent forward for Halfhyde to get a full view of the damage. 'Me bum,' she said.

'Yes. I recognize it, Victoria.'

'Glad to hear it. Take a closer look, go on.'

He did so. 'Hand marks,' he said in some astonishment. 'Who did that, or is it indiscreet to ask?'

'No, it's not. Mrs Weder bloody Ublick. In bloody church, would you believe it? Bloody hurt too, I can tell you. And I tell you something else for dead certain sure, mate: I'm pulling out from helping that bloody dick. You can say what you like, mate, that old Watkiss can be bloody assassinated any time he likes, I'm not taking no further bloody part in it.'

Halfhyde was grinning. 'And that's fact, you said it?'

'Eh?' she said, still facing away from him.

'Never mind, Victoria. Just cover your posterior, Bum, if the word conveys more to you. I'm expecting a man from the Foreign Office.'

*

At 10.45 that morning Mrs Weder-Ublick was already seated in a pew in St Thomas' Church. A front pew, where she could be seen – and in any case her station in society as a clergyman's widow demanded that she should sit in a front pew. She looked about herself without appearing to do so. A dropped hymnal, a stone in her shoe, that sort of thing. The congregation was a normal one, she thought. Dignified persons, ladies and gentlemen, for the common people went to chapel, not church, in England – it was different in Germany where the Old Lutheran

Church was perfectly respectable. As in the Old Lutheran Church, the congregation of St Thomas was neatly dressed in morning coats, spats, tall hats on the pews alongside them, starched high collars and neat cravats with pearl-headed pins; they all looked alike, resembling – for the church was very full – sardines in a tin. Not the ladies: the fineries of the fashionable ladies set them apart one from the other, especially as to the hats. The church resembled a very high-class milliner's establishment, no doubt situated in Palmerston Road if not Bond Street in London. Her mind wandering a little as she watched without success for the large figure – it couldn't possibly be missed were it there – of Canon Rampling, she wondered how it had ever come about that it had been permitted that Southsea's most exclusive thoroughfare had been named after such a person as Lord Palmerston. A good Prime Minister, yes, and a patriot. But by all accounts a lecher. Years before, upon an earlier visit to England without her husband, Mrs Weder-Ublick had been invited to dine at a stately home, Brocket Hall, and in speaking to another guest, a flighty woman unaware of Mrs Weder-Ublick's strict principles and ecclesiastical connections, had shown her the billiards room and in a whisper, and giggling a little, had also indicated the billiards table itself where Lord Palmerston had died whilst making love to a servant girl. Mrs Weder-Ublick wondered if the dear Queen had ever been informed of *that* episode. Now, the episode and the memory of the woman's giggle made her think of Miss Penn, and she shuddered.

At 11 o'clock precisely the Reverend William Scale emerged from his vestry and, joined by his retinue with bowed heads, went to his stall and the service began.

There was still no Canon Rampling.

When the service ended, and after Mrs Weder-Ublick had put twopence in the collection bag proffered by a sidesman who had the look of a retired admiral, all red face and white whiskers and his breath smelling of cigars and whisky, the Reverend William Scale proceeded alone down the length of the nave, his surplice a-swing behind him as he strode, but strode slowly and with reverence, to take up his station just outside the west door.

The congregation began to move past him for their hands to be shaken and their health enquired after, or a gentle rebuke to be administered for not having been seen in church the Sunday before. Mrs Weder-Ublick, as the procession moved with the speed of a tortoise under the total control of the vicar, began to seethe with impatience; but at long last she got there.

'Good morning, Mr Scale,' she almost gushed. 'Such a *very* nice service – and such an interesting and helpful sermon.' She waited to be thanked by the vicar, and then continued. 'Er . . . I was wondering . . . is Canon Rampling – '

'Detained by Her Majesty, I'm sorry to say,' Mr Scale fibbed. 'Most unfortunate, but of course not to be helped. Her Majesty's requirements are paramount.'

'Oh, of course. Er . . . evening service – '

'I'm afraid I can't say, dear lady. I'm uncertain as to Canon Rampling's movements.' Another fib: Canon Rampling had in fact been most explicit. By now embarrassed, Mr Scale turned and grasped the hand of his next parishioner. Mrs Weder-Ublick took the hint and moved on, her face flaming. Not even the expected invitation to the vicarage for coffee. It was really scandalous that her expressed wishes should have been so totally and rudely ignored. It would quite obviously be no use attending evening service and Mrs Weder-Ublick was damned if she was going to do so and risk incurring another brush-off.

She walked back along Old Portsmouth's High Street towards the Keppel's Head Hotel. As she went she pondered, not for the first time since yesterday, certain words uttered by that deplorable Penn woman when, before the well-deserved beating amid a flurry of disturbed petticoats, Mrs Weder-Ublick had asked her why she had appeared to be spying upon her: Mrs Weder-Ublick was certain she had not come for worship.

'It's that old bugger,' Victoria had said frantically. 'That barmy brother of yours, Watkiss – '

'What about him, may I ask?'

'Gone and got me into this bloody mess, that's what! All because of them bloody natives.'

'I think,' Mrs Weder-Ublick had said, 'that you'd better explain *fully*.'

'You think what you bloody like, mate, I'm not saying anything more.' She had suddenly realized that any revelations would incur the fury of St Vincent Halfhyde, to say nothing of the Foreign Office, and Scotland Yard, and even the Queen herself. 'And you can shove that up yer corsets,' she had added viciously and had given, not entirely by intent, a kick that had taken Mrs Weder-Ublick hard in a tender spot. But even the beating, which she would have had in any case, quite failed to make her utter. There was a basic toughness about Miss Victoria Penn, as Mrs Weder-Ublick was forced to realize.

NINE

That Sunday afternoon, shore leave was piped aboard the *Almirante Smith*. On insistence from Admiral Watkiss it was piped in the proper manner of the British Navy, even though in the Spanish tongue, by swarthy bosuns' mates moving about the ship above and below, blowing piercing noises upon their bosuns' calls and uttering time-honoured words not unknown even in the days of Vice-Admiral Lord Nelson and his hardy tars returning after his glorious death at Cape Trafalgar to enjoy the many and varied blessings of the land to be found in the thousands of alehouses of Portsmouth Town.

'Do you hear there. . . . Leave to both parts of the starboard watch from four bells in the afternoon watch to four bells in the first watch tonight. Leave to bona fide natives until seven bells in the morning watch tomorrow. Any rating adrift over leave will be brought before the Officer of the Watch on his return aboard. Do you hear ther. . . .'

The words 'bona fide natives' did not, as might have been thought, refer to the Chileans but to such ratings as had their homes in Portsmouth, of whom there were none. Nevertheless, the words were included because they always had been, in British warships at any rate, since time immemorial, or nearly, and Admiral Watkiss was a firm and staunch believer in tradition, which was not only nice for its own sake but was a highly useful way of maintaining discipline. When the pipe was uttered close to his quarters he listened to it, not understanding a word of the Spanish but listening just the same.

The pipe was heard also by Petty Officer Steward Washbrook who didn't understand it either, or not all of it – he had acquired some Spanish – but did understand its purport. He had already obtained his Commander-in-Chief's permission to proceed ashore, leaving Admiral Watkiss in the care of his leading hand, a native Chilean, Leading Steward Escobar.

'Take care, Washbrook,' Admiral Watkiss had said. 'Don't lose control of yourself through drink and attract the attention of the naval patrols or you'll find yourself back on all those charges again, I shouldn't wonder.'

'Yessir. I'il be very careful, sir.'

And Washbrook would be; for a start, he would go ashore in his Chilean uniform, mingling with the rest of the ship's company so that he would in no way stand out. In the British Navy, memories were long, and Her Majesty the Queen had never before been accused of being as tight as a gnat's arse in public and in a loud voice, which was much more serious than the embezzlement of wardroom funds. Yes, much care would be taken, certainly. Petty Officer Steward Washbrook would not have gone ashore at all had it not been for Maisie Mutch, a youngish woman with whom he had continued to correspond at intervals since leaving Portsmouth (in a hurry) for Chile to join the staff of the C-in-C. Maisie Mutch worked in a public house named the Crown and Jackstaff in an alley leading off Arundel Street in Portsea, a fairish walk from the dockyard but worth it.

As a petty officer, Washbrook was excused another of Admiral Watkiss' foibles: as in any British warship, the junior ratings – leading hands and below – did not simply step ashore down the gangway even though the ship was alongside the berth: they went ashore in boats. Not real boats but metaphorical ones, imaginary ones. Already the earlier pipe had been supplemented by another, one that indicated the time at which the libertyboats, as they were called, would leave the ship. Catching the libertyboat meant falling in for inspection by the Officer of the Watch before going down the gangway. It was neater that way; and if a man was late in falling in he had thus missed the boat and had to await the next one, which might be two hours hence.

There was a good deal of Chilean muttering about this innovation; more muttering when Petty Officer Steward Washbrook was seen to walk down the gangway unimpeded and uninspected by the Officer of the Watch just because he was a petty officer. It wasn't fair that a mere steward, a man whose rate was known variously to the British Navy as po bosun or piss-pot jerker, should have preferential treatment, but such was the British way. Washbrook waited on the jetty for the Chileans to join him: even though they might be hostile, he wished for that anonymity in a crowd, at least until he was out of the main gate. And of course he could always pull his PO's rank if necessary.

As it happened, there was no difficulty. Chattering in Spanish, the Chileans moved through the gate on to the Hard with Washbrook concealed in their midst. He turned left into Queen Street, freeing himself from the smell of garlic.

*

The Keppel's Head Hotel was something of a rendezvous: the evening before, Mr Mayhew of the Foreign Office had arrived there off the railway train from Waterloo and, being a superior person of high rank in the diplomatic service, had dined alone in his room, waited upon by the elderly soup-stained waiter himself. During and after his dinner he had studied documents from a Gladstone bag similar to Detective Inspector Todhunter's, immersing himself in the very serious business of foreign threats to the life of Admiral Watkiss. These threats were being taken with immense weightiness: nothing must be allowed to disturb Her Majesty in her jubilee year, especially during the great occasion of the fleet review.

Next morning, while Mrs Weder-Ublick was in church and Mass was being said aboard the *Almirante Smith*, Mr Mayhew walked into the dockyard just down the road and was checked by Sergeant Sadley.

'Good morning, sir. May I enquire your business, sir?'

'Foreign Office,' Mr Mayhew answered briefly.

'Oh – yessir.' Sergeant Sadley saluted. Mr Mayhew obtained directions as to where the *Taronga Park* was berthed and walked on into the yard. He mounted the gangway shortly after Miss Penn had covered herself modestly.

He tapped at the cabin door and was admitted.

His initial encounter was with Miss Penn.

'Oh, it's you,' she said, he being expected and she recognizing him from the long voyage to Chile many months earlier. Leaning backwards she called out to Halfhyde, 'Bloke from the Foreign Office, mate.'

Halfhyde appeared from the doorway into his sleeping cabin. Mr Mayhew was welcomed aboard. Halfhyde said, 'You've come about Admiral – '

Mr Mayhew raised a hand and made a business of clearing his throat as though to obliterate any naming of names in case of eavesdroppers. 'The less said the better, Captain Halfhyde. I should remind you that . . . certain matters are confidential, and – '

'You may speak with perfect freedom aboard my ship, Mr Mayhew, I assure you.'

'Ah. That's as maybe, Captain. Er . . . perhaps Miss Penn . . . ?'

Halfhyde sighed. Mayhew had been like this all the way out to Valparaiso and leopards didn't change their spots. He said, 'Oh very well. Victoria?'

'Yes, mate?' She had decided to act the innocent. If Halfhyde wanted to chuck her out, he would have to say so.

He scowled, knowing her ways, reading her like a book. 'If you'd be good enough?'

She flared up at him. 'Look, mate. If you want me to bloody make myself scarce, why not bloody say so, eh? I know what I'm supposed to do when the bloody Foreign Office turns up. Bugger off, right?'

Mr Mayhew cleared his throat again. That appalling woman, his face said. The appalling woman pushed past him, went out to the deck, and banged the door shut behind him so that it smote his back and he lurched forward. 'Well, really,' he said.

Halfhyde grinned. 'Think nothing of it. She's Australian.'

'Ah, yes. Yes, of course. Colonials . . .' Mr Mayhew didn't elaborate but his manner spoke for him: colonials were neither one thing nor the other and were certainly beneath the dignity of the Foreign Office. The Colonial Office itself was not in the same bracket as the Foreign Office or the India Office and persons of inferior social status were commonly admitted to it as mere civil servants and not as diplomats. One had perhaps to make allowances for all colonials and especially Australians. And in any case he remembered Miss Penn all too well . . .

He opened his Gladstone bag. He brought out a sheaf of papers, which he shuffled with an air of importance, one that went well with his morning coat and striped trousers, his umbrella and the Gladstone bag of secrets. He lost no time thereafter in coming to the point, which Halfhyde found unusual. 'The threat is positively identified, Captain,' he said. 'That is to say, we have positive knowledge that a band of disaffected Chileans are currently in this country for the purpose of assassinating Admiral Watkiss. Not only that: they are believed to be already here in Portsmouth.' He paused, watching the effect of his announcement, though tending to look two ways at once on account of a squint.

'Then it's really going to happen?' Halfhyde asked.

Mayhew nodded. 'That seems to be quite definite, I fear. Her Majesty – '

'Never mind Her Majesty for now, Mr Mayhew. Have you any names?'

Mayhew looked angry at the curt dismissal of the Queen. 'Yes, we have, Captain Halfhyde. With memories of our sojourn in Chile those names are perhaps not surprising. Not that we have the names of all the participants, the underlings, the actual assassins-to-be. We have the principals.'

'And they are?'

Mr Mayhew took his time: he was a man who liked drama, and being the conveyor of startling news. Shuffling his documents again and peering at them in double focus through gold-rimmed pince-nez, he said, 'One of them is Colonel Opago. The other is General Puga.'

'Ah,' Halfhyde said.

'You remember them, Captain, obviously.'

'Indeed yes.' The Chief of Police in Santiago, and the Commander-in-Chief of the Chilean Army, the latter a much-tasselled man who had been, under the old administration, the opposite number of Admiral Watkiss. Both had suffered as a result of Watkiss' activities. These had been the men upon whom Halfhyde had reflected earlier, the very ones whom Watkiss had outwitted to the extent that they had very nearly been induced to arrest each other in the immense hoo-ha that had enveloped Santiago and Valparaiso as the previous administration had sought to find and arrest Admiral Watkiss on a charge of attempting to put a large spoke in the Chilean wheel on behalf of the Queen of England – acting in the interest of the British Empire rather than that of the Chilean president. And after the recent *coup*, both officers had been deprived of their appointments. It was no wonder they were now after Watkiss' blood; at the same time they would be able to cock a very large and satisfactory snook at the Queen, currently cocooned across Spithead in Osborne House.

Mr Mayhew, to whom one didn't mention the word snook, went on before Halfhyde could utter. 'As I have said, Captain, we don't know the identities of what one might call the cat's-paws. But to know of the principals is half the battle. We should be able to nip the threat in the bud very smartly.'

'How?' Halfhyde asked.

'How?' Mr Mayhew didn't like being asked direct questions. 'At this stage I can't say precisely how. Matters must . . . er . . . develop towards a capture, you know. These things can't be rushed and to, for instance, seek to have Colonel Opago and General Puga arrested in a hurry would be . . . er . . . of little use. The niceties have to be observed as you'll appreciate.'

'You mean it's better to wait till the assassin's revolver is actually aimed at Admiral Watkiss?'

Mayhew shook his head. 'No, in any case they could use a knife. Or anything else – poison in his food, that sort of thing.' He had quite missed Halfhyde's point. 'In any case, that will not be your responsibility and you need not concern yourself with that part of it. The chase and apprehension of the bandits is to be left to Todhunter and Scotland Yard. The diplomatic side of it, naturally, will be mine.' He paused. 'Thus we come to your part, Captain Halfhyde.'

'I'm all agog, Mr Mayhew.'

There was a sharp look. 'I beg your pardon?'

Halfhyde waved a hand. 'Never mind.'

'This is not an occasion for levity, Captain Halfhyde.'

'Indeed not. Her Majesty must on no account be discommoded.'

'Exactly. And to that end the *Taronga Park* and yourself are to be most importantly used.' Mr Mayhew bent closer to Halfhyde, speaking almost into his ear and very furtively.

*

The Crown and Jackstaff was crowded, largely with seamen from the foreign ships that had arrived in the port to do honour to the old Queen of England, the milch cow of Europe as she had been called – she was great-aunt or grandmother to virtually all the crowned heads from Germany to Russia. As well as Germans and Russians there were Frenchmen with pansy-looking pompoms on the tops of their caps, there were Italians and Spaniards and Greeks, the latter vainly demanding *ouzo*, there were Japanese with slit eyes and stunted forms, there were Americans from a battleship, the USS *Earl D. Susler*. All this, plus such sprinkling of British seamen and marines as could fight their way in through the foreigners.

But no Maisie Mutch.

Washbrook made enquiries of the landlord, who expressed astonishment at the Chilean uniform. 'What you doing in that rig, then, eh?'

'Chilean Navy,' Washbrook said briefly. 'PO Steward to the Commander-in-Chief, that's me. Now, what about Maisie?'

'Well. Come to think of it, she did mention as 'ow she'd 'eard from you in Chile. I'm very sorry to say there's bad news, matey.' He gave Washbrook the facts straight: only ten days before the *Almirante Smith* had arrived in Spithead, Maisie Mutch had fallen victim to the horse bus that plied between the dockyard's main gate and the outlying village of Cosham to the north of the town. The fatality had occurred at the top of Arundel Street itself, not far from the Crown and Jackstaff. Maisie Mutch had fallen when climbing aboard and the horse had drawn a wheel over her head.

'Go on,' Petty Officer Steward Washbrook said in tones of disbelief. 'She never!'

'Fact, mate.' The landlord leaned across the bar, shoved a measure of rum across. 'On the 'ouse.'

'Bottoms up,' Washbrook said absently, draining the glass. 'Dead, you said?'

'As a doornail, mate. And buried.' The landlord sucked in his cheeks. ''Orrible sight, like strawberry jam. Just after she'd finished work, too, it were.' Lowering his voice he added, 'Mother's ruin, that's what did it. I'm ever so sorry, mate. Not bin in for a long while you 'aven't, but I do remember you was gone on 'er, like.'

'Yes.' Petty Officer Steward Washbrook cursed beneath his breath. He'd been relying on Maisie Mutch; now he would have to start afresh, always difficult for a seafarer whose time in any port was limited. He returned the landlord's favour with another rum, had another himself and then thought: sod it. The bottle offered quicker and handier solace. One more rum, then he went on to Brickwood's beer, the mainstay of the British Navy when in Pompey. After a while he became aware of a small, dark man who had sidled up alongside him as he stood at the bar. He looked round and met the man's eye. The man gave him a wink.

Washbrook said, 'Wotcher, mate.'

The man disregarded the greeting. He said, 'You like a drink, yes?'

'Got one.'

'One to follow, yes?'

'Don't mind if I do. Brickwood's XXXX.' He added, 'Pint.'

The order was passed, the glass lined up. The small man said 'You wear the naval uniform of my country, which is Chile.'

Washbrook stared and belched. The small man stepped back a pace. Brickwood's beer was as strong on the breath as in the glass. Washbrook said, 'That's right, mate, I do. And 'oo might you be if I might make so bold?'

The small man shrugged his shoulders so deeply that his face almost vanished between them. 'I represent my country, señor. Or mate, perhaps? You are not Chilean?'

'No, I'm not bloody Chilean.' Something of Admiral Watkiss had rubbed off on the steward. 'Mate'll do if you bloody must. But just *'oo* are you, eh?'

'A member of a mission from Santiago, sent as a courtesy to Her Majesty your Queen, señor mate.'

'Oh, ah. Cos o' the jubilee, eh?'

'Yes, that is correct.' The small man watched the swift descent of the Brickwood's and without asking bought another. Washbrook was pleased; thoughts of Maisie Mutch were receding, though she was useful as an excuse: sorrows were there to be drowned. He volunteered some information.

'Chilean rig's cos I'm serving aboard the dago flagship, see? *Almirante Smith*. Special job, like. PO Steward to the Commander-in-Chief 'isself.'

The small man seemed impressed. 'That is so, yes?'

'It's so all right,' Washbrook said grimly. 'Old bugger's British, see, asked for me special, God 'elp me. Old Watkiss, 'e's three parts round the bend and coming up the straight for air.'

'That is so?' the small man asked politely. Washbrook stared into his glass, reflecting on the horrors of life under the Chilean C-in-C. The small man said nothing further about the *Almirante Smith* or about Admiral Watkiss but he did buy more drink, which was satisfactory. After a while he said, 'I like you, my friend. I like you much.'

'Ar.'

'To me you have the appearance of an honest man.'

Petty Officer Steward Washbrook looked surprised. 'Do I?'

'Very much, yes. Tell me, my good and honest friend. Are you interested in the ladies? To be perhaps more precise . . . in the services of a woman?'

'Yes,' Washbrook said. 'Not 'arf.'

TEN

Next morning Admiral Watkiss, about to leave the flagship for the London train and his Admiralty appointment, duly made by the handy offices of Halfhyde, was woken by Leading Steward Escobar.

'*Almirante*, it is seven bells, señor.'

Admiral Watkiss heaved his nightshirted body round in the bed (not bunk; flag officers didn't sleep in bunks). He tweaked at his nightcap, the bobble of which seemed intent upon entering his mouth. He glared at the trembling steward. 'What the devil are you doing here?'

'I bring your tea, *Almirante* – '

'Where the hell's Washbrook?' A leg was thrust out of the bed. To the order of his Admiral, Escobar removed the bedsock.

'*Almirante*, he is – '

'Oh, balls and bang me arse, man, no doubt you're about to trump up some sort of excuse for him. Get me my monocle.'

Leading Steward Escobar gaped: his English was basic and did not include monocle. Admiral Watkiss brought his other foot out of bed and stamped it. 'Oh, God give me strength! Don't you damn well understand English? *Mon – oc – le*. Over there, on my chest-of-drawers.' He pointed. 'Oh, what a blasted fool you are, like all blasted dagoes! *Eyeglass*.' He made eyeglass motions around his right eye and Leading Steward Escobar, scared out of his wits, got the point. He picked up the monocle on its cord and handed it over. The C-in-C thrust it into his eye. Escobar stood as though transfixed by the sight of the snakes, hearts and other emblems tattooed on his Admiral's arms. Watkiss glared through the monocle. 'Now then. Washbrook hasn't returned from shore leave, has he – I knew it! No, don't damn well argue with me, you've had no permission to speak and to speak without permission is an offence against Queen's Regulations, the Articles of War, and the Naval Discipline Act and never mind that this is a damn dago ship – that's fact, I said it. When Washbrook does return, *if* he does since he may have been arrested by the naval patrol, tell him I'm going to have him blasted well flogged round the fleet. Tell him that from me, what's-your-name – '

'Escobar, *Almirante*. Carlos – '

Admiral Watkiss seemed to vibrate. 'Oh, for God's sake, you fool, I didn't ask your blasted name! Get out.'

'*Si Almirante*.' Leading Steward Escobar, sweating like a pig, turned away thankfully. Admiral Watkiss drank tea, then called the steward back.

'What's-your-name. The tea's too strong. Make some more.'

*

Petty Officer Steward Washbrook also awoke somewhat later but, unlike his Commander-in-Chief, woke with a woman in his bed, the woman promised by the member of the mission from Santiago. Up to a point Washbrook had been disappointed in the woman, who had drooping breasts, few teeth, dank hair and a black eye that had appeared when activity in the bed had dislodged the eye patch that she had worn like Admiral Lord Nelson but with a difference. However, it had been the usual seaman's fate of any port in a storm and her services, such as they were, had been provided free by the generosity of the small man from Santiago and you didn't look gift whores too closely in the mouth.

Washbrook's awakening was bleary and it took time for him to sort out fully in his mind the events of the previous night. Certainly the woman with whom he was in bed was not Maisie Mutch: Maisie Mutch – he remembered – had been killed by the horse bus. Stone dead, her erstwhile employer had said. The room he was in was not Maisie Mutch's room. Well, all that was easy enough to sort out, it being, death apart, the kind of situation that had been not unfamiliar to

Petty Officer Steward Washbrook in the past. Different women, different places of performance.

But there was something else; or rather, some*one* else: the small, dark Chilean, currently not present. Washbrook found it hard to believe that the small man was a diplomat, if that was what was implied by his being a member of a mission to the Queen of England from Santiago. Washbrook did not see the Queen consorting with such as the small dark man. His experience as steward in the wardrooms of the fleet had brought him into contact, albeit as a mere servant, with the sort of people likely to have been diplomats had they not instead become naval officers: in a word, nobs. The small dark man was no nob. He had, however, been pretty flush with cash. No less than one hundred golden sovereigns had been passed to Petty Officer Steward Washbrook in a bag of chamois leather.

Washbrook hoped it was still with him, and left the strange woman's bed to check. It was; it was safe beneath his trousers. Washbrook made to get back into the bed, then decided, as the woman began snoring, to look at his watch. Dragging it from his Chilean uniform pocket, he found the time was eight-thirty.

'Blimey,' he said aloud, in a panic now. That old Watkiss, he would be going mad; Leading Steward Escobar was fairly useless in the performance of his duties. Washbrook, forbearing to wake his night-time companion, rushed into his uniform, left the room, blundered about on a sleazy landing, found some stairs carpeted with stained drugget, descended to a narrow hall and exited from the front door which opened directly on to the street, or alley – he recognized the alley, for the Crown and Jackstaff was just a few doors down.

He passed it, moving quickly. And he thought about Admiral Watkiss; thinking, his heart beat like a drum, a muffled drum sounding out a tattoo like they used when a deserter was being hanged. Or a murderer. Or someone who was in the pay of a foreign power. Petty Officer Steward Washbrook, having taken gold, was in the pay of a foreign power, or so he believed. There was another sum yet to be paid, payment being due when he, Washbrook, had carried out his part of the bargain, after which he would be, if not exactly a murderer himself, then certainly an accomplice. An accessory before the fact, he believed the peelers called it. Probably after the fact as well.

The Chilean had been precise. Washbrook, in return for monies both received and due, was to help bring about the demise of his loathed Commander-in-Chief. This was to be achieved in a manner yet to be promulgated: he would be contacted in due course – very soon, in fact. The Chilean would himself board the *Almirante Smith* in the guise of a shoreside stevedore supplying luxuries to officers of flag rank – liquor, cigars, fresh fruit, silken shawls and perfumes and other items most suitable as gifts for ladies who might bestow favours in return.

Petty Officer Steward Washbrook, hastening towards Aggie Weston's and Edinburgh Road and Queen Street *en route* for the main gate into the dockyard, shook with a terrible apprehension. Of course he'd been drunk – tight as a newt in fact, but memory did come back in fits and starts. He had committed himself to a dreadful crime. Naturally, he wasn't going to carry it out – oh, no! At any rate that was what he had determined upon last night – take the money, the down payment which was a fortune to make even an admiral lick his lips, then retreat aboard the *Almirante Smith*, not go ashore again, and then in due course sail back to Valparaiso. He had determined upon this course despite the utterance of threats, which at the time had seemed so unreal as not to be seriously set against the glitter of very present gold. In the light of day, those threats were much more real. The slitting of throats had been stressed, and the arm of Santiago was very long. It came to Petty Officer Steward Washbrook now that there might be much danger in a return to Valparaiso. Indeed, it would be quite lunatic, assuming Admiral Watkiss to be still alive.

What could he do to get out from under while, ideally, still retaining the one hundred gold sovereigns?

*

'I am Admiral Watkiss, Commander-in-Chief of the Chilean Navy,' Watkiss announced importantly to a flunkey at the Admiralty. 'I have an appointment with the Second Sea Lord. Kindly inform him that I am here.'

'Yessir. If you'll be so good as to wait one moment, sir.'

Admiral Watkiss blew out an impatient breath. 'Oh, very well.' It was always the same with the blasted Admiralty, he reflected, they couldn't believe the evidence of their own ears and had always to check what had been told them, as though they had an impostor to deal with. A useless bunch really, men who polished chair-seats with their backsides, men who had never known a violent storm at sea or faced the broadsides of an enemy fleet. Watkiss paraded up and down, brandishing his telescope at nothing in particular, screwing his monocle into his eye in preparation for outfacing the Second Sea Lord, and pondered on the nonsense about threats from the disaffected Chileans: by this time the man Todhunter's story had been backed by Halfhyde and by the naval command at Portsmouth, but Admiral Watkiss had believed none of it. He could scarcely be got at aboard his own flagship; his ship's company might be useless dagoes, inefficient and unseamanlike and probably cowardly if ever they were called upon to fight, say in a skirmish against another South American hotchpotch state such as Argentina, or Peru or whatnot . . . they might be – they were – all of that; but (with the possible sole exception of Captain del Campo) they were loyal to himself. He was their Admiral and they looked up to him, respected him, were indeed, he believed, quite fond of him really. Oh, he had his foibles, he knew that, no use denying it – but they took it in good part and understood that he was that good old British institution, a character. Seafarers, even dago ones, always had a kind of reverence for characters. . . .

Oh, he was safe enough, it was a load of balls and bang me arse. Take Washbrook, for example: true, the man was a blasted rogue to a great extent, would cheat his grandmother out of tuppence-ha'penny and was accustomed to helping himself to his, Watkiss', whisky, restoring the level of the bottle with water – or had until he'd been caught out and threatened with being thrown overboard into the filthy waters of Valparaiso Bay. A scamp, but devoted to his Admiral's service. Good stewards always were; loyalty was their watchword. Washbrook would defend his Admiral to the death, braving any would-be assassin's gun or knife or bomb.

'This way, sir, if you please, sir.'

The flunkey had returned. Admiral Watkiss followed him up an ornate staircase on the walls of which hung portraits of admirals past: the great Lord Nelson of course, Lord Rodney, Lord Howe, Cochrane, Collingwood . . . Sir Ramsey Fetherstonehaugh who had lost half his fleet in a storm in the Bay of Biscay in the fifties but had earned his place on the staircase because he had lost himself as well and was not, after his gallant death, to have blame cast upon his memory. At the head of the staircase waited a person whom Watkiss considered a popinjay, an officer of the navy's paymaster branch, secretary to the Second Sea Lord who, not having a seagoing appointment, was not entitled to that other branch of popinjay, a flag lieutenant.

Admiral Watkiss was ushered into the Second Sea Lord's presence by the popinjay.

'The Commander-in-Chief of the Chilean Navy, sir.'

'Watkiss.' The Second Sea Lord hoisted his body perfunctorily from his swivel chair and almost immediately sank back again. He stared. 'My dear fellow – why the telescope?'

Watkiss bridled. 'Why *not* the telescope, my dear sir?'

'It's – oh, well, never mind. Sit down and put the telescope on the floor beside you. Now then – important business, I believe it was said? I hope I'll not appear rude, Watkiss, my dear fellow, but Her Majesty's jubilee has given me an immense amount of extra work. I found it hard to fit you in, frankly.' He brought out a gold turnip-shaped timepiece. 'I can give you fifteen minutes and I'm afraid that's all.'

'Well, I shall do my best not to detain you longer, Admiral,' Watkiss said ungraciously. 'But really, I – '

'I have the Chaplain of the Fleet due in fifteen minutes. A question of Her Majesty's choice of hymns for the service aboard the *Lord Nelson* after the review.'

The Chaplain of the Fleet, Watkiss thought, a ready ear for his suggestion of a Salvation Navy? At the Second Sea Lord's invitation he sat down and brought out a file of documents. He started on the matter of his back pay. 'As you know, Admiral, I am in addition to being the C-in-C of the Chilean Navy a post captain on the retired list of the Royal Navy. I – '

'Oh. Has that been settled?'

'Yes.'

'I understood that it had not.'

'I assure you it is. In any case, you seem to be aware of my situation – '

'It's been brought to my notice upon a number of occasions, Watkiss – '

'And it's now been settled,' Watkiss stated firmly. 'Not before time I may say.'

'My information is that it has *not* been finally settled.'

Admiral Watkiss grew heated. 'Oh, balls and bang me arse, my dear sir, it was settled when I was undergoing that wretched business in Santiago, being accused, falsely accused, of all manner of things by those blackguards of the previous administration, a set of blasted nefarious – '

'Yes, yes. Persons who, as you know, I think, are intending to assassinate you. Frankly, I believed that this threat might be the reason for your visit here, Watkiss.'

'Well, it isn't. I don't believe any of that, the buggers would never dare. No, it's not that.' Admiral Watkiss waved some of his papers. 'It's the question of my back pay in the rank of captain. I have received none to date. A not inconsiderable sum is owing to me and I wish the matter to be settled while I am in British waters. I ask you to be good enough to authorize the payment of this sum. *That* is the purpose of my visit.' Watkiss sat back with his arms folded and a truculent look on his face. 'Well, my dear sir?'

The Second Sea Lord sighed, but inwardly. He said, 'It's not a matter for me – '

'Oh, yes it is. I – '

'My dear Admiral, at this particularly important time I am quite unable to deal with matters affecting pay. You'll have to refer to the Paymaster Director-General. Get him to sort it out.' The Second Sea Lord gave a thin smile. 'Pull your rank. Not as a post captain in Her Majesty's Fleet but as Commander-in-Chief of the Chilean Navy. I'm sure he'll be found co-operative.'

'I haven't the time, as you should know, to traipse from office to office like – like some damn telegraph boy – '

'Then I suggest you send your flag lieutenant to conduct – '

'I haven't *got* a blasted flag lieutenant,' Watkiss snapped. In

Santiago, he had pressed his case for a popinjay but had been refused and it was a sore point: a popinjay was useful as someone to be sworn at, someone to use as a whipping-boy. 'The blasted dagoes are too mean, the whole damn fleet's run on a shoestring.' He simmered for a few moments, saw the Second Sea Lord glance again at his timepiece surreptitiously drawn from a pocket, and realized that he would get nowhere currently with his claim for his back pay: he would have to go and see the Paymaster Director-General and prise the sum owed out of his money-bags. For now, he must hasten to press his next objective.

He did so. 'There is something else, Admiral.'

'Ah? Then please make haste with it, Admiral.'

Watkiss compressed his lips; he disliked being rushed. 'I have had an idea, and since you are about to talk to the Chaplain of the Fleet, I find this a good opportunity of getting your own views on the matter.'

'Yes?'

'Yes. I propose,' Admiral Watkiss said, screwing his monocle, which had fallen to the end of its cord, back into his eye, 'to form a Salvation Navy.'

The Second Sea Lord gaped.

Admiral Watkiss said, 'Along the lines of the Salvation Army, don't you know. General Booth. In Darkest England and the Way Out.'

'I beg your pardon?'

'Oh, a pamphlet written by the man Booth. Of course, to call himself a general is ridiculous effrontery, we all know that. But the pamphlet contains some good, sound stuff. I – '

'You've read this pamphlet, Admiral?'

'No,' Admiral Watkiss said impatiently. 'But I've heard of it, you see. I've – er – had discussions with Canon Rampling, who as you no doubt know came to England with me aboard my flagship and is currently in attendance upon Her Majesty in – '

'Yes, yes. A Salvation Navy . . . an interesting idea – '

'Cut down drunkenness in the fleet. Buttress the idea of God and His discipline. Sow the seeds of rebellion against dishonesty such as the petty pilfering of stores and equipment – '

'Yes, I – '

'And,' Watkiss went on inexorably, 'to *do good*. Some good anyway . . . leave one's mark on the British fleet as a person whose one thought was for the moral fibre of seamen. Also perhaps welfare,' he added. 'The man Booth fights, for instance, against the evils of prostitution, or so I believe. If the men of Her Majesty's fleet could be – er – weaned away from the temptations to be found in the world's cesspits, then good would have been achieved I fancy.'

'Ah – yes. An uphill task, of course.' With thankfulness in his heart the Second Sea Lord observed his door opening: his secretary entered to announce the arrival of the Chaplain of the Fleet. The Second Sea Lord stood up and held out a hand to Admiral Watkiss.

Watkiss shook it ungraciously, angry at being cut short. 'No doubt you'll mention my idea to the Chaplain of the Fleet,' he said stiffly.

'No doubt.'

Admiral Watkiss picked up his telescope and left the room. He left the Admiralty building, then remembered the Paymaster Director-General and went back in again. No appointment, but he would soon see about that. Commanders-in-Chief were not two a penny and were not to be pushed around by clerks.

He was still in the Admiralty when, to his surprise and gratification, he was given a message that his presence would be welcome back in the Second Sea Lord's office. Two interviews in one day! He preened.

*

The Second Sea Lord had spoken of the Salvation Navy to the Chaplain of the Fleet, the Venerable Archibald Prout, who had laughed heartily, vibrating a well-nourished stomach with his mirth. 'A lunatic suggestion, do you not agree, Admiral?'

'Of course I do.'

'A sort of Admiral Booth.' The chaplain frowned in thought, crossing his gaitered legs. 'I've heard of Watkiss, you know.'

'Who hasn't? More trouble to the navy than a cartload of monkeys. In my opinion he's always been on the brink of his sanity, though I shouldn't say that about the Commander-in-Chief of a foreign navy – a friendly country, now they've had a change of government.' The Second Sea Lord paused expectantly. 'Well, what do we do about the Salvation Navy?'

'Without upsetting Watkiss – and the Chileans?'

'Exactly. One must be circumspect. We want nothing to go wrong in Her Majesty's jubilee year, especially whilst the Chilean flagship's in port. For all I know, Watkiss may have sold the Salvation Navy to Santiago, though I admit he didn't say so.'

The chaplain nodded and inserted a finger between his neck and the constriction of his clerical collar. 'Tricky, very tricky, I should simply say that the idea's being considered, Admiral.'

'At the highest level,' the Second Sea Lord said. 'And then we forget all about it?'

The Venerable Archibald pursed his lips. 'Not forget all about it, I would venture to suggest, Admiral. *Shelve* it. A matter for very deep consideration . . . then we can always blame the Treasury for stinginess.'

'Excellent,' the Second Sea Lord said with relief.

After the departure of the Chaplain of the Fleet, the Second Sea Lord had another visitor, a totally unexpected one who had sought audience through the very highest quarters – the Palace via the Foreign Office – and therefore could not be denied the Second Sea Lord's time. This visitor was from the Chilean Embassy and was plainly in a very disturbed state indeed, almost hissing with suppressed – barely suppressed – indignation and affront. He had a very great deal to say and he said it forcefully and with the production of several sheets of thick, expensive paper each with a bright red seal at its foot. These documents had the appearance of affidavits.

Having listened and read, with his heart sinking into his boots, the Second Sea Lord dismissed his visitor with a promise that his diatribe would be treated with the utmost urgency and seriousness and would be acted upon most sternly. Then he sent for his secretary with a demand that Admiral Watkiss, if still in the building – the Second Sea Lord recalled his own advice as to the Paymaster Director-General – was to be asked to come again to his office before leaving for Portsmouth.

*

'So you've spoken to the Chaplain of the Fleet,' Admiral Watkiss said, beaming happily. 'I'm really most grateful, my dear sir. May one ask what his reaction was?'

'It's being considered,' the Second Sea Lord said briefly.

'At a high level, I trust? No shilly–shallying? I know what the blasted clergy are like if you don't. All gas and gaiters, that's the established Church and its unctuous pillars.' Watkiss was riding the crest of a wave now and he warmed to his theme. 'I envisage the Salvation Navy as being far from unctuous, really down to earth and comprehensible to the lowest seamen on the messdecks. I believe – '

'Admiral, I've not asked you to see me about this – this Salvation Navy idea – '

'Not?' Watkiss was taken flat aback. 'Then may I blasted well ask – '

'I assure you it will be considered at the very highest level. We must wait and see. What I wish to talk to you about is something rather different. Potentially more serious at this time of Her Majesty's review.' The Second Sea Lord got up from behind his desk and, closely targeted by Admiral Watkiss' monocle, went to a big window opening over Horse Guards' Parade where a detachment of Her Majesty's Foot Guards were being surveyed by a slim young officer mounted upon a black horse. Without turning round the Second Sea Lord addressed Admiral Watkiss.

'Admiral, there has been a representation from the Chilean Ambassador.'

'Really,' Watkiss said disagreeably.

'To put no finer point upon it, a complaint about you.'

Admiral Watkiss reddened dangerously. 'About *me*? Is that what you said?'

'Yes.'

'Oh, what balls. What confounded cheek! I've done *nothing* that could possibly call forth a complaint, especially from a dirty little – '

The Second Sea Lord swung round and lifted a hand peremptorily. 'I advise you not to compound the complaint. I understand that "dirty little something or other" was a phrase used in the hearing of the First Secretary from the Chilean Embassy – '

'If it was used, then it was used purely descriptively,' Admiral Watkiss broke in distantly. 'The little bugger – '

'Yes, yes, *yes*! I don't deny that foreigners can be irritating at times, but one must be diplomatic in your position, Admiral. Besides, there is another matter. I understand you have put the captain of your flagship under arrest – '

'Oh, del Campo, yes. Not arrest exactly. I've confined him to his quarters, that's all, and told him only to come out on pain of blasted death, not that I'd actually carry that out, I'm known to be a humane man. Only I *will not have* blasted inefficiency and a total lack of any vestige of seamanship ability.' Admiral Watkiss was growing more and more truculent, seeing himself the victim of a Chilean conspiracy. 'How would *you* like it if your flagship was to enter Portsmouth under the *very eyes* of Her Majesty with the blasted port- and starboard-hand channel buoys draped from your fo'c'slehead like – like a blasted whore's washing? How would you like *that*?'

'Well, of course – '

'And I'll tell you another thing,' Admiral Watkiss went on energetically, picking up his telescope and flourishing it. 'I believe . . . you've spoken of the threat to my life emanating from those unspeakable, despicable blackguards, have you not? Well, I see this damn lying as part and parcel of that, an attempt to assassinate my reputation as – as a man of principle and decent dealing, an officer determined to uphold the best traditions of the British Navy – '

'The Chilean Navy in your case, Admiral.'

'What?' Admiral Watkiss stared. 'Oh, kindly don't split hairs, Second Sea Lord, I detest that sort of thing. I repeat my charge, that the blasted dagoes are out to poison people's minds against me – '

'I think that's scarcely likely – '

'Oh, you do, do you? May one ask why?'

'Because the two factions are on opposing sides. It is the accredited Chilean Ambassador who is making the complaint. It is the discredited persons of the previous administration who are threatening your life, Admiral.'

'Oh. Well, don't you see, that's typical blasted dago? The

buggers are like that, forked tongues like serpents, can't be trusted out of your sight – '

'Admiral, I – '

'With respect, Second Sea Lord, I have a very great deal to say yet and I'd be obliged if you'd do me, as Commander-in-Chief of the Chilean Navy, the courtesy of listening without interruption. After all, my reputation as a fair and respected officer is at stake . . .'

*

The interview over, Admiral Watkiss, seething with fury, almost apoplectic with it, took a hansom cab to Waterloo station and thence the railway train to Porstmouth. From the station he took another cab, past Sergeant Sadley into the dockyard. The cab was directed to where the *Taronga Park* was lying alongside. Admiral Watkiss, bustling up the gangway, was observed by Victoria Penn, who called out a warning to Halfhyde. 'It's the old geezer, mate. Coming aboard.'

There was only one old geezer in Victoria's book. Halfhyde emerged from his cabin in time to meet Admiral Watkiss at the head of the ladder from the after well-deck.

Watkiss was breathless. 'Halfhyde, my dear fellow. A pleasure to see you.'

'And to see you, sir.' Halfhyde threw a stern look at Victoria; he had caught a suppressed giggle.

'Kind of you to say so. I dare say you're busy – I realize that, of course. Her Majesty . . . but I'd much appreciate a word in your quarters.'

'Most certainly, sir. Er – in private?'

'What? Of course, you fool . . . oh, I understand, my dear fellow, your woman. I don't mind her.' Watkiss was magnanimous in his hour of need. 'She may as well know how blasted badly those buggers at the Admiralty have treated me. As bad in their own way as the dago buggers.'

'Language,' Victoria said. 'Remember there's a lady bloody present, mate, eh?'

'I'm sorry. Now, Halfhyde, if I may intrude upon your time.'

Halfhyde, believing that something very drastic must have occurred to make Watkiss so unaccustomedly polite, ushered him into his quarters and called for his steward. Whisky was ordered and brought in on a tray, and was consumed by Admiral Watkiss very thankfully.

A little refreshed he said, 'My dear fellow, would you believe it, I've been the subject of a complaint by those dagoes! Stupid buggers are so blasted thin-skinned, don't you know. Can't take a ticking off. Especially that dolt del Campo . . . doesn't like being confined to his quarters, though I should have thought he'd be happy enough to be relieved of his responsibilities and sit around in an atmosphere of pansy scent like a whore's parlour.' He gave a cough. 'My apologies, Miss – er.'

'Penn,' Victoria said, doing her best to keep a straight face. 'Sounds like yer being misunderstood, mate, eh?'

'Yes,' Admiral Watkiss said, sounding pathetic. 'I'm grateful that you at all events understand me. I've always done my best, you know. I've tried to keep up standards, after all.'

'You bet,' Victoria said encouragingly. 'What have they been on at you about, eh?'

'They appear to think I was rude and – and overbearing was, I think, the word used. That Second Sea Lord . . . blasted nincompoop I call him, Halfhyde – '

'*Did* you call him that, sir?'

'Yes.' Admiral Watkiss had a beaten look. 'Perhaps I should not have done. What do you think, Halfhyde? As you know, I've always valued your opinion.'

'I would say it was possibly indiscreet, sir.'

'I dare say you're right,' Admiral Watkiss said dejectedly. 'I might perhaps have put it differently. But, you see, the bugger had fobbed me off about my claim for my back pay, he'd been mealy-mouthed about my idea for a Salvation Navy, and he seemed to believe all this claptrap from the blasted dagoes. It was natural for me to call him a nincompoop since he is one, and as you know, I'm a man who tries always to speak the truth without fear or favour and on the whole I'm pretty forbearing, I've always thought.' He held his glass aloft for a refill; this was forthcoming. More pathetic than ever, he said, 'You're my mainstay, my dear fellow. You've never failed me yet and I trust you won't damn well fail me now. It would be monstrously disloyal and ungrateful when I'm in so much blasted difficulty brought upon me by jealous persons. Do you know what?' As Halfhyde and Miss Penn waited in consuming curiosity, Admiral Watkiss dropped his bombshell. 'That nincompoop . . . thoroughly taken in by that jackass del Campo and the dagoes from the Chilean Embassy . . . even used my well-meant idea of a Salvation Navy against me . . . said I'd been hallucinating, what blasted cheek, and that I'd been under strain and wasn't well.' Spilling whisky, he raised his free arm and shook a fist in the air. 'The buggers are going to put me before a blasted medical board, a set of damn quacks to sit in blasted judgment on my blasted sanity!'

ELEVEN

'Ah, Todhunter.'

Detective Inspector Todhunter rose from his luncheon table and stood respectfully: the Foreign Office was a most important institution and its gentlemen were of the very highest social class; in addition he knew Mr Mayhew. 'Yes, Mr Mayhew, sir, how can I be of assistance?'

'I take it you've finished lunch?'

'Oh yes, sir, indeed I have.' Mr Todhunter had not, in fact, yet had his pudding, which was jam roly-poly and one of his favourites, just as it had been his old mother's, but one did not allow even jam roly-poly to come between oneself and one's duty to accede to the wishes of the Foreign Office. 'I am at your service, Mr Mayhew, sir.'

'Yes. There are certain matters . . . you'll kindly come to my room. But clandestinely.'

Mr Todhunter gave a start. When gentlemen bade you come to their bedrooms clandestinely, certain constructions could well be placed upon their motives; but surely not in Mr Mayhew's case? No, of course not. Mr Todhunter, to whom as a detective suspicion came naturally, recovered himself. 'I understand, Mr Mayhew. I shall of course take all precautions.'

Mr Mayhew nodded, turned away and strode briskly from the dining-room. That day's luncheon was attended only by Mrs Weder-Ublick, Todhunter apart. Mr Mayhew nodded to the lady and gave a tight bow. Mr Todhunter reflected that both he and Mr Mayhew were known to Mrs Weder-Ublick from their former sojourn together aboard the *Taronga Park* to be associates (of a sort) and that therefore Mr Mayhew had felt it safe to have a brief conversation without arousing any curiosity or suspicion. In the interests of being clandestine, Mr Todhunter, seeing the jam roly-poly on its way to the table, decided to have it and thus allow a decent interval between Mr Mayhew's departure and his own. He ate, as did Mrs Weder-Ublick, and having eaten left the dining-room, making for the gentlemen's lavatory. With his lunch he had drunk three glasses of water: his old mother had always instilled into him the advantages of taking liquid (non-alcoholic), and of what she had termed a good flush through. This time, there was the added element of being clandestine. His visit concluded, Mr Todhunter took his bowler hat from the hatstand in the hall and went out on to the Hard, moving towards the dockyard gates. After a few yards he gave a propagandic tongue-click of self-annoyance, for you never knew who might be within earshot, and turned back into the Keppel's Head. Very neatly done, he thought with some pride, just what his Chief Super would have recommended. He went upstairs, ostensibly to fetch some forgotten object from his bedroom, then cautiously deviated and tapped on Mr Mayhew's door.

The door was opened immediately, rather startling Mr Todhunter, who took an involuntary step backwards. Mr Mayhew looked annoyed. 'You've taken your time, Todhunter,' he said.

'Very sorry indeed, sir. I thought – '

'Yes, well, never mind. Come in.'

Mr Todhunter stepped inside, holding his bowler hat respectfully across his chest.

'Sit down, Todhunter, and listen.' Mr Mayhew indicated a leather-cushioned chair near a wardrobe. This reacted when Mr Todhunter sat down, making a noise unfortunately rather vulgar for which any apology would only have made matters more pointed. But Mr Mayhew appeared not to have noticed.

'Admiral Watkiss,' he said.

'Yes, sir?'

'I've received word by the telephone from Whitehall, Todhunter.'

'Whitehall, yes, sir.' There was reverence in Mr Todhunter's tone.

Mr Mayhew said, 'Disturbing word really, though useful in a sense. It seems that Admiral Watkiss is to go before a naval medical board at 10 a.m. tomorrow, perhaps, though this is not stated, to assess his fitness to take part in the review. There seems to be some doubt as to his – er – general health.'

'I see, sir.'

Mayhew gave a thin, wintry grimace that might have been an attempt at a smile. 'I rather doubt you do, Todhunter, but be that as it may. The fact is – and this runs in parallel, to my mind, with Admiral Watkiss' – er – illness, or shall we say could be said so to do.' The Foreign Office man broke off and looked confused, as well he might, Todhunter thought for he also was in a state of some confusion. 'Where was I?'

'Admiral Watkiss' illness, Mr Mayhew, sir, and a parallel.'

'Oh, yes. Now, I've come to believe for certain reasons that I'm not at present free to divulge, that Admiral Watkiss is likely, if found fit, to be under the greatest threat during the course of the fleet review itself.'

'The Chilean threat, do you mean. sir?'

Mr Mayhew looked impatient. 'Of course. What else for heaven's sake? For one thing, and this is self-evident and is not in any way secret information, an assassination carried out in the presence, the very presence, of Her Majesty, would have much more impact than any clandestine act, do you not agree?'

'Oh, yes, Mr Mayhew, sir, very much more impact without a shadow of a doubt. But, if I may, sir, I ask myself another question, and it's this: why should the Chilean renegades *wish* to make such an impact? With respect like, sir.'

'What?'

'I mean, sir, their main objective, their *only* objective to the best of my knowledge, sir, is Admiral Watkiss himself?'

'Yes and no,' Mr Mayhew answered.

'I see, sir,' Mr Todhunter said doubtfully.

'I think I shall break no secrecy by giving you my own views and interpretations, Todhunter, and this I shall do.'

'Thank you very much, sir.' Todhunter looked immensely grateful and flattered.

'I believe, and of course I'm not at liberty to quote chapter and verse, as you'll realize – '

'Of course, sir – '

'I believe that there are, or could be, what one might call wheels within wheels.'

Mr Todhunter was listening attentively. 'Yes, sir.'

'Trade, you know. Trade is very important – trade with Chile. Supplies of, oh, very many things. Guano, nitrates, copper and silver ore . . . gold, manganese, tanned leather goods and so on. Also our British exports to Chile – textiles, oils, combustibles, mineral products, machinery. You must understand the importance of all this.'

Mr Todhunter's bottom had crept to the very edge of his chair: he was agog. 'Oh, yes, Mr Mayhew, sir, indeed I do, most certainly.'

'To us. And to the Chilean government.'

'Yes, indeed.'

'It would be a sad day if matters should go awry. These Chilean renegades, the instigators of the threat to assassinate the Commander-in-Chief of their own country's fleet, could *wish* for that. Could *plot* for that.'

'Er . . .'

'Note that I said *could*. Not *are*. That is an important distinction, Todhunter.'

'Oh yes, indeed, sir, I'm aware of that.'

'Perhaps I should explain.' The diplomat furrowed his brow; explanations, candid ones at all events, came hard to the Foreign Office, but he tried. 'It is my view, my own view, not in any way the official view – so far as I know – that the renegades may wish to regain power through the actions of their anonymous agents currently here in Britain, indeed almost certainly in Portsmouth, by showing up their supplanters in power in Santiago as unable to protect even their own naval C-in-C. Show them up before the whole world. Now, in my own view that would have, or could have, a most serious effect on trade, and the new administration in Chile would also take the popular blame for the ensuing impoverishment of all classes. We, the British, after such an affront to Her Majesty in her jubilee year, and especially during her presence at the review, would doubtless abrogate all trading agreements. Foreign nations would be likely to follow suit – foreigners, Todhunter, are like apes, they tend to copy great nations, would you not agree?'

'Oh yes, sir. Foreigners are funny, there's no doubt about that. My old mother, she used to – '

'Yes. Well, Todhunter, that's my summary and I intend to act upon my assumption that the assassination attempt will be made after the *Almirante Smith* has taken up her station in the review lines – and most likely of all at the very moment that Her Majesty is passing the Chilean flagship. And so I intend to circumvent such a *dastardly* act of cowardice. I shall take the steps necessary to frustrate it.'

'Yes, I see, sir. May I – '

'If the medical board passes Admiral Watkiss as fit, I shall instruct Captain Halfhyde to embark Admiral Watkiss aboard the safety of his own ship, Todhunter.'

'The *Taronga Park*, sir? And Admiral Watkiss will attend the review aboard the *Taronga Park*, sir, is that the idea?'

'Yes. And since he insists, apparently, that he is a post captain in the Royal Navy, then I shall arrange that he attends as such, an appropriate disguise I fancy which he can scarcely refuse to adopt. On the other hand . . . it may well be better, safer, if he attended as something else altogether. But we shall see.'

Mr Todhunter nodded, but cautiously and with reserve. There was, in Mr Todhunter's view, a high degree of barminess around; for one thing, knowing Admiral Watkiss as well as he had come to in times past, he doubted very strongly that Watkiss would allow himself (as a Chilean?) to be prised away from his flagship . . . but, of course, Mr Mayhew would no doubt have the means of persuasion; no one would wish to be assassinated, naturally.

*

The arrangements for the Queen's tour of the slums of Portsea Island had been put in hand some months previously. These things took time and organization; the tour was not to be an informal one. The Queen was adamant that it was not to be and she had been terse with her Prime Minister, Lord Salisbury, when he had murmured about the unwisdom inherent in approaching the poor too closely. He had hinted at the prevalent diseases emanating from slum dwellings and he had pontificated briefly on the rise of Socialism, an evil thing that Her Majesty should keep decently clear of. He had referred to Keir Hardie.

'Who is he, Lord Salisbury?'

'An agitator, ma'am.'

'Will he be in Portsmouth?' the Queen asked.

'Not to my knowledge, ma'am. He . . . agitates mostly in Scotland as I understand. In any case, he can be kept away by the police force.'

'Well, then! What a fuss about nothing, Lord Salisbury.' The Queen stared at the Prime Minister through her raised lorgnette. 'You are becoming a fusspot, Lord Salisbury, as bad in many ways as Mr Gladstone. The tour will be properly conducted. We consider that to be a mere politeness to the common people, who *expect* to see us in formal surroundings and properly escorted. We must never forget that our position depends on the people themselves, upon their goodwill – which we understand is immense. So much cheering and waving when we appear in London. No, we shall *not* disappoint the poor of our premier naval port. They are all such *very* loyal souls.'

So the full fandango was mounted for the Tuesday. On Monday afternoon, horse trucks were attached to a special train from Waterloo to carry the horses of a Sovereign's Escort of the Life Guards, which was to be commanded by one Major Ames said, at six foot eight inches, to be the tallest officer in the British army. A half-battalion of foot guards found by the Coldstream occupied the passenger section of the horse train. This escort would be supplemented on the day by two companies of the Border Regiment stationed in the town, and by a guard of seamen in belts, chin-stays and gaiters plus rifles with bayonets fixed, routed out from the barrack hulks in the dockyard. A detachment of the Royal Marine Light Infantry would bring up the rear of Her Majesty's procession, and from Southsea Common, as she disembarked from a launch at the Clarence Pier, a battery of the Royal Marine Artillery would fire a Royal Salute, thus alerting the poor of Portsmouth that they were about to be inspected. And as, on that Monday afternoon, the troops and sailors and marines of the Portsmouth Command were marched up and down on the common, shouted at by sergeant-majors and drill-sergeants and gunners' mates from the barrack hulks, Petty Officer Steward Washbrook, still biting his nails, was approached, clandestinely, by a would-be assassin.

*

Having been given encouragement and moral support in his distress by Halfhyde and, in her own way, by Miss Penn, Admiral Watkiss had repaired aboard the *Almirante Smith*, back to his normal bounciness. He was not, he had said to Halfhyde, going to be brow-beaten by any blasted Second Sea Lord and still less by any doctor or, as he put it, any damn naval surgeon masquerading as a doctor.

'I've asked to be examined, if the buggers must examine me, by the Medical Inspector-General himself. They were evasive about that, just like them . . . I may find myself fobbed off with some blasted fleet surgeon, but in any case I'm not going to damn well co-operate, damned if I am.'

'Good on yer, mate,' Victoria said. 'Just you keep your spirits up and don't let 'em sit on you, eh?'

'I have no intention of allowing anything of the sort, young woman, I assure you. And I'm not going to crawl to that pansy bugger del Campo either.'

'That's the stuff,' Victoria said, grinning. As Admiral Watkiss set foot on the gangway in order to leave the ship, she leaned forward and kissed him. Watkiss was so astonished that he was for once speechless. As he went down the gangway he overheard the young woman's loud remark to Halfhyde: 'Thought the poor old geezer could do with a bit of love, mate.' The remark didn't entirely spoil the kiss itself; it was a long time since Admiral Watkiss had been kissed, although for one dreadful moment when he had first met Captain del Campo he had believed the little bugger was about to ingratiate himself with a kiss . . . Of course to embrace in public was common and just showed her breeding or lack of it, but it had been most kindly meant he was sure. And it did quite a lot for his ego on that bleak day, just to know that he was still kissable.

In a softened mood he went aboard his flagship. No side party to greet him, no commander to salute him aboard. Naturally, in the circumstances, no Captain either. Admiral Watkiss' eagle eye noted untended lines, hanging judases drooping over the battleship's side and a splodge left by a seagull right where his foot took the quarterdeck. However, he said nothing: it just might be better if he watched his step until after this stupid medical board was out of the way. He went himself to Captain del Campo's quarters and pushed past the sentry on the entry port. He found Captain del Campo asleep in an armchair and unceremoniously woke him up.

'You can come out now,' he said ungraciously. 'But remember – no more smashing into blasted buoys. Understood?'

'*Si, Almirante. Muchas gracias, Almirante.*'

The little bugger, Watkiss thought, had almost turned himself into a reef knot. But he, Watkiss, had behaved well, done the right thing, it was absolute balls and bang me arse to say he was sick or under too much strain. But he did wish, in retrospect, that he hadn't made so much of a to-do about his alternative status as a post captain RN. He now had more than a suspicion he was being boarded under that rank and nationality; they couldn't really have boarded him as an admiral of the Chilean Navy.

Making for his own quarters he found a man lurking by the door into his steward's pantry. This person, a dago by the look of him, was talking to Petty Officer Steward Washbrook.

'Washbrook.'

'Yessir – '

'Who's that man and what the devil is he doing aboard my flagship?'

The man answered for himself, giving a greasy smile. 'Señor *Almirante*, I offer luxuries for officers, cheap to admirals for the great honour of serving ... powerful perfumes, tablets of much scented soap – aphrodisiacs such as Spanish Fly – other toiletries and cosmetics – '

'Get out.'

'But señor – '

'*Get out of my sight – and get off my flagship*! If you don't vanish before I've counted to five I'll have you damn well castrated by the ship's butcher.'

Before the man vanished, Watkiss caught a very curious look passing briefly between him and Washbrook. Admiral Watkiss ground his teeth angrily. Typical of Washbrook, always on the lookout to make a dishonest penny . . . no doubt he'd bought some of the dago's filthy soap and would sell it to his Admiral on the return voyage at a huge profit to himself. Aphrodisiacs, indeed!

*

Certainly Petty Officer Steward Washbrook had that huge profit in prospect but it was not to be earned from the sale of soap. He was very much on the horns of his dilemma. He had not withdrawn from the bargain; if he did so, and if he uttered a single word in the wrong place, then he knew very well that his throat would be cut. He knew that for a certainty; the Chileans were like that, they kept their threats. His throat would be cut, if not here in Pompey then in Chile. Or even at sea, on the voyage back to Valparaiso. Murder was so easily done at sea, and bodies were so easily and cleanly disposed of, and it was a pound to a penny the assassins would have another accomplice, maybe more than one, aboard the flagship. Washbrook's life wouldn't be worth a fish's tit, which was an expression he'd picked up from Admiral Watkiss.

But actually to murder Admiral Watkiss, a fellow Briton! The old sod had asked for it, of course he had, but even so Petty Officer Steward Washbrook shrank from murdering him in cold blood. The hangman's noose was a very tight thing, and final. No appeal, no miss-musters, no second chance.

Petty Officer Steward Washbrook sweated into his white duck tunic with the blue badges of his rank on his arm. Chancing his arm – that was what sailors called the act of crime. Guilty, and away went the PO's crossed anchors and good conduct stripes, not that Washbrook had any of the latter after that business with the Queen and the embezzlement of wardroom stores. But stuff his rank; it was his bloody neck now. Or his throat. The enormity of what he'd committed himself to smote him suddenly like a wet haddock, the haddock simile coming to him because old Watkiss had always been partial to a nice, fresh haddock. Would haddock – come to think of it – disguise the taste of curare, of which a packet had that day been handed over for use as Washbrook, with his intimate knowledge of his Admiral's ways, thought best and safest?

But could he bring himself to do it, watch the awful contortions of a human being in his death throes? And could he skate out from under afterwards? The Chilean agent had gone into ways and means that had sounded more or less foolproof, but now they didn't seem so foolproof after all. Washbrook, if he wasn't very fly indeed, was going to get it in the neck.

The neck again! Washbrook felt his neck as if for the very last time. Terror struck like a shaft of lightning. Bugger it, it had been the drink to blame. For the first time in his life Petty Officer Steward Washbrook regretted his habit of thirst. From now on he would lay off the bottle. If he had time, that was. If only he had someone to talk to, someone in whom he could confide and seek advice. But you couldn't confide about murder, not really you couldn't, except perhaps to a reverend, a Bible basher.

'Bloody hell,' Washbrook said to himself aloud. That Canon Rampling . . . he was staying in Pompey with a fellow reverend – the ever-open steward's ears of Washbrook had, during the voyage from Valparaiso, picked up that bit of information. The bloke, the reverend bloke, at St Thomas' – that should be easy enough to find.

Why hadn't he thought of that before? Rampling had seemed a decent sort of cove, big and jovial, generous with his tips, a sort of father-figure.

He was the obvious one. The only one, seeing as Maisie Mutch had been squashed flat.

Petty Officer Steward Washbrook thought fast. Old Watkiss wouldn't allow him to go ashore again, not after he'd been adrift over leave and left His Nibs to Leading Steward Escobar. Not without a proper reason. Washbrook racked his brains.

Onions.

Old Watkiss, he was partial to onions, like he was partial to haddock. Washbrook in fact had a stock of onions in the Admiral's personal store, because there was always the devil to pay if he ran out, but he needn't have them for long. Acting with the speed of light Petty Officer Steward Washbrook made his way to the Admiral's store where the sack of onions lay. He hefted the sack to the upper deck, made his way unseen (for the gangway staff were smoking cigars in the quartermaster's lobby) to a lifeboat, lifted the heavy canvas cover, and shoved the sack into the boat. No one ever checked the lifeboats and once the ship was at sea again the sack could very easily be shoved overboard and no one would ever know. This done, Washbrook went along to the Admiral's quarters to report an omission of duty that could very quickly be put right as a result of a run ashore.

TWELVE

'You're a blasted useless fool, Washbrook.'

'Yessir. Sorry, sir.'

'Oh, what's the use of being blasted well sorry? What's done is done and I have to suffer for it! What a blasted apology for a steward you are. How you ever came to be rated petty officer in the British fleet I shall never know. About as much blasted use as a bishop in a brothel, aren't you?'

'Yessir. But if I go – '

'Oh, hold your tongue, Washbrook, do. It so happens it doesn't matter this time. I shall be dining with Captain Halfhyde aboard his ship. Tomorrow's a different matter. You'll go ashore first thing after my breakfast and buy onions. Is that clear?'

'Yessir. If I may suggest it like, sir, I can go this afternoon, sir – '

'Oh no you can't. I shall require a bath before leaving for the *Taronga Park* and I can't damn well trust you to be back in time to see the damn bathwater's available and *hot*, one can't trust those blasted Chilean engineers to do anything right. No, you'll go tomorrow.'

'Sir, if I – '

Admiral Watkiss raised his telescope. 'Oh, don't damn well *argue* with me, Washbrook. Just do as you're told and be thankful I'm a reasonable man.'

*

The launch bearing Her Majesty neared the disembarkation pontoon at the Clarence Pier. From Southsea Common the Royal Marine Artillery barked out its Royal Salute. In the launch, proceeding inwards over a choppy sea and with the channel still bare of its port- and starboard-hand buoys, Her Majesty was being prepared for the business of getting out on to the pontoon. Over her black bonnet had been rigged a length of ribbon, like the griping-band of a seaboat, to hold it in place against the wind coming from the south-west quarter. The trip had not been very pleasant and the Queen, feeling the onset of *mal-de-mer*, had been tiresome although naturally no one would have spoken the word. She had berated her lady-in-waiting, a duchess also suffering from the motion. She had been sharp with the terrified midshipman in command of the launch. But as ever she kept a stiff upper lip and merely grunted bad-temperedly when two beefy seamen under the charge of a petty officer with a ginger beard placed themselves about her person and lifted her off her feet to set her down on the pontoon which bore a red carpet over its normal seaweed and barnacles. Her Majesty was then assisted up some iron steps similarly covered. When she reached the pier's deck, a band provided by the Royal Marine Light Infantry blared out 'God Save the Queen' and all present, including the Lord Lieutenant of the county, the Mayor of Portsmouth, the Chairman of the Board of Guardians, the Bishop of Winchester, the Portsmouth garrison commander, the Naval Commander-in-Chief, the Governor of Portsmouth Gaol, some miscellaneous minor dignitaries and the sub-dean of the Chapels Royal (but not, after all, Canon Rampling) all snapped to attention and saluted their monarch and her loyal tune.

When all this was over the Queen spoke urgently in an aside to her lady-in-waiting. The lady-in-waiting was seen to be in some embarrassment but she coped nobly and approached the sub-dean of the Chapels Royal who immediately understood and conferred, also *sotto voce*, with one of the minor dignitaries. While the guard and band remained rigidly at attention, the scarlet-clad officers still with their swords presented, the Queen was placed in the bath chair that had now been carried up from the launch, and was wheeled away by the lady-in-waiting to a hidden place indicated to the sub-dean by the local dignitary. This was an unfortunate delay and was attributable to the cracking of the royal chamber pot during the crossing from

Osborne House, the pot in question being of naval pattern as used aboard the royal yacht, and described in the Naval Rate Book as pot, chamber, with two gold bands and crown, for use of HM The Queen. The late Prince Consort had had only one gold band.

When Her Majesty was ready, she was transferred from the bath chair to an open carriage drawn by two black horses, and the procession got under way.

*

'Oh, the Admiral's steward from the *Almirante Smith*, yes. What does he want?' Canon Rampling clicked his tongue; annoyed at being left out of the royal tour of Portsmouth's needy he was communing quietly with his Maker and asking forgiveness for the sins of annoyance and jealousy: the sub-dean of the Chapels Royal had been ordained a good ten years after himself and yet he was part of the retinue and it wasn't fair. He addressed the Reverend William Scale's parlourmaid again. 'What did you say, Hawkins?'

'I said 'e didn't say, sir. Just said it was private.' The girl added, 'He seemed in a state, sir. Upset.'

Canon Rampling sighed; but a lack of charity was another sin and the matter might be important. It might concern Admiral Watkiss who was in a sense a parishioner, a floating one. 'Oh, very well,' he said, 'perhaps you'd better send him in.'

Petty Officer Steward Washbrook was brought in and the servant was dismissed. Canon Rampling stared thoughtfully. The man was undoubtedly upset, very upset, quite green as to his complexion, and he was shaking. 'Well, Washbrook, what is it? Has something happened to Admiral Watkiss, is that it? Is he unwell?'

'No, sir. Not yet, sir.'

Rampling raised his shaggy eyebrows. 'Not yet? I don't think I quite follow, Washbrook. Kindly explain, and tell me how I can help.'

'Yessir.' Washbrook cleared his throat noisily. Never before had he invoked the Church and he was uncertain as to the proper procedures. After a few moments he blurted it out. 'Confessions like, sir.'

144

'Confessions? My good man, I'm not a Roman! We of the Church of England don't normally hear confessions, and there's a perfectly good RC padre aboard the *Almirante Smith*, is there not?'

'Yessir, but not being a candle meself, like, I preferred to approach a Church of England gennelman like you, sir. A gennelman of the cloth. English like. And you always such a kind and thoughtful gennelman, sir, what is respected by all, including even them candles, sir.'

Canon Rampling closed his eyes for the second time at the disrespectful reference to the Church of Rome but forbore to offer a rebuke, for the man was clearly distressed and anyway he had been much pleased by the testimonial, a rare thing in his experience. In a kindly voice he enquired, 'Are you in some personal difficulty, Washbrook?'

Washbrook blew out a long breath of relief at having got this far; the old Holy Joe seemed very friendly. 'Not 'arf, sir,' he said.

*

The poor of Porstmouth were dressed in their collective best bib and tucker in honour of Her Majesty, grateful for her kindly interest in their welfare. Bunting had been rigged everywhere by the town council, flags of all descriptions hung from lampposts and windows, the Union Flag of course predominating and the flag of the German Emperor nowhere to be seen, for it was well known that the dear Queen detested the Kaiser, never mind that he was her grandson. Loyalty was everywhere; it was nice to have someone to cheer at, wave flags at. Two known Socialists had been arrested on trumped-up charges and would be held in custody until after the tour. The hordes of small urchins had had their noses wiped and had been generally cleaned up and threatened with all manner of retribution if they should let their parents down in front of the Queen. They had been spoken to particularly about not urinating in the street and not using their normal language in Her Majesty's hearing. They had all promised to behave; if they were good, the old lady might chuck them a ha'penny.

It was a really splendid occasion. The brass blared out soldierly tunes; 'Goodbye Dolly Gray' boomed its way past the Town Hall, and further on in Commercial Road the Landport Drapery Bazaar, buried behind its loyal display of flags and notification of a forthcoming bargain week, was treated to a spirited 'Soldiers of the Queen', and then, as the Royal Marine Light Infantry in rear faded towards Arundel Street, the stirring strains were heard of 'We Don't Want to Fight, But by Jingo if We Do, We've Got the Ships, We've Got the Men, We've Got the Money Too'.

Bosoms everywhere along the route swelled with pride and many a manly eye was wiped as the old Queen passed by, looking, it was later noted in the *Portsmouth Evening News*, a trifle morose. But this the poor of Portsmouth understood and sympathized with: it was hard for an old lady on her own, still missing the comforting presence of Prince Albert and known to have many disagreements with the Prince of Wales, who like all sons – didn't they just know! – was a bloody pain in the arse at times. Her Majesty had much to put up with though her lot must have been much happier since she'd got rid of that Mr Gladstone, this being a reflection on the part of the Conservatives present.

The cheers, naturally, were deafening. Even though they must have been used to it, the horses of the Life Guards grew restive as the head of the procession turned into Arundel Street, off which led sundry insalubrious roads of slum dwellings. On the turn Major Ames was unseated and rolled away from the horses' hooves in almost the very spot where Maisie Mutch had been squashed by the wheels of the horse bus. At this Her Majesty looked very annoyed and was seen in discussion with her lady-in-waiting. As the procession turned into one of the alleys there was a total log-jam and the Chief Constable rode forward to sort it out. A certain amount of strong language was uttered and the adjacent urchins looked delighted. They took immediate advantage.

'Garn, if me dad 'eard me talk like that, 'e'd take a belt to me arse!'

'One o' them sodjers said fuck.' This was greeted with a storm of approval. A policeman was heard to use the equally

146

disapproved-of bugger, which called forth more delight. Then a furious mother went into action, fat arms flailing at juvenile ears; joined by others, she secured victory. The urchins grinned and dodged but wisely took account of the threat to have their mouths washed out with vinegar. The Life Guards and the rest of the military, plus the seamen, rode or marched ahead past the turning while Her Majesty's carriage was drawn into the alley towards the homes of the poor, the Mayor of Portsmouth walking by its side together with the Lord Lieutenant, the Bishop of Winchester and the Chairman of the Board of Guardians.

The lady-in-waiting was seen to pass a handkerchief, no doubt impregnated with eau-de-cologne, to Her Majesty, who held it delicately beneath her nose.

From her carriage, she leaned forward graciously and addressed a stout woman wearing an apron made from a sack. 'How very nice,' she said, 'for us to be made so very welcome.'

The woman curtsied clumsily. 'Yes, Your Majesty, thank'ee, Your Majesty.'

'How very nice to talk to you. That wretched boy is picking his nose.' The stout woman turned in horror, the boy was assailed and the carriage moved on as his protests rent the air. The Queen nodded and bowed to right and left and then, half way along and quite close to the Crown and Jackstaff, called for the Bishop of Winchester who hastened to her side, he having been intercepted by the loyal flag-waving of the people. He was somewhat out of breath, his mitre was awry and he was clasping his crook, not as God's instrument to shepherd straying sheep, but more as a club, a weapon of defence.

'Your Majesty. . . .'

'What proportion of the people in the Portsmouth area of your diocese, Bishop, are regular churchgoers?'

The Bishop drew a figure from the air. 'Ninety per cent, ma'am.'

'Really? That's very good news. But tell me, what are you doing about the others?'

'The others, ma'am?' The Bishop had been caught off his guard.

'That is what I asked, Bishop, the others, those who do *not* attend regularly.'

The bishop, who had in fact done nothing, preferring to allow discretion to his many parish clergy, dredged up another answer. 'I do the will of God, ma'am – '

'So we would expect. That is very right and proper. But pray, what is the will of God in this matter?'

The bishop opened his mouth in an ungainly gape, lost for a suitable reply to what he considered a stupid question, for it must be obvious that God would want everyone to attend church, but God came to his assistance very fortuitously when one of Her Majesty's horses relieved itself with an embarrassing splodge. The Queen instantly turned her face away and small boys dashed towards her carriage with buckets and shovels: horse manure sold for a penny a bucket to the residents of Southsea with large gardens.

The procession moved on, reached the end of the street and turned left along a similar street. No ha'pennies had been cast from the Queen's carriage and she left behind her murmurs of discontent from the urchins at such stinginess. Such were the outraged comments of one barefoot youth that his mother took a swipe at him with a hefty hand. 'That's enough o' that, you grasping little bugger,' she said. ''Er Majesty 'as *Buckingham Palace* to keep up! Just you sod orf before she 'ears yer.'

*

Admiral Watkiss took no part in the procession having other engagements that day, and of course as a visitor from a foreign country the poor of Portsmouth were none of his concern, so he wouldn't have been included anyway, but it still rankled. It would have been a tremendously valuable opportunity to press home his idea of a Salvation Navy, a concept that the Queen, as a devoted churchgoer, could not have failed to appreciate. But perhaps another chance would come.

He had been woken with his cup of tea by Petty Officer Steward Washbrook, prior to the latter going ashore on his ostensible onion hunt. Making the tea in his pantry, Washbrook's mind had been on the packet of curare stowed at the back of the Admiral's store cupboard, of which he, Washbrook had the key. If he was to do it . . . in the tea, the whisky, the haddock, the onions? A cold shiver coursed along Washbrook's spine: of course he wasn't going to do it. Of course he wasn't . . . was he? Necks were necks but throats were throats and life was sweet, at any rate when death from one hand or another loomed so nastily. With luck, the reverend would sort it all out.

He had taken the tea tray in, tea and a digestive biscuit. 'Four bells, sir,' he said.

'Go away, Washbrook.'

'Yessir, certainly, sir.' Washbrook coughed discreetly. 'Best get up, sir. Them medical gennelmen, sir – '

'Get to hell out of my cabin, blast you!'

'Yessir.' Washbrook left quickly. Cantankerous old sod, deserved to be taken down a peg, he did, but maybe not all the way down to Davy Jones' locker.

Gloomily, Admiral Watkiss drank his tea and ate the biscuit, making crumbs in his bed. All this damned hypocrisy about his health, it was ridiculous. It was not him but the Second Sea Lord who needed a medical board.

Seething with indignation, Admiral Watkiss got up, shaved, bathed, breakfasted in his dressing-gown, then got himself up in his full uniform as Commander-in-Chief of the Chilean Navy, just to be difficult, since he was aware he was being boarded in his rank of post captain in the Royal Navy. He was damned if he was going to co-operate in any way at all.

When he was in all respects ready he sent word to the gangway. His barge was brought alongside and he was piped, more or less, over the side. Captain del Campo and Commander Latrinez were present, as was their duty when their Admiral was going over the side. Admiral Watkiss returned their salutes but did not address them. Commander Latrinez had some breakfast egg on his uniform jacket.

The barge took the Commander-in-Chief across the short span of Portsmouth Harbour to the jetty at Gosport. There was a delay while the ferry was berthed to discharge its load of civilians and Admiral Watkiss chafed as his barge was forced to lie off and his foreign uniform became the cynosure of many interested eyes. There were a few comments, persons wondering who or what he was. He muttered something about blasted civilians, pimply clerks and so on.

Disembarking, he strode along the landing stage and engaged a cab to take him to the Royal Naval Hospital at Haslar.

*

At about the same time as Admiral Watkiss was arriving at Haslar Hospital, Petty Officer Steward Washbrook had reached the nub of his anxieties and was waiting in a nervous state for Canon Rampling to pronounce.

Rampling was horrified, disbelieving. 'Goodness gracious me, you can't possibly be serious! Can you?'

'I can an' all,' Washbrook said. 'Every word's true, sir, true as I sit 'ere, sir. In the confessional box like.'

'Confessional?'

'Yessir, confessional.' Washbrook stressed the word. 'You said, like – '

'I said, and said it quite clearly, that I am not of the Church of Rome, Washbrook. You can't regard me as – '

'You're a religious gennelman, sir, beggin' your pardon. A *reverend* gennelman. Responsible to God, like.'

Rampling stared in agitation, seeing the way things were going. 'Responsible to God, Washbrook?'

'Yessir. For not revealing what's bin told you in the confessional, sir. Under seal, sir. Like them Customs blokes.'

'Oh dear, oh dear, what a dilemma, Washbrook! You've no right to do this, you know, you should have taken my advice and approached the RC padre aboard. Yes, I realize you're not a ca – Catholic, but still.' Rampling dithered, blowing out his cheeks in distress. A soul was a soul, of course, but then Admiral Watkiss had a soul as well and in the eyes of God was equal to Petty Officer Steward Washbrook, a concept that Watkiss might not find agreeable, but that was beside the point.

'Are you,' Canon Rampling asked desperately, 'seeking sanctuary, or something like that?'

'Something like that, sir, yes.' A word came to Washbrook. 'Forgiveness, sir. As well as . . . hanged if I ain't gorn and forgot the word, sir.'

'Absolution?'

'I expect so, sir, yes. That'd be it.'

'But really, Washbrook . . . absolution comes after the event, not before it. Surely you can see that? To receive absolution in advance, and then to go and commit the act, that's simply ridiculous and would certainly not commend itself to God.'

'Well, maybe not, sir. You're the gennelman what knows all about that, the *God* side like. So I reckon I'd best just settle for that sanctify . . . what you said.'

'*Sanctuary.*' Alarm sounded in Canon Rampling's voice. 'Are you suggesting that you might be offered sanctuary here in the vicarage? Because – '

'Oh no, sir. There's the Admiral's bath. And his onions, what I haven't bought yet, sir. And there's them Chileans.'

'Then what *do* you want?'

'I want God's advice, sir. Through you, sir – your advice really, I s'pose. Me neck or me throat is what it bloody – beg pardon, sir – is what it comes down to. I'm a troubled man, like, what wants to be put right. So long as it's safe, see. And you can't tell anybody else, sir. Not Admiral Watkiss, nor Captain Halfhyde, or that Todhunter. Not any o' the peelers, sir. It's in the confessional, see, whether or not you're a b – a candle. I read somewhere . . . if a priest breaks the seal, like, the seal of the confessional, he fries in everlasting 'ell, poked at by the devil with a red-'ot pitchfork, till 'e's proper knackered. That's what I read, sir. Now, you don't want to risk that sort o' lark, do you, sir, eh?'

*

Detective Inspector Todhunter rose late and with a start: to oversleep when on a job was a crime in the eyes of his Chief Super and rightly so. Todhunter gave himself a small smack on his wrist, a tribute in a way to his old mother, who used to smack him like that years ago when he'd been a naughty little boy. Smacked, he got out of bed. The room still had an unfortunate smell, not to say a disgusting stench. The day before had seen the arrival of the horse train from Waterloo with the mounts of the Life Guards embarked, and Todhunter had done his duty which was to see to it that no harm came to

Admiral Watkiss or even the Queen; he had contacted the station master and the military officer in charge of the train and he had gone aboard the horse trucks the moment the animals themselves had been disembarked and he had rootled about searching for bombs and other explosive devices, and for Chileans, because you never knew with foreigners, they got up to all manner of dirty tricks, like monkeys. They could have concealed a man with weaponry for all Todhunter knew and his action was a brave one. The trouble was that the horses of the Life Guards had been unclean in their habits and the aroma had clung to his blue serge suit which was the only one he had with him and he had gone to bed, glad enough of the negative result of his search, but supperless since he had felt unable to enter the hotel dining-room with his attendant stench.

This morning he was due aboard the *Taronga Park* to apprise Captain Halfhyde of the new plan of campaign as devised by Mr Mayhew. And for the same reason as last night, he once again missed his meal. No porridge, no fried eggs and bacon, no toast and marmalade. Mr Todhunter, never fond of horses since a police one had kicked him on his bottom during a riot inspired by the Socialists outside the Canning Town Public Baths, now disliked them more than ever.

Leaving the Keppel's Head breakfastless he saw Mrs Weder-Ublick walking along the Hard in the opposite direction from the dockyard gate. He pulled out his watch from his waistcoat pocket: yes, he had time in hand. Might as well just see what Mrs Weder-Ublick was up to, if anything. Deprived now of the temporary assistance of Miss Penn, he had been neglecting Mrs Weder-Ublick and it might still be useful to know what she was doing in Portsmouth . . . there was that perhaps very relevant business of her antipathy towards her brother.

He followed, very discreetly, making a pretence of reading a newspaper that he had exchanged a penny for with a boy outside the hotel. It happened to be the *Morning Post*, which was a bit of a slip because the *Morning Post* was read only by the gentry and he should have known his place and bought the *Daily Telegraph*, but he put his unprofessionalism down to the intense hunger that was gnawing at him and producing indigestion, which was unpleasant and soured his stomach. When he observed Sergeant Sadley coming towards him on his bicycle, he waved the *Morning Post* in a gesture of negation, meaning that he did not wish to be recognized or saluted. Sergeant Sadley took the hint but was unable to stop himself sitting rigidly to attention as he cycled past.

Mrs Weder-Ublick seemed to be heading towards Southsea. St Jude's Church again?

*

Canon Rampling's advice – or God's advice through his local agent – had been firm and authoritative. Petty Officer Steward Washbrook had a duty to his Admiral, to humanity and to God. On no account was curare (or anything else lethal) to be administered to Admiral Watkiss. The possible cutting of throats was to be accepted as payment, or retribution, for his wickedness in having agreed to further the Chileans' designs. The taking of life was the worst of all sins, and Canon Rampling had been able to throw back at Washbrook the awful red-hot pitchfork and the frying in hell. Canon Rampling, however, had given his promise that he would not make any revelations to the authorities – just so long as Washbrook agreed to bring the packet of curare intact to St Thomas' Vicarage to be held in the safekeeping of Canon Rampling, who intended to flush it down the WC, a splendid affair built specially to the order of the previous incumbent by Thomas Crapper & Sons of Chelsea.

'You agree to this, Washbrook?'

'Well, yessir,' Washbrook answered reluctantly. It would mean more jiggery pokery with the onions in order to secure permission for another run ashore, but he would probably manage. 'But what about them Chileans, sir?'

'You must tell them you've lost the packet, Washbrook.'

'They won't believe that, sir.'

Canon Rampling hummed and ha'ed. 'Possibly not. But they won't be sure, you see. It'll give you leeway, Washbrook. In the meantime I shall try to think of – of something else.' He frowned in thought. 'It may be advisable, perhaps, if I were after all to speak to Detective Inspector Todhunter, a private word – '

'But sir – '

Rampling held up a hand. 'You have come to me for advice, Washbrook. You will do well to leave the affair in my hands now. Todhunter is a reasonable man, and I would present you as an innocent man who has been lured into evil by evil men. No doubt you were – er – inebriated at the time – in fact, I remember you said you were – '

'Oh yes, sir,' Washbrook said eagerly. 'Pi – '

'Yes, yes. Well, the demon drink has been responsible for so much of the world's misery and sin, Todhunter will naturally understand that. I shall tell him, if that is what I decide is the best thing to do, that you came to me with a confession and that subsequently you delivered the curare to me. That will stand you in very good stead. Yes, I really do believe that that is the proper thing for me to do.'

'It won't preserve me throat, sir,' Washbrook said, sounding desperate. 'What do I – '

'Your throat, I would venture to suggest, Washbrook, will be very adequately taken care of by Detective Inspector Todhunter who has the whole process of the law supportive at his side. There remains just one more thing.'

'Yessir?'

'The question of the one hundred sovereigns. It would be just as well if they were removed from your possession, I think. If I were to be able to tell Todhunter that you had made a donation to ecclesiastical funds he would be much impressed with – with your lack of evil intent shall we say. Of course, he may order the money to be impounded at Scotland Yard, but that is a bridge to be crossed later.'

Canon Rampling got to his feet: the interview had taken time and he was conscious of trespassing upon the generosity of his host the Reverend William Scale, whose good lady was being kept out of her drawing-room. The interview was now at an end. Canon Rampling accompanied Petty Officer Steward Washbrook to the front door, laying the hand of friendship and trust upon the latter's shoulder and adjuring him to be of good heart now that the Lord had been apprised of his problem. He had just parted from his supplicant when he became aware of a square-shaped woman advancing beneath a large hat along the street and he recognized Mrs Weder-Ublick, though not in time to beat a retreat.

He was caught, no possible escape.

Mrs Weder-Ublick smiled and halted. 'Osterley,' she said. 'At last!'

'Well, well,' Canon Rampling said as heartily as possible. 'I do declare it's Mrs Weder-Ublick – '

'Hermione, Osterley.'

'Ah.'

*

Admiral Watkiss had been shown into a small waiting-room at the end of a draughty corridor along which bodies, dead or alive he knew not, were being pushed on wheeled stretchers by sick-berth attendants in white coats. As in the Admiralty, there was pictorial evidence of past senior officers, in this case of the medical branch. Fleet surgeons and medical inspector-generals looked down upon Admiral Watkiss from behind a wealth of whiskers, mostly white. Watkiss glared back at them as if daring their successors to pronounce him anything but fit and well and able to perform his duty as he always had done. They all looked well past it themselves and in any case Watkiss had scant time for naval doctors, if that was what they cared to call themselves which he did not. Poultice wallopers, quacks, that was all they were, with an inordinate fondness for the bottle. Admiral Watkiss had crossed swords in the past not only with Dr Baeza of the *Almirante Smith* but also with another wretched doctor who had refused his direct order to employ leeches on a patient and had had to be removed from the surgery under arrest as a result.

In the waiting-room Admiral Watkiss glared round at blank green-painted walls and sniffed the stench of some sort of antiseptic – carbolic, of course. He was taking a deep sniff when a sick-berth petty officer entered and addressed him.

'Captain Watkiss, sir?' The man stared at his uniform, looking puzzled. Admiral Watkiss put him right, frigidly.

'Chilean, eh. Rightyo, then, so long as the name's Watkiss. Come this way, if you please, sir.'

He turned away and Admiral Watkiss followed, having the feeling he was going to his execution, not of course that he intended accepting any verdict that he didn't approve of himself. Blasted doctors!

THIRTEEN

There were two medical officers in the room to which Admiral Watkiss was taken. They were seated at a big desk. One of them, the senior of the two wearing four gold rings on his cuffs with scarlet cloth between them, sat behind the desk; the other, with only three rings, sat at the side. The junior one stood as Watkiss entered; the senior one did not, but he gestured Watkiss to a chair set opposite him and then, with his arms folded across his chest, spoke.

'Captain Watkiss.'

'*Admiral* Watkiss.'

'You have been referred to us in the rank of captain, Captain Watkiss.'

'Oh, very well, then,' Admiral Watkiss said huffily. To disagree too strongly might prejudice his claim to back pay from the Admiralty, and secretly, inside himself, he felt that to be a post captain of the British Navy was really superior to being an admiral in the Chilean one. 'Have it your own way,' he added, raising his head so that he could look down his nose in disdain for quacks.

'Yes. Now, Captain Watkiss, will you please describe your symptoms.'

Admiral Watkiss glared. 'I haven't got any blasted symptoms.'

The two doctors exchanged significant looks and the senior one cleared his throat. 'You have been referred to us – '

'Yes, I'm aware of that, thank you, not being mad or stupid, and I consider it to be utter nonsense. I'm perfectly fit and healthy. There's no damn thing wrong with me at all – '

'You must allow us to be the judge of that, Captain Watkiss. That is what we are here for. I – '

'You can save your blasted valuable time, then,' Watkiss snapped. 'I repeat, I'm perfectly fit.'

There was another exchange of looks, then the senior doctor picked up a small bell on his desk and rang it. At once a sick-berth attendant entered the room and before he knew what was happening a thermometer was thrust into Admiral Watkiss' mouth. He snatched it out again. He was reprimanded. 'Captain Watkiss, you are now under medical orders. Kindly receive the thermometer.' The instrument was replaced. Admiral Watkiss ground his teeth against it but it was of strong construction. After sixty seconds during which both doctors maintained a total silence, the thermometer was removed, consulted and pronounced upon.

'Temperature normal, sir.'

The senior doctor nodded and the sick-berth attendant left the room with his thermometer. Both doctors looked a shade baffled but not for long. Doctors, Watkiss thought, always had something up their sleeves to make them look intelligent. Questions were asked.

'Have you suffered from headaches, Captain Watkiss?'

'No.'

'Do you ever have a full feeling in your head?'

'No, never.'

Both sets of eyebrows were raised. 'Never at all?'

Caution came to Admiral Watkiss; this was possibly a trick question. Doctors, like Chileans, were wily. Perhaps it was usual for people to suffer sometimes from the feeling of a full head and to deny the condition totally might be the wrong answer. 'On occasions, yes.'

'When?'

'When some damn fool does something blasted stupid, that's when.'

Again the exchange of looks. 'Ah, yes. I see. Does this full feeling come on often, Captain Watkiss?'

Watkiss assumed a long-suffering look. 'I've just said, have I not, that it does *occasionally*. That is what I meant, occasionally.'

'But perhaps it has happened more frequently lately?'

'I refuse to answer that question.'

The senior doctor picked up a pen and noted something on a form; Watkiss believed he had written down 'yes' as the answer to the question. He was about to utter a sharp comment when the doctor got in first. 'Why do you refuse to answer, Captain Watkiss?'

'Because I refuse to commit myself to – to anything. Because I believe that some blasted idiot, some nincompoop in the Admiralty, is jealous of me and wishes to prevent my taking part in the review of Her Majesty's fleet – that's blasted well why and you can shove that in your pipe and smoke it, blasted quacks, what damn use are you, I'd like to know, skilled in blasted poultices and bandages and bottles of coloured water done up as blasted medicine and nothing else. Couldn't – '

'Captain Watkiss.' The voice was not loud but it was very firm. It was also cold with anger. 'Have you finished your tirade?'

'I haven't *had* a tirade. I have merely stated what you are and what you are not and that's fact, I said it.'

'It's fact *because* you said it?'

'Yes.'

'I see. Now, I feel sure you would wish to apologize for your remarks? As an officer and a gentleman?'

Admiral Watkiss opened his mouth and closed it again. In his view the doctor was a blasted lunatic but he had better be humoured and this undignified affair brought thereby to a swifter conclusion. 'Oh, all right, as an officer and a gentleman. Yes, I apologize.'

'Thank you, Captain Watkiss.' The four-stripe doctor leaned across his desk and looked hard at Watkiss, staring right into his eyes which were unfortunately a little bloodshot, matching the network of small broken veins on his cheeks and around the nose. 'I understand that in your capacity as Commander-in-Chief of the Chilean Navy you have confined your flag captain to his quarters?'

'Oh, that bugger. Yes.'

'And that you threatened his life if he should emerge?'

'Possibly. I really can't remember. A C-in-C has an enormous amount to do, you know.'

'Yes.' Once again a pen was dipped into the inkwell and another note was made. This done, the senior doctor looked up at Watkiss. He said, 'This has been a preliminary investigation only and not a full medical board. I am recommending that you should go before such a board . . . and this board, in view of the imminence of the fleet review by Her Majesty, will convene in one hour's time.'

*

'I so often think,' Mrs Weder-Ublick said reminiscently, 'of our voyage to Chile together in the *Taronga Park*. No doubt you do.'

'Yes. Oh, yes.'

'A happy time . . . Osterley.'

'Yes, indeed . . . most happy.'

There was a silence. Then Mrs Weder-Ublick asked, 'And that man of yours. Your former churchwarden. Is he with you still?'

'Tidy? Oh yes, indeed he is, though he's quartered at the moment in the YMCA.'

Mrs Weder-Ublick raised her eyebrows. 'The YMCA?'

'Yes, dear lady . . . Hermione. The YMCA in fact takes men of all ages. And Tidy finds the atmosphere most pleasant. The temperance aspect, you know.'

'Oh, quite. Drink is such a sin. When I think of all the terrible misery . . . when I was with the mission in Africa, you know – the natives used to indulge, over-indulge I should say, in some potion fermented from coconuts – '

'Kava?'

'No, Osterley.' Mrs Weder-Ublick assumed her schoolmistressy or missionary tone. 'Kava is a term applied both to a shrub, *Macropiper latifolium*, and to a drink – yes, certainly a drink, Osterley – but prepared not by the Africans but by the Polynesians who prepare it from the roots of the shrub. The shrub,' she added in order to keep the conversation going, for Canon Rampling was not being very forthcoming and seemed *distrait* for some reason or other, 'has a succulent stem and large cordate leaves.'

'Really, really.'

'Yes . . . nature is most interesting, do you not think?'

'Oh yes, indeed. God's work, of course.'

'Yes, of course. We must always offer thanks for – for all that He has provided for us.' What on earth was the matter with Osterley? She hadn't come here to talk about nature or even about God, deeply though she might, and did, revere the Lord and all His Works. No; her present mission was to establish what Canon Rampling's future plans might be. She hoped to convince him that to remain in England would be the very best thing for him. And she had hoped for an ally in Churchwarden Tidy, who as a good Yorkshireman had his reservations about life in Chile. This Mrs Weder-Ublick knew.

She was about to try to bring the conversation back from God and His works towards the mundane matters of human life when Canon Rampling, disturbed by the curious juxtaposition of her visit immediately upon that of Petty Officer Steward Washbrook, whose own mission appeared to be to assassinate the brother of the lady now sitting in the chair so lately occupied by the would-be assassin himself, spoke again, though on account of his word given to Washbrook, he felt unable to prepare the good lady for the worst.

'As of course you know, dear lady – Hermione – your brother Admiral Watkiss is at present in the port.'

'Yes, he is.' The tone was non-committal but Canon Rampling fancied the enmity was still there: too much had been said in the past abour her marriage to a blasted Hun, too many indignities had been heaped upon her in her distant childhood by a brother who had detested her and who had customarily laid upon her alone all the blame for escapades and torturing of the cat *et cetera*. Canon Rampling sighed; enmities were disturbing things. He tried again; his simple remark seemed to have brought the conversation to another end.

'Admiral Watkiss . . . a man of ideas, you know.'

'Really.'

'Yes, indeed he is. He and I . . . we have discussed, not deeply as yet but mighty oaks from little acorns grow . . . you've heard the saying – '

'Yes.'

'Yes, of course.' Canon Rampling closed his eyes for a moment, wishing Mrs Weder-Ublick would go; he sought for an excuse to eject her but none came. Mrs Weder-Ublick seemed to inhibit the brain's workings. He went on with a touch of desperation, 'What we have discussed is the possibility of forming a Salvation Navy. Along the lines of the Salvation Army – '

'Goodness gracious me!'

'Quite. A large and perhaps strange concept – '

'I didn't mean to imply that, Osterley. What surprises me is that my brother should be interested in spreading the word of God rather than the word of himself, if you follow. It's not in the least like him. But the idea, the concept – yes, I think that is splendid. I take it you agree?'

'Oh, yes, most certainly, as a churchman. I – '

'Drink and sin, Osterley.' Mrs Weder-Ublick leaned forward until she was virtually touching Canon Rampling's black frock coat. 'Strong language and women of ill repute.'

'Ah.'

'Those are the attributes of sailors, Osterley. Men with little principle, here today and gone tomorrow. Like the soldiery only much, much worse. I do think the idea of salvation for them is a *very* noble idea . . . I repeat, my surprise is the fact that my brother should have thought of it.' She paused. 'Do you think he is suffering from – er – well, you understand, at a certain age men can get ideas, some sort of mental confusion perhaps – '

'No, dear lady, Admiral Watkiss is . . . still a very forthright man with his powers of concentration fully intact.'

'And you also are truly keen on this idea?'

'Er – yes. Yes, indeed. Most commendable.'

'Exactly. We appear to be in accord, Osterley. Now, how do you propose that we should proceed?'

'We?' Canon Rampling's heart had sunk into his boots. He had committed himself to the wretched woman's service in a sense. She would not rest but would pursue him day and night with urgings about their common cause.

She would; she underlined it, losing no time. 'Yes, we. We must work together on this. I shall be thinking hard about it, you may be sure. I shall ask God for His blessing upon our efforts. My late husband would have been delighted.' She paused, looked hard at Rampling, who was showing signs of agitation. She asked, 'What is the matter, Osterley?'

Canon Rampling said weakly, 'I'm very sorry, dear lady, but I fear I have to go back to Chile with your brother.'

*

The full board had convened. Six in all, plus a clerk for the clear purpose of taking notes in shorthand. Admiral Watkiss looked sourly at the clerk; if it hadn't been for blasted Pitman . . . Admiral Watkiss was always suspicious of having his words quoted back at him; once they had been uttered, that was surely enough for anybody.

The six doctors, however, were the important persons and Admiral Watkiss was very glad to see that five of them appeared to be in the last stages of decrepitude. One, a fleet surgeon, had an ear-trumpet handily placed before him on the long green-baize-covered table; another shook with fairly obvious palsy. All five were white-whiskered although the head of one of them was completely hairless, like an egg Watkiss thought. One was smoking a meerschaum pipe and filling the room with rather nasty-smelling tobacco, cheap stuff, rather like the *periques* of uncut tobacco issued to the ratings aboard the men-o'-war, long in shape and known throughout the service as pricks. Another somewhat ostentatiously sniffed at a kind of tube which he thrust up each nostril in turn, whilst another with an exceptionally pale and unhealthy face made frequent use of a bottle of smelling-salts as though he were about to faint.

What a bunch, Admiral Watkiss thought. But he should have no difficulty with them. Like himself, they would be old-fashioned, accustomed to a more robust navy than the soft-bellied nincompoops controlling the present-day fleet.

The sixth member, however, was a different kettle of fish: the one with the four gold rings who had interviewed Watkiss earlier. And it was this doctor who started the proceedings by quoting from some dismal report, evidently from two sources: the Admiralty, and the Chilean Ambassador to the Court of St James; the doctor announced this in full and after he had done

163

so there was some muttering and whispering amongst the members of the board.

The deaf doctor raised his trumpet and applied it to his ear. 'What was that?' he demanded in a squeaky voice.

'Never mind, doctor.'

'But I do mind, doctor! I'm entitled to hear the evidence and all relevant submissions.' He tapped a thin hand on the green baize, obviously upset.

'Oh, very well, doctor.' A note was hastily scrawled on a piece of paper and passed along. The deaf doctor read it, then brought out a vast silk handkerchief and blew his nose loudly. 'What a thing,' he said. 'What are people coming to?' Admiral Watkiss wished he could have read the note.

The report of the preliminary interview was then read out, loudly for the benefit of the doctor with the ear-trumpet.

'Temperature taken, found to be normal. The patient denied having had headaches and any feelings of fullness in the head. He denied having any symptoms.'

The doctor with the palsy spoke up. 'No symptoms at all, doctor?'

'No, doctor. None at all.'

'How very strange! What's the matter with him – hey?'

Before this somewhat relevant question could be answered, the deaf doctor voiced a query. 'Are his bowels regular?'

Admiral Watkiss glared in fury: what right had this bunch of lunatics to enquire into his most personal functions? In a loud voice he said, 'My blasted bowels have nothing whatsoever to do with you.'

His voice had been loud enough to reach the deaf doctor without the need for repetition. This doctor said, 'The relevance of any question is entirely a matter for the board, Captain Watkiss.' He peered down at his notes. 'Or is it Watkins? Watkins would be more usual, I fancy. H'm?'

'No, it's Watkins,' Admiral Watkiss said. 'Oh, damn and blast, I mean Watkiss.' He shifted his rotund body about in immense indigation: they were confusing him intentionally; and the exchanged looks were very significant indeed.

'Watkiss, then. Funny name,' the deaf doctor said then went back to his point tenaciously. 'Are your bowels regular?'

'*Yes!*'

'Ah. Can't be much wrong with him in that case,' the deaf doctor said, and thereafter seemed largely to lose interest in the whole thing. The other doctors, however, had not. In their view bowels and their functioning were of lesser importance than other aspects of their victim's life and behaviour. Admiral Watkiss was asked if he were an abstemious officer.

He rustled angrily. 'Of course not, what a stupid question.' He added, 'Naturally, I do not drink to excess, and seldom when at sea.'

'Quite. All very natural,' the pale doctor said unexpectedly. 'I always say that a teetotaller is a very unnatural thing and abhorrent to any seaman. There are worse vices and – '

'Yes, doctor, but no reference was made to teetotalism, merely to abstemious behaviour,' the senior doctor said. 'I consider the two things to be entirely different.'

'Rubbish,' the pale doctor said, applying himself once again to his bottle of smelling-salts.

'Thank you, doctor, we shall pass on to other matters,' the chairman of the board said crisply. 'Now, Captain Watkiss. We have already been into the question of your treatment of Captain del Campo, have we not, and – '

'A mere matter of discipline,' Admiral Watkiss said, 'and the discipline aboard my ships is and always has been a matter for me alone and is nothing whatsoever to do with you or any other blasted doctor – '

The senior doctor held up a peremptory hand. 'One moment, Captain Watkiss. Discipline is one thing; to go beyond the normal limits is quite another. I – '

Admiral Watkiss had started to vibrate, always a bad sign with him. 'Oh, balls and bang me arse!' he said. 'What utter drivel and rubbish! What do you know of discipline, may I ask? Am I to understand that you have battled against the westerlies, attempting to take a ship ,under sail around Cape Horn in face of appalling weather – snow and ice and gales – in face indeed of the most appalling dangers known to mankind? Have you done that? If you blasted well had, you'd know that there's no room for namby-pambyism at sea. Any captain must at all times exercise the utmost control of his ship's company and to do that requires the sanction of punishment – so there!'

He sat back, arms folded and a smirk of triumph on his face. He'd got them this time. There was a silence, broken only by the odd cough as the stupid idiots tried to sort that one out, and by a plop as the deaf doctor dropped his ear-trumpet. Then the chairman spoke.

'Portsmouth Harbour, Captain Watkiss, is not a rounding of Cape Horn. I suggest – '

'It's not up to you to suggest anything, doctor. Am I to take it you consider it normal and proper that my flagship should enter a British port with the blasted channel buoys draped about my fo'c'sle, thus making me a jackass in front of every seaman in sight, to say nothing of the anguish it must have caused Her Majesty? Do you consider that unmeriting of the severest punishment? If you blasted well do,' Admiral Watkiss added energetically, 'then you must be blasted well mad, and that's fact, I said it!'

'The boot may be found upon the other foot,' the chairman said in an acid tone. 'I am trying to ascertain what your state of mind was at the time you – er – ordered Captain del Campo to go below. Can you enlighten me?'

'No, I can't. I don't make a habit of noting down my state of mind in the deck log.'

'But surely – '

'Oh, God give me strength! You can write down that I was cross.'

'What did he say?' the deaf doctor asked.

'I said I was cross,' Admiral Watkiss shouted.

'Cross? That seems a mild enough emotion. Were you not, perhaps, in a tantrum?' This was a sly interpolation from the palsied doctor.

'*I was not in a tantrum!*' Admiral Watkiss answered angrily, exhibiting all the signs of one. He simmered down. 'Oh, call it angry if you wish. So would you have been if, say, some nitwit had knocked a – a pair of blasted tweezers into an opened-up stomach or such. Am I not right?'

There was a laugh from the bald doctor. 'Good heavens, my dear fellow, it happens all the time. No point in getting cross,

166

you just have to yank the offending object out, that is assuming it hasn't gone too deep.'

'Which,' Admiral Watkiss stated, 'is what I did – yanked the offending object out before it, or in this case he, had a blasted chance of going deep. I am so glad you see my point at last.'

But it appeared they hadn't, quite. More probing questions followed. The Chileans had been most upset by what had been inflicted upon Captain del Campo, and indeed had raked up all manner of complaints from the past: how Admiral Watkiss had flouted Chilean custom in Valparaiso by ejecting from his flagship the normal quota of women who came aboard as laundresses but at the same time performed other functions for the ship's company in port; there were many examples quoted of the rudeness of Admiral Watkiss to his Flag Captain and Executive Officer; his threats of keel-hauling and being made to walk the plank and being hanged from the fore upper tops'l yard were brought out. And many other things.

Then came the nub, the real Machiavellian purpose of the medical board, the members of which, in the opinion of Admiral Watkiss, were obviously in the pay of the Chilean Embassy, all rogues together. It was put by the chairman.

'Captain Watkiss, it has been considered in – er – certain quarters that you may be . . . shall I say, temperamentally unfit for the very onerous task of Commander-in-Chief . . . that perhaps you would in fact be much relieved if your place was taken, at least for the period of the fleet review, by – er – by someone else.'

Admiral Watkiss stared glassily, taken flat aback now. He asked in a croak, 'Which someone else?'

'The only other Chilean available – '

'*Other* Chilean? You make it sound, my dear sir, as though I'm a blasted dago myself! I am *not* a dago.'

'Chilean. Indeed, your use of the word dago was another ground of complaint . . . but to answer your question: the only sufficiently senior Chilean available is, of course, Captain del Campo.'

Watkiss was for a moment speechless. He gave a strangled gasp and then he started. He was not going to hand anything over to Captain del Campo, not even a fried egg. He was not

167

going to be declared mentally unsound – and he could now see clearly the way matters were proceeding – by a bunch of blasted quacks. He said as much. He said in a voice of fury, 'You may think I am unversed in medical matters but let me tell you I'm blasted well not! If I'd known your blasted names before I attended, I'd have looked you up in the Medical Register. As it is, I'm willing to bet any sum you care to name that not a blasted one of you is a blasted doctor. You're a bunch of quacks, blasted charlatans, and I'm not having my good name sullied by a bunch of – of *poseurs* passing themselves off as – '

'Captain Watkiss – please – I think you have said more than enough and – '

'I've only just blasted well begun,' Watkiss said loudly. 'I wager that in all your cases your medical degrees consist solely of *bachelor* of medicine. Not *doctor*. Possibly also bachelor of surgery. Do any of you deny this?'

There was an embarrassed silence; no one answered the question.

'There you are, then! Not a blasted qualified doctor among the lot of you!'

'I beg to differ, Captain Watkiss,' the senior doctor, or quack, said. 'Yes, we are bachelors of medicine certainly, but that does not mean we are unqualified. We are all of us licensed to practise medicine and surgery . . . and really, do you imagine for one moment that the Admiralty would have appointed us surgeons to Her Majesty's fleet if such was not the case?'

'I can't speak for the blasted Admiralty,' Watkiss said with dignity. 'I have always considered them to be useless nincompoops who do their best to make things quite impossible for those of us who are at sea. But am I now to take it that none of you is in fact a *doctor*?'

There was another silence.

'Come on,' Admiral Watkiss said, trying to conceal his glee. 'Answer the question, if you please.'

The chairman, after glancing along the table to right and left, did so with obvious reluctance. 'We are not doctors of medicine. None of us has the degree of MD. But that is purely academic, and it is the normal courtesy to address us – '

'Kindly do not attempt to evade the issue, or I'll have you . . .

h'mph.' Admiral Watkiss changed tack. 'You now admit you're not doctors. Just as I blasted well thought, and I don't know why I've been wasting my time since I have no intention of taking the slightest notice of your blasted verdict.' He got to his feet and bounced out of the boardroom.

FOURTEEN

Detective Inspector Todhunter, relinquishing his shadowing of Mrs Weder-Ublick when he had seen her admitted to St Thomas' Vicarage by no less a person than Canon Rampling, turned back for the dockyard to resume his progress towards the *Taronga Park*. Perhaps later on he would have a word with Canon Rampling who might perhaps have some useful information about the lady. When he had drawn level with the Keppel's Head Hotel it began to rain and Mr Todhunter deviated into the hotel and his bedroom in order to put on his galoshes: his old mother had always warned him not to get his feet wet and risk chills, and old habits died hard.

Galoshed, he set off once again for the main gate where in accordance with his orders he remained unrecognized by Sergeant Sadley even when his Scotland Yard pass was offered and scanned. Sadley, Mr Todhunter thought, was a good man, very reliable. He went on towards the *Taronga Park*, avoiding the noisy, dangerous steam engines as before. There was much on his mind; still he had discovered no leads to the would-be assassins of Admiral Watkiss, which was a panicky thought. If Admiral Watkiss should be assassinated, then his stock would drop sharply with his Chief Super and that would never do.

His approach to the *Taronga Park* was seen from the decks and someone above was not as discreet and efficient as Sergeant Sadley: a shout floated across the dockyard.

'It's the dick, mate.' Victoria waved a hand. 'G'd day, mate. Or is it? Reckon it rains as much here as in bloody Liverpool, eh?'

Mr. Todhunter raised his bowler hat. 'Good morning, Miss Penn. Is Captain Halfhyde aboard?'

'Too right 'e is. Busy, I reckon, with some bigwig naval bloke. But come on up, have a cup of tea in the saloon, eh?'

Mr Todhunter climbed the ladder from the dock wall and entered the saloon. Victoria followed him in and tea was brought by the steward. Victoria said, 'Cosy, eh?' She snuggled up to him on the settee running beneath two port-holes. Uneasily, he shifted a little sideways.

'What's up, mate? Unclean, am I?'

'No, no, Miss Penn, of course not.' Mr Todhunter was very embarrassed.

'Got me new scent on. Bought it at the Landport Drapery Bazaar. Like it, do you?'

It was very strong and carried, in Todhunter's view, certain obvious connotations. 'Very nice,' he said. Miss Penn moved closer and Mr Todhunter's body impinged on the arm of the settee. He could go no further without seeming very rude indeed. Miss Penn giggled and said, 'Don't mind me, mate, you know me, I can't bloody help it.' Todhunter prayed inwardly for the bigwig naval bloke to conclude his business with Captain Halfhyde and be gone. But time passed slowly and after the fourth cup of tea there was a clatter of horses' hooves on the dockyard wall and a cab drew up. Out of it got Canon Rampling with a worried look on his large face.

*

The members of the medical board had retired, like a jury or like the officers forming a court martial, to consider their verdict. While Admiral Watkiss was taken back to the waiting-room they had congregated, in a spacious room with panelled walls, a view across Spithead towards the Isle of Wight, and yet more portraits of venerable naval surgeons plus, this time, a bevy of angry-looking women in the garb of matrons with starched collars and cuffs and magnificent head-dresses also starched. All these faces, whiskered or beneath veils, stared down gloomily upon the deliberators as though willing them to do their duty sternly, without fear or favour.

Each doctor held a glass in his hand: sherry for some, gin for others. Cigars had been lit and there was an air of informality. The discussion at first was fairly general: they had had an unaccustomedly hard forenoon and they felt a need to relax. They talked of the rise of Socialism, the way it was making the common people get above themselves; thank God, the palsied doctor said piously, it would never penetrate the fleet with its pernicious dogmas. The tars were immensely loyal and would remain so. They were all agreed on this. They spoke of their grandchildren, this being a safe subject; wives, of course, were unmentionable in the wardrooms of the fleet. An officer was married, not to a wife, but to the service, the service of the Queen. Of course they spoke of Her Majesty, reverently as though in church. She was wonderful, an inspiration to everyone in the Kingdom and in the wider Empire overseas. The deaf doctor, who was nearing retirement, was, in addition to his other duties, not onerous ones, an honorary physician to Her Majesty and thus could speak with authority though never, of course, in a medical sense which would in any case have been impossible since he had never actually attended her.

After a while they spoke of Admiral Watkiss.

'They don't like him at the Admiralty,' the palsied doctor said, shaking badly. 'Always been a confounded nuisance, so they say.'

'A nephew of mine served under him once,' the bald doctor said. 'Apparently he had all the starboard ladders in the ship marked Captain Only. . . .'

'When he commanded the *Devastation* he had all the water-tight bulkheads burnished so that they looked splendid but were no longer watertight,' the pale doctor said. 'But I understand that such is not entirely uncommon.'

The senior doctor, finishing his gin, called the members together into the medical board they were supposed to be. 'What are we going to do about him?' he asked.

One doctor stated flatly that Watkiss was a madman and ought to be certified as insane but such was, as the palsied doctor pointed out, beyond their present brief. 'The most we can do,' he said, 'is to recommend that he be relieved of his command. That's what the Chileans want, isn't it? The British Admiralty itself has no jurisdiction over him – '

'Not as Commander-in-Chief of the Chilean Navy, no. But as a captain on the retired list of the Royal Navy, which is what

he's come before us as . . . well, that's a different kettle of fish.'
This was the senior doctor. 'We can, I think, put in a
recommendation that he be given treatment here at Haslar in
that rank, just until the review's over.'

'But we can't *do* anything for him, can we?'

'No, of course we can't.' The senior doctor sounded irritable:
he had to catch a train back to London. 'But that's not the
point. The point is that it would satisfy the Chileans, which is
what we're here for.'

There was a series of grunts. The palsied doctor gave it as his
opinion that they were being misused. 'I don't see why we
should dance to Santiago's tune, you know.'

The deaf doctor said, 'Hear, hear,' and added, 'What did he
say?'

The palsied doctor's sentiment was repeated into the ear-
trumpet. The deaf doctor said, 'Oh, I entirely agree, yes.
Especially in this, the year of Her Majesty's jubilee. I'm quite
sure the Queen would never approve any giving in to foreigners.'

'Quite so, doctor. But I fear we're no further ahead. What do
we do about Watkiss?'

'Do we really need to do anything?' the pale doctor
demanded peevishly. 'Watkiss isn't very different from the
general run of post captains and admirals, they're all a pretty
bloodthirsty and demanding bunch who believe the sun shines
out of their backsides. I don't see why we of the medical branch
should be made the cat's-paws of the Chileans,' he added in an
aggrieved tone. 'We have to remember Watkiss is *British* after
all. I think we owe him some loyalty.'

'He's a very rude man,' the palsied doctor said querulously.

'Very rude indeed, certainly – '

'Coarse language every other word – '

'Insulting, too. The way he stormed out was quite appalling
and I – '

'Accusing us of being damn quacks!'

'Yes, doctor, that was of course unforgivable – '

'Except in the case of a lunatic, a man who's lost his wits and
is no longer responsible for his actions. I still say, declare him
unfit for further service. Even in a Chilean ship.'

'And give in to the damn Chileans?' the palsied doctor burst out. 'Surrender to a bunch of – of – well, not dagoes of course, but you know what I mean.'

They did; all of them. The British stuck together, even though one of them might be in the employ of the Chileans. The mood of the members of the board swung towards Admiral Watkiss, warts and all, except in the case of the disagreeable doctor who had considered Watkiss to be mad and who looked like being a dissenter.

'All this nonsense the Second Sea Lord mentioned in his report,' he grumbled. 'This Salvation Navy business. If you ask me, that's the notion of someone who's taken leave of his senses – '

'Oh, nonsense, my dear doctor,' the chairman interrupted. 'It's very commendable indeed.'

Except for the disagreeable doctor they all agreed to this as well. Religion was the mainstay of the fleet, the firm rock upon which discipline was founded. But the dissenting doctor insisted on furthering his point. 'I happened to be speaking to a padre only this morning. I mentioned the Salvation Navy . . . he said it was totally ridiculous, absolute poppycock. He said that if a rating needed God, who better than himself to confide in? I think that was pretty conclusive. Straight from the horse's mouth, don't you know.'

No notice was taken of this; padres were not the best of witnesses, usually failing to understand the need for strict discipline aboard a ship, and in any case regarded by the older seamen as being Jonahs, figures of ill omen and bringers of bad weather and tragic happenings, akin to corpses being retained aboard rather than sewn decently into their canvas and committed to the deep. There was further discussion, the expression of views tending to go round in circles. A number of the doctors began yarning; one drifted off into sleep. Finally the senior doctor looked at his watch, clicking his tongue in annoyance: he had a luncheon appointment with the wife of the captain of a first-class cruiser currently in Chinese waters. . . . He said loudly, 'Gentlemen, I recommend that we have Captain Watkiss back to be informed of our verdict. May I take it this is agreed?'

'What was that?' the deaf doctor asked. 'What did he say?'

The Chairman said it all over again, into the ear-trumpet. The deaf doctor looked bewildered. 'Have we reached a verdict, doctor?'

'*I* have, doctor. Captain Watkiss may be rude and overbearing but that does not make him mad – besides which, he is British. There is another point and a most important one. Declared unfit to serve, Captain Watkiss would raise the most monumental shindig and we would all be put to a very great deal of trouble. We do not, I think I can say for all of us, wish to have the great occasion of Her Majesty's jubilee review spoiled?'

There was a chorus of assent.

'Very well, then. Gentlemen, we shall take a stand for Britain. We decline to be dictated to by Santiago. Captain Watkiss is perfectly fit.'

'Hear, hear.' Tables were thumped with enthusiasm. It was a popular enough verdict on the whole, with just a few reservations.

*

'I happened to meet Mr Mayhew, Mr Todhunter,' Canon Rampling said. 'He informed me you were going aboard Captain Halfhyde's ship so here I am.' He wiped sweat from his face. 'There is a most important matter that I must bring to your attention as soon as possible.'

'Cup of tea first?' Victoria asked.

'I thank you, Miss Penn, but no. I have but recently drunk a cup of coffee, and I – '

'That's all right, mate, no need to explain, some of us need the po more than others if we overdo it.'

Canon Rampling had gone scarlet. 'My dear young lady . . . words fail me.' He seemed to be gasping for air. He appealed to Todhunter. 'The matter is most urgent. I must ask you to step outside on to the deck for a few moments.'

'Meaning,' Victoria said, 'that you don't want me around, eh? I'll save the dick the trouble of shifting his arse. I got other things to do, thank you very much.' She flounced out of the saloon, trailing the Landport Drapery Bazaar's scent. When she was safely out of earshot, Canon Rampling bent towards Mr Todhunter's ear. 'It has to do with Admiral Watkiss,' he said. 'Admiral Watkiss and his steward, the man Washbrook.'

*

'Ah, Captain Watkiss. Kindly sit down.'

Watkiss lowered himself into the chair set before the long table. He had a truculent look, having disliked being kept waiting by a bunch of doctors. He breathed hard down his nose in a long-suffering way but said nothing.

'We have made our decision, Captain.' The chairman smiled. 'Or should I say Admiral?'

'Yes, you should.' Admiral Watkiss was about to say more but realized in time that to be addressed as Admiral could very well be a good sign. 'About time too,' he said sharply. 'I have a great deal to do before the review can take place.'

'Yes, indeed. Well, you'll be relieved to know that we have found nothing wrong with your health – '

'Relieved my bottom!' Admiral Watkiss stared angrily. 'It never for one moment crossed my mind that you might find otherwise, since I'm perfectly fit as I blasted well told you at the start of all this nonsense – '

'Yes, well. Allow me nevertheless to congratulate you upon a clean bill of health, Admiral Watkiss. However,' the chairman went on, determined to get his dig in, 'I am left wondering if you're prepared to accept our verdict?'

'Of course I am! Why ask? What a blasted stupid question.'

'But – a bunch of what was it – quacks?'

'Ha.' For a moment Admiral Watkiss was nonplussed, but it was a short moment. 'I call that hair splitting.'

'There is more than a hair's breadth between a qualified medical practitioner and a person unqualified to practise medicine. In other words a quack, which is what you accused us of being – '

'Oh, I may have used the word perhaps,' Admiral Watkiss said with an off-hand wave of his arm that revealed his tatooed snake and sent his golden Chilean tassels flying in circles, 'but naturally it was used only in jocular vein. Damn silly if you've taken umbrage.'

'Oh no, no, we rise above that sort of thing, Admiral. So we take it you do accept our decision?'

'Yes, yes.' Admiral Watkiss started to get to his feet, then sank back again. The pathetic quacks presumably expected to be thanked for their efforts. 'I'm most grateful, gentlemen. Most grateful. It's one in the eye for the blasted pimps at the Admiralty. Yes, most grateful, and I need hardly say, I imagine, that if ever I should be in a position to be of some service to yourselves, then you may call upon me.' He knew that they were not in the least likely to but the generous gesture had been made.

They all rose to their feet; the chairman accompanied Watkiss to the door and along the corridor, a friendly hand upon his shoulder. 'It was kind of you to express your appreciation, Admiral. We in the medical profession are not averse to a word of thanks now and again.'

'Oh. Well, natural enough no doubt.'

'Yes indeed.' The chairman gave a discreet cough; there seemed to be something behind it, something unexpressed in words, a nuance accompanied by the hint of a suggestion. Admiral Watkiss remembered that doctors were accustomed to receive presents from grateful patients, usually at Christmas: the odd pair of grouse, perhaps, from the squire, turnips or a rabbit from the cottager, that sort of thing in a country practice. In a town, some first-rate brandy or port or a case of whisky in extreme cases . . . and the actual report to the Admiralty had yet to be written.

He gave an ungracious grunt. 'If there is anything in particular – '

'Yes. Gin, perhaps?'

'Oh, very well.'

'May we say a case, perhaps? Not Chilean. Plymouth – Coates'.'

'Yes, all right.'

'Thank you so much, Admiral. A very generous gesture.'

Quack had possibly been an indiscreet term.

*

Detective Inspector Todhunter now had something on to which to cling like a leech. 'What a stroke of luck, sir,' he said to Canon

Rampling. 'One that must be acted upon without delay. I shall speak to Captain Halfhyde, of course, then – '

'But I promised Washbrook I would inform only yourself, Mr Todhunter. I have not reported the facts even to Mr Mayhew. I gave Washbrook my word.'

'Which you have kept, sir! You have informed only me. If I find it necessary in the interest of the law to inform others, then your word remains inviolate.'

'Yes, I see.' Canon Rampling looked dubious nevertheless: it didn't seem quite right but of course the law was the law and Detective Inspector Todhunter was its tool. 'But do please take the very greatest care. I am in no doubt that the man Washbrook harbours no evil intent whatsoever and has simply been swayed by Chilean gold.'

'Quite so, sir, quite so indeed. My Chief Super has always stressed the power for evil that lies in gold, and Washbrook is by no means the first innocent to fall into its clutches. I shall see that he is protected from his folly, in so far as it lies within my power to do so.'

'And your power, Mr Todhunter – '

'Just may not have the scope, sir, but we shall have to see. Our first duty, of course, is to the safety of Admiral Watkiss against the vile assassins, you'll agree with that, I know.'

'Oh yes, indeed I do. A very terrible crime – assassination.'

'Yes, sir.' Mr Todhunter smoothed down his blue serge jacket. 'And liable at this moment of history so auspicious for Her Majesty to give rise to a most serious international incident.'

'Yes, I take your point.'

'If it should succeed that is, sir.'

'Yes, quite.'

'Thus, sir, it behoves me to take all steps possible.'

'Yes. I do see that, Mr Todhunter.' Poor Washbrook: he might well be dropped in the soup yet. Canon Rampling was much disturbed in his mind. Had he broken the confessional? But as he had stressed to Washbrook, he was no Roman. Still, the principle was much the same and a promise was a promise and although what Todhunter had said was strictly true, it might be a sin in the sight of the Lord to break a promise by proxy. Washbrook had pointed out the punishments, the devil with his red-hot pitchfork and so on, but Canon Rampling reminded himself that he and not Washbrook was the man of God and, frankly, he was not at all certain (he should be but wasn't) about the existence of the devil as other than a very nasty threat. Anyway, that was the hope he nourished: he was not without sin, minor sin of course, any more than any other human being.

When the bigwig visitor had left the ship, Detective Inspector Todhunter went up for words with Halfhyde. In addition to the now inhibited chincanery of Petty Officer Steward Washbrook, he informed Halfhyde of the Foreign Office dictum as promulgated by Mr Mayhew that Admiral Watkiss was to attend the review aboard the *Taronga Park*.

'In God's name, why?' Halfhyde asked.

'Reasons of security, sir.'

'Admiral Watkiss' security, Mr Todhunter, I presume? Not mine. My ship could become a target, couldn't it?'

'Well, sir, since you raise the query, I would hazard a guess that the answer might well be "yes". But only if the assassins get to hear, sir. So full secrecy must be observed.' Todhunter paused. 'I understand that it is in Mr Mayhew's mind that Admiral Watkiss should come aboard your ship not as an admiral in the Chilean Navy, but perhaps as a captain in the British one, or, again, possibly as, well, something else, sir.'

'What something else?'

'Mr Mayhew has not informed me as to that aspect, sir.'

'I see. Does Admiral Watkiss know of these arrangements, Mr Todhunter?'

'I think not yet, sir, no.'

'Who's going to inform him?'

'As I gather, sir, Mr Mayhew himself. With the weight of the Foreign Office behind him.'

Halfhyde grinned. 'Admiral Watkiss will not be pleased, I fancy. But why all this cloak-and-dagger? If Washbrook was to do the deed with the use of curare in the porridge or whatever – and the Chileans, we must surely assume, don't know he's confessed – they aren't going to mount an actual and very visible attack during the review?'

Mr Todhunter assumed a judicial air. 'It is a case of taking all precautions, sir. Just in case like. The Chileans are like all foreigners, sir, as you'll agree I'm sure, very slippery customers. Very slippery indeed, sir, like snakes.' Mr Todhunter used his hands to depict a snake. 'You grasp them in one place, and they wriggle out of your hand. We must be very circumspect, sir, and up to all the crafty dodges foreigners can think up. There is not only Admiral Watkiss. There is also Her Majesty the Queen to be thought of. The hand of the assassin must not come close to Her Majesty. Which leads me to the point, the important point, Captain Halfhyde, sir, that the royal yacht with Her Majesty embarked will pass close to the *Almirante Smith*, which is one of the reasons why Admiral Watkiss is to be removed – '

'Tell me, Mr Todhunter – does the Queen know of the threat of assassination?'

Detective Inspector Todhunter drew in his cheeks; he was quite shocked. 'Why, Lord bless my soul, sir, I should hope not! In my humble opinion it would be a criminal act in itself to bring anxiety to an old lady at such a time of rejoicing over what should be a happy occasion.'

Halfhyde nodded gravely, concealing a grin. 'Of course, Mr Todhunter. I apologize for the very thought. But tell me this too: is it really considered likely that the assassins would go into action close alongside the royal yacht?'

'It has to be taken into account, sir. If them – if those Chileans do get to hear that Washbrook has grassed, talked like, sir, why, their anger will know no bounds. No bounds at all, sir. And slippery like they are. . . .' Todhunter once again stated his views on the wiliness and untrustworthiness of foreigners and added that the fury that in his experience always accompanied frustration might lead the assassins to take great risks in order to achieve their objective and that nothing whatsoever could be ruled out.

FIFTEEN

'I shall not abandon my command and that's fact, I said it. You exceed your blasted authority, Mr Mayhew.'

'I beg to differ, Admiral. I have the full authority of the Foreign Office to act – '

'Oh, balls and bang me arse, man – '

'To act as I see fit.' Mr Mayhew was losing his temper fast. 'Not as *you* see fit, Admiral, and I – '

'What balls – '

'It is *not* – what you said. It is fact. I have the authority of Her Majesty's Principal Secretary of State for Foreign Affairs and – '

'Oh, for God's sake hold your tongue and get off my ship.'

'I – '

'You come aboard and insult me by suggesting I might abandon my command, you give me some cock-and-bull story that *my own steward* is involved in this dastardly threat to my life – never in my whole life have I heard such monstrous bilge – have you never heard the word *loyalty*, no, don't blasted well answer, of course you haven't, don't know the blasted meaning of the word I shouldn't wonder!' Admiral Watkiss was bouncing up and down with anger. 'Do as you've been ordered and get off my ship *this instant* or I'll have your balls for breakfast, just see if I don't!'

Admiral Watkiss brandished his telescope, just missing the end of Mr Mayhew's nose. He looked extremely dangerous; Mr Mayhew seized his silk hat and fled, muttering angrily to himself about obvious lunatics and making a mental note that the members of the medical board that had pronounced

Watkiss sane should be subject to much questioning by the Medical Inspector-General of the Navy.

*

A bell rang peremptorily in the Admiral's pantry and Petty Officer Steward Washbrook obeyed the summons, hastily shoving the packet of curare into his pocket rather than leave it lying around; he had been interrupted in the middle of shifting its stowage since you couldn't be too careful until the stuff had been taken ashore to the reverend's custody.

'You rang, sir?'

'Don't be a blasted idiot, Washbrook, of course I rang.'

'Yessir. Sorry, sir.'

'And don't *cringe*. I like respect and instant obedience but not *cringing*. Anybody would think I was some kind of blasted tyrant.'

'Yessir.' There was something odd about the Admiral: he had never before objected to cringing, an attribute that came naturally to Petty Officer Steward Washbrook; officers usually expected it.

'Am I a tyrant, Washbrook?' Watkiss asked suddenly.

'You, sir?' Washbrook managed to look astounded. 'Oh, no, sir, no, not a tyrant at all, sir.'

'Quite. I agree. I'm a reasonable enough man.'

'Oh, yes, sir, a very reasonable man, sir – '

'Gentleman.'

'Eh?'

'Gentleman. Not man. And don't say "eh" to me like that, you're not addressing the lower deck when you speak to me. Now: have I ever been *un*reasonable, Washbrook?'

Washbrook, whom circumstances had made a good actor, looked shocked. 'Oh, no, sir, never, sir.'

'Quite. Or bad-tempered – except of course when you've been a blasted idiot and buggered up something, like breakfast or my bed.'

'No, sir, never bad-tempered, sir, except when you just said like, sir.'

'When you've damn well asked for it.'

'Yes, sir, that's it, sir.'

182

'I'm normally of a kindly disposition?'

'Very kindly, sir.'

'And generous?'

'Oh yes, sir, generous.'

'I do not make unreasonable demands upon you?'

'Oh no, sir, never, sir.' What was the old bugger up to?

'You've been happy in my service? As happy as any blasted steward has any right to be?'

'Oh yes, sir, very happy, sir.' Washbrook was back to cringing again now but this time Watkiss didn't appear to have noticed.

'In short, Washbrook, I've been a good master?'

'Very good indeed, sir.'

'Yes, I see. So you'll summarize my virtues, Washbrook.'

'Your virtues, sir?' Washbrook looked blank.

Admiral Watkiss shifted impatiently in his chair. 'Oh, damn you to hell, you blasted idiot, my good points.'

'Oh. Yessir.' Washbrook's head was swimming by this time although in all conscience he should be used to the old sod by now. He concentrated hard, sensing that the matter was important and that he must watch himself in case he left out a good point. 'Kindly, sir.'

Admiral Watkiss nodded. 'Yes. Go on, Washbrook.'

'Yessir.' Washbrook frowned in thought, shifting his stance a little as he did so.

'Stand still, blast you, don't damn well fidget when speaking to your Admiral.'

'Sorry, sir.' More concentration. 'Generous, sir.'

'Yes.'

'Reasonable, sir.'

'Yes.'

'Not a gennelman to make unreasonable demands like, sir.'

'No.'

Washbrook thought hard, his tongue protruding a little way through his lips. Watkiss said testily, 'Oh, come on, you fool.'

'Yessir,' Washbrook said with a touch now of desperation. 'Not a tyrant, sir.'

'A good master.'

'Yessir. Very good indeed, sir.'

'A good master who cares for the men under his command,' Admiral Watkiss stated.

'Very caring indeed, sir, yes.' Washbrook thought of something new that ought to go down well. 'An orficer an' a gennelman, sir.'

Admiral Watkiss glared down his nose. 'What a blasted impertinence for a man of your sort to say that to me! *Of course* I'm an officer and a gentleman!'

'Very sorry indeed, sir.'

'So I should damn well think! However, I am all those things, Washbrook, am I not?'

Bloody old paragon I don't think, Washbrook thought. He said, 'Oh, yessir. All them things, sir.'

Admiral Watkiss got to his feet and stared up at his steward, his monocle now clasped into his eye-socket. 'In that case, you – you damn blackguard, why the blasted hell have you pocketed dago gold in return for agreeing to commit the abominable crime of assassinating your Admiral?'

'Oh, my God, sir,' Washbrook said, shaking like a leaf, 'I didn't know you knew, sir. I'm very sorry, sir.'

*

Petty Officer Steward Washbrook rubbed at his rear end and felt a nasty bruise on his forehead. His kindly Admiral had been very angry and very brusque: his kindly Admiral's arm had shot out and seized him and had turned him round with a swift and brutal movement that had taken him unawares. His Admiral's foot had contacted his bottom and in staggering to the door he had caught his head on a piece of the Admiral's furniture. He had then made his escape, followed by his kindly Admiral's yells of anger. He was now in a lather of sweat and anxiety; and reverends were right out for the future, except of course for curare delivery . . . after that, never again would he place his trust in the Church, not the Church of England – he had a bloody good mind to go candle and sod the lot of them. So much, he thought savagely, for the bloody confessional. There was just one good thing in the outcome: Admiral Watkiss had let slip the information that Detective Inspector Todhunter had believed his story as related to Canon Rampling and the police did not intend arresting him. He still had a part to play, and he had a nasty feeling he would be playing it for his life. He was not to let on to the Chileans that he had talked; they would then continue to place all their reliance on the packet of curare and their quarry would be safe for long enough. Once Admiral Watkiss felt safe, then Washbrook was to be the link between the law and the miscreants and would inveigle them into the handcuffs of Detective Inspector Todhunter.

'And make certain you do as you're damn well told, you blasted rogue, Washbrook, or I'll have fire-bars clamped to your blasted feet and have you dumped in the blasted harbour and that's fact, I said it.'

It was sheer coincidence of timing that led to Petty Officer Steward Washbrook having a visit within the next hour from the Chilean who had contacted him earlier with the means of carrying out the assassination. This person had insinuated himself up the gangway, slipping a small amount of money into the hand of the sentry, who had happened to notice him in the intervals between picks at his nose. Thus admitted, the assassin made his way to the Admiral's pantry. He startled Washbrook rather badly.

'Oh, it's you, is it?'

'Yes. You have not yet administered the poison?'

'Gimme a chance, mate!' Washbrook said. He was wondering if he should take the opportunity of making an immediate report to his Admiral so that the Chilean could be arrested right away; but that would still leave other Chileans who would suspect something and they would think up another scheme; and in any case Washbrook deemed it wiser on the whole to stick rigidly to the orders as issued by Admiral Watkiss. Do anything out of turn and the old sod would go potty. So all he said was, 'Got to seize me moment, like, see? Mustn't go orf at 'alf cock.'

'Arf cock?'

'Jump the gun, like. Act before I'm ready. As 'is stoo'ard, it's best left to me.'

'Very well, señor. But make no mistakes.' A hand was drawn remindingly across a dark-skinned throat. 'You will not have the second thoughts?'

'Me? Second thoughts? Oh, no, mate, not me! I've give me word and – '

'You detest your terrible Admiral. That makes it easier, yes?'

'Yes, mate, dead easy in that respect. I hate the old skinflint. Never get a decent word out of the old bugger, never a word of thanks for all I do for him. Just abuse, that's all. Cruel, he is, really. Mean and cruel and bloody stuck-up, thinks 'e's God. Said so once. I 'eard him going for the officer of the watch – mind you, the oow was just a dago . . . no offence meant I'm sure, mate . . . and old Watkiss, 'e said that as captain of a British ship on foreign service he'd represented 'Er Majesty the Queen and as 'Er Majesty the Queen was the 'ead of the Church of England she represented God . . . so the old sod was thus to be regarded as God, see. Acting God, any'ow. Course, since the oow was a da – Chilean, sorry, and so was the ship, it didn't really mean all that much, not really, but I reckon you see what I mean. The da – Chilean nearly shat 'isself, being that close to God. Superstitious lot, you blokes, eh?' Petty Officer Steward Washbrook had much enjoyed emptying his mind of Watkiss' self-applied virtues. Kind, generous, reasonable, caring, a good master – they had all tended to stick in his throat but he'd known of course that it was vital his throat should unstick. He reflected now that the packet of curare *could* come in very handy like, but of course that devious-minded reverend would be waiting for it and if he failed to make delivery within the next hour or so then the arresting hand of Detective Inspector Todhunter might well be feeling his collar.

'Just you leave it to me, mate,' he said to the Chilean.

*

In Osborne House in the Isle of Wight, all was now ready for the seaborne procession of Her Majesty to Cowes Roads for her embarkation aboard the *Victoria and Albert*. The great review was to take place the next day; already most of the warships with their black hulls and buff-coloured upperworks had either steamed grandly out of Portsmouth Harbour past Fort Blockhouse and the Round Tower and Clarence Pier, through the swept channel where fresh buoys had now been placed in position following the entry of the Chilean battleship – either that, or they had steamed directly into their allotted anchorages in Spithead and the Solent from Plymouth and Chatham or from the widespread British Empire – from Gibraltar and Malta, from the West Indies, from Hong Kong and Singapore, from the loyal colonies of Australia and New Zealand, Canada and South Africa.

'It will be the most *splendid* occasion, my dear dean,' Her Majesty said. She was sitting in the sun and conversing with the sub-dean of the Chapels Royal, an old crony.

'Very splendid indeed, ma'am. Let us hope nothing occurs to mar its splendour.'

The Queen gave him a sharp sideways look. 'Do you think it likely it will, dean?'

'I was thinking of the weather, ma'am.'

'Ah, yes.' Her Majesty was always subject to a little *mal-de-mer*. 'But whatever the weather, we shall take it in our stride on this occasion. We are, after all, a seafaring race, are we not? A breed that is not easily cast down. We are so glad Mr Gladstone is no longer our Prime Minister,' the Queen added as though the presence of Mr Gladstone could of itself have induced queasiness. 'He would completely have failed to rise to the splendour of our fleet and the nobleness of our Empire, bringing it all down to the level of a public meeting in support of the Liberal Party. Very dull, those Liberals, do you not find?'

'Very dull indeed, ma'am. Very dull.'

'And *contentious*.'

'Very contentious, ma'am.'

'We hope we shall be accorded a good view. The after deck is not as advantageous as the bridge where the captain is.'

'Ma'am, I am certain – '

'Yes, dean, you may be but we are not.'

'I do understand, ma'am.'

The Queen gave a grunt of irritation and clicked her tongue. The trouble was the royal bath chair, which could not be manoeuvred up the ladder to the bridge of the royal yacht; nor could Her Majesty climb the ladder whilst disembarked. This was not, of course, on account of a possible display of the royal underwear to male persons standing below the open steps of the ladder, for the British tar was a chivalrous person and could be relied upon to avert his eyes, though the Queen was woman of the world enough to realize that a discreet peep might be taken at, say, the Princess of Wales or the Duchess of York. No: it was simply because of Her Majesty's lack, in these her later years, of much agility and it would be disastrous for her to fall. And there was no room on the ladder for more than one person at a time, not alongside in a helping stance that was. And Her Majesty had flatly refused the offer of her First Sea Lord that she be hoisted on the jib of the derrick with a broad canvas band around her bath chair.

'Like a donkey,' she had said and that had been that.

After the grunt and the tongue-click, conversation languished and the sub-dean racked his brains for something to divert the Queen. He found it. He said, 'I was talking recently, ma'am, to an old friend. . . .'

'Really?'

'Canon Rampling, ma'am. You spoke to him a few days ago – '

'Yes, I recall the occasion. The man who mistook nanny for myself! Such a stupid thing to do.'

'Yes, ma'am. Canon Rampling was much abashed . . . but when we were talking an interesting subject arose, one that I think will amuse Your Majesty.'

'Yes?'

'The Admiral commanding the Chilean Navy, ma'am, aboard the *Almirante Smith*. He – '

'The ship that smashed into those buoys?'

'Yes, ma'am, a slight contretemps with the navigation I am told – '

'A *most dreadful* exhibition.'

'Quite so, ma'am.' The sub-dean gave a cough. 'The Admiral – Admiral Watkiss – '

'Watkiss? An unusual name for a Chilean, is it not?'

'Ma'am, Admiral Watkiss is not a Chilean. He is British. He was once a captain in your navy.'

'I see. Fancy joining the Chilean Navy! Well, dean? What were you going on to say, pray?'

'Admiral Watkiss, ma'am, has had an idea. He has put to Canon Rampling, also I understand to the Second Sea Lord,

188

that it might be possible, and indeed desirable, to found a Salvation Navy along the lines of the Salvation Army. Do you not find that interesting?' He waited for Her Majesty to guffaw; she had quite a sense of humour when something tickled her, and she was known to have a loud laugh. But the dean waited in vain and was astonished at her reaction.

'What a very splendid idea,' she said.

'Ma'am?'

'This person, what was his name?'

'Watkiss, ma'am. Admiral – '

'He must be a very *feeling and benevolent* person. You know how very much store we set by the welfare of our dear soldiers and sailors, how deeply we believe that religion must play a very important part in their lives, which are at times hard. We consider this to be a very excellent idea. We trust you are giving it your support, dean. Also the archbishop.'

'Well, ma'am – '

'We shall be most interested in learning more. Salvation Navy . . . it has such a splendid ring, do you not agree? If the archbishop thinks fit, we would, if asked, be pleased to lend the idea our royal patronage. Frankly, we believe our sailors to be more in need of it than our soldiers. Our soldiers are always in enjoyment of the land's comforts. Our sailors are not, dean. So *un*comfortable upon the sea. The raging of the waters, the terrible buffeting of the wind. Such a life leads to excesses when land is reached. Drink and other things, dean.'

'Quite so, ma'am.'

'If God is brought more closely to them in the world's ports much of the evil would be removed, we believe. Yes, a most noble concept.' The Queen paused, reaching a hand down absently to fondle her attendant Sealyham. 'We would much like to speak to this Admiral Watkiss, dean.'

'Yes, ma'am. Canon Rampling could convey your wishes. But if I may remind Your Majesty, there is little time left before tomorrow's ceremonies, and – '

'Yes, dean, we are aware of that. And immediately after our review of our fleet we go to Balmoral by the train. But I see no reason why the Chilean captain should not take charge of his ship without this Admiral Watkiss being on board?'

The sub-dean said, 'That is not my province, ma'am, but the Chilean captain – the channel buoys, you remember?'

'Hoity-toity, dean! Buoys are replaceable, soiled souls are not. Admiral Watkiss is to be commanded to present himself on board the *Victoria and Albert* to accompany us for the review, and we shall talk together.'

*

Lieutenant Seaton had boarded the *Taronga Park* in order to convey a message to Halfhyde; but Halfhyde had gone ashore, having crew business to conduct at the local shipping office of the Board of Trade adjacent to the Camber, the area of the harbour reserved for merchant vessels. In his absence, Lieutenant Seaton was met by Miss Penn.

'It's you, is it,' she said loftily. 'I wouldn't have dared show me bloody face if I'd been you. Not after the other night I wouldn't.'

'A misunderstanding, that's all – '

'Misunderstanding me arse! Tried to grab me tits you did, in that cab.'

Her voice had risen. Lieutenant Seaton hissed, 'It would be better if you were to keep your voice down, you little trollop.'

She faced him with her hands on her hips. 'Ho, so that's it, is it? Trollop, am I? Paid for your bloody tucker and all! You bloody blokes seem to think you're God's gift to women. Let me just tell you, mate, that I'd sooner consort with the bloody scum of bloody Sydney than with your sort, all gold stripes and brass buttons and not enough confidence in their bloody cocks to woo a woman proper but resort to bloody rape. Lucky for you there was no bloody copper around.' Seeing that the crew had largely stopped work and that every ear was a-flap, she made an effort and simmered down. 'Anyway, what you come aboard for, eh?'

'To pass orders to Captain Halfhyde.'

'Gone ashore. Leave a message if you bloody like. Sooner act as messenger meself than have you come back, mate.'

'Very well then. Kindly inform Captain Halfhyde that I am to board his ship at 0800 tomorrow, and accompany him for the passage of the review lines.'

'Any particular reason, is there?'

190

'None that I shall reveal to you, Miss Penn. And a very good day to you.'

Giving a formal salute he turned away for the gangway to be pursued by Miss Penn's voice at its shrillest. 'Best watch it while you're aboard, mate; if Captain Halfhyde sees you trying it on he'll do a Watkiss and throw you bloody overboard!'

*

'I'm afraid your blasted Foreign Office must play second fiddle, Mr Mayhew. Her Majesty's wish is her command, or didn't you know that?'

Mayhew held on to his temper. 'Of course I'm aware of that, Admiral. But – '

Admiral Watkiss shook his telescope. 'Oh, blast you, there are no damn buts when Her Majesty the Queen speaks! I have every intention of going aboard the *Victoria and Albert* tomorrow, and none whatsoever of taking any blasted notice of you or the damn Foreign Office, so there.'

Tight-lipped, the Foreign Office man once again took up his silk hat and stalked out of the Admiral's quarters. The wretched Watkiss had a point, that was undeniable, but the Foreign Office view was that in the circumstances the Queen's command ought to be set aside in the interest of her own safety. To allow her to be put in close proximity to the target of a threatened assassination was really quite unthinkable, yet it was currently being thought. Mr Mayhew would return to London and Whitehall by the first available train and see that urgent representations were made to Her Majesty's advisers. But frankly he had little hope; Her Majesty was at times a most obdurate old woman and she seldom changed her mind. As Mr Mayhew had said, quite strongly, to the proposed victim of the assassins, it was up to him to get the Queen off the hook by, perhaps, feigning illness at the last moment; but he had met with no success in that direction. The proposed victim was cock-a-hoop.

When Mayhew had vanished from his quarters, Admiral Watkiss extended all his fingers fan-wise, put the little finger of his right hand to the thumb of the left, and, pointing towards the door through which Mayhew had gone, conveyed the whole lot to the end of his nose. 'Blasted clerk,' he said witheringly. 'Damn pimp!'

He rang for his steward. It was Leading Steward Escobar who appeared. 'Where's Washbrook?' Watkiss demanded.

Leading Steward Escobar mumbled something in a mixture of English and Spanish which Admiral Watkiss interpreted as indicating that Washbrook had gone ashore. 'Oh yes, onions,' he said. 'Bring whisky. Quick about it. And don't go and make a balls-up of it.'

When the whisky came Admiral Watkiss drank a solo toast to Her Majesty. What a remarkable woman, what insight . . . it was a tremendous honour that he had been accorded. To actually accompany Her Majesty on the review of her fleet! Watkiss' one worry was, naturally enough, Captain del Campo, who could certainly be relied upon to do something extraordinary with his ship. However, on this occasion, such would have to be accepted. At least he, Watkiss, would not be aboard when Captain del Campo either slewed the *Almirante Smith* across the exit channel and hit Fort Blockhouse fair and square, or put his helm the wrong way in Spithead and sailed away past the review lines into total and deserved disgrace.

After two stiff whiskies Admiral Watkiss rang again, and again Leading Steward Escobar appeared. By the usual mixture of English and Spanish and a number of gesticulations around the head and the neck and the bottom of his uniform trousers, plus the sign of the cross made in front of his chest, Admiral Watkiss conveyed an order for the Roman Catholic padre to report to him immediately. He was to bring a prayer-book and Bible with him. Before attempting to converse intelligently with the Queen about the Salvation Navy, it was necessary for Admiral Watkiss to mug up on God and all His works and in the absence of Canon Rampling Roman Catholic instruction would have to be made the best of.

SIXTEEN

Canon Rampling was also to be aboard the *Victoria and Albert* the next day, in attendance – at last – upon Her Majesty, taking up temporarily his one-time role as a chaplain in the British fleet. He was much looking forward to this even though he had been apprised by a telegraph from the sub-dean of the Chapels Royal that Admiral Watkiss had been bidden to the royal presence for a dissertation on the curious idea of a Salvation Navy.

Being at a loose end, and not wishing to become a burden to his host and hostess the Reverend William and Mrs Scale, he decided that afternoon to walk along to the dockyard and board the *Taronga Park* for a word with Halfhyde and perhaps to glean some information as to any developments in regard to the threat to Admiral Watkiss, which had caused him much concern especially as to whether or not he should as a humane act have warned Mrs Weder-Ublick that her brother was, or might be, in grave danger. Not that she had seemed to have any more time for that brother than she had whilst *en route* for Valparaiso so long before; yet Canon Rampling recalled that she had suddenly developed a family feeling when she learned that Watkiss was being harassed by the then Chilean government, whose *coup*-displaced adherents were even now forming the threat of assassination. . . .

H'm.

Not that there was anything Mrs Weder-Ublick could do to circumvent that threat, of course. Such was not a woman's work.

As luck, or misfortune, would have it, Mrs Weder-Ublick

was encountered coming out of the Keppel's Head Hotel. Canon Rampling was once again too close to dodge.

He lifted his clerical hat. 'We meet once more, dear lady. Hermione. Twice in two days, how strange.'

'How very *fortunate*, Osterley.' She was breathing rather hard and, looking at her closely, Canon Rampling noticed that she was distressed.

'You are worried, dear lady. Can I help in any way?'

'It's my brother,' she said. History was repeating itself, he felt sure, and he was right. 'I've been spoken to by Detective Inspector Todhunter. He asked a number of questions, strange ones I thought. About my brother's contacts in Chile. Of course, I was unable to help. But in the end I asked him what it was all about.'

'Ah. And he told you?'

'Yes. I really don't know what to think. You're aware of – of enmity I suppose you could call it, between my brother and myself. But I've never wished him harm, you know. I've never wished him dead. Now I find this most upsetting.'

'Naturally . . . Hermione. But you may be quite sure that the authorities are doing all they can. I happen to know this, but you'll understand that I mustn't . . . er . . . reveal too much.' Canon Rampling was most certainly not going to tell her about Washbrook and the packet of curare, now delivered and deposited in the safe at the vicarage, awaiting Scotland Yard's instructions. That would never do.

He uttered more words of sympathy and Mrs Weder-Ublick dabbed at her eyes with a frilly handkerchief. She mumbled something indistinct and more tears flowed. She was plainly distraught and as a clergyman he must do his duty. He said kindly, 'If I can help in any way at all . . . you must feel free to confide in me, you know. It always helps to share one's sorrows.'

She laid a hand on his arm. 'Dear Osterley,' she said. 'You are *such* a comfort. I feel like some fresh air to clear my mind. A walk, perhaps, along the sea front if you wouldn't mind?'

Well – he'd offered his support and he must give it. His proposed visit to the *Taronga Park* must wait; it was not, after all, important. He offered an arm courteously to Mrs Weder-

Ublick and she took it and they set out towards the sea front, just like any middle-aged married couple. Canon Rampling's heart sank: thin end of the wedge?

But that was when Mrs Weder-Ublick saw the Chilean.

*

It had been the sheerest chance. There might have been nothing in it at all, though Mrs Weder-Ublick was certain the man was an assassin. Why else should there be a civilian Chilean in Portsmouth? The ship's company of the *Almirante Smith* would certainly not be allowed ashore out of uniform and they wouldn't have any plain clothes with them in any case. Was she, Rampling asked, certain of the suspect's nationality? She was; she had been in Chile for quite long enough to recognize one of its citizens *instantly*, and such a person naturally stuck out like a sore thumb in a place like Portsmouth with its smart, clean bluejackets and sober civilian population dressed according to their class. Of course he was a Chilean. He was ill-kempt.

The Chilean was walking towards Queen Street. Mrs Weder-Ublick, while Canon Rampling dithered with uncertainty, took immediate charge and went at a brisk pace towards the Metropolitan Police guard on the main gate of the dockyard. She made a breathless report to Sergeant Sadley, who had just taken over from a fellow sergeant. 'I see, madam. You are certain that this man is a Chilean, are you, madam?'

'Yes. I have only a moment ago said so to Canon Rampling. I believe it is possible he may be one of the desperadoes who are threatening my brother's life – '

'Your brother, madam? May I enquire who – '

'Admiral Watkiss of the Chilean Navy,' Mrs Weder-Ublick said impatiently. 'Will you please – '

'Admiral Watkiss.' Sergeant Sadley was making notes in a book he had drawn from his pocket. 'You are the sister of Admiral Watkiss?'

'I have just said so!' Mrs Weder-Ublick snapped.

'I see, madam.' Sergeant Sadley licked at the end of his pencil. 'And he is your brother. Yes, I follow. And you believe you have set eyes upon one of the would-be assassins – '

'Yes. Will you please – '

'Just a tick, madam. It's my duty to note everything down, see. Now, which way did this person go?'

Mrs Weder-Ublick pointed along Queen Street. 'That way, and do *hurry* or he'll have vanished.'

*

Mr Mayhew had scared Whitehall badly; the Queen must most certainly not be put at risk. Lord Salisbury came down personally by the train from Waterloo Station to speak to Her Majesty. Before the audience at Osborne House, he had words with the Commander-in-Chief, Portsmouth Command, a crusty admiral whose almost constant wheezing and whose frequent use of a bottle of chemicals designed to ward off asthma attacks indicated that he was close to retirement from active service. Lord Salisbury made the point that the Watkiss-preserving stratagem of putting him aboard Halfhyde's ship incognito was now in danger.

'In that connection, Admiral,' Lord Salisbury said, 'why was it considered necessary for Watkiss to be present at all at the review? Would it not have been safer had he *not* been present?'

'Yes,' the Admiral wheezed briefly.

The Prime Minister looked puzzled. 'Then why – ?'

'The Watkiss factor, Prime Minister.'

'Ah. You mean – '

'I mean he would have given trouble. He would have stormed about the place uttering threats and general nonsenses and he would have given the game away in advance by drawing attention to himself – that's why. As you may have been informed in the past, Prime Minister, there is no accounting for Watkiss. The fellow is filled to the waterline with bullshit.'

'Bullshit, Admiral?'

'Bullshit, sir. But I'm fully behind you in any attempt to make Her Majesty change her mind about having him aboard the royal yacht.'

Lord Salisbury left the Commander-in-Chief's imposing residence, an immense Georgian building filled with secretaries of the navy's paymaster branch, stewards and seamen, the latter forming the crew of the Admiral's barge, and at times of his carriage, and was conveyed in a cab to the gunwharf where a naval picquet-boat waited to take him across the water to Cowes and Osborne House. His audience with Her Majesty was far from propitious: the Queen was adamant. Lord Salisbury felt obliged to inform her of the threat to Admiral Watkiss.

She was horrified. 'A person of such excellent intentions! How *vile.*'

'Yes, ma'am, vile it certainly is. But – '

'And he is British. It wouldn't be so terrible if he were a Chilean. These people are in the habit of doing such things to their own people, are they not, Lord Salisbury?'

'Well – '

'But a Briton – and in our own country! Really, Lord Salisbury, it is *monstrous.* I take it Admiral Watkiss is being accorded every possible protection by our police and armed forces?'

'Certainly, ma'am, certainly, you may be assured of that.' Lord Salisbury gently eased away the attention of Her Majesty's Sealyham, which was investigating his left leg. The dog gave a growl and vanished beneath the Queen's black skirts. Lord Salisbury, covering up the incident, went on hastily, 'Your Majesty, it is your own safety that concerns your government. If you are to place yourself close to Admiral Watkiss, then danger may very well come to your person, and that – '

'Nonsense, balderdash, Lord Salisbury. These wretched assassins would never dare. To suggest some attack on our royal yacht, in the *very midst* of our battleships and cruisers and gunboats is totally absurd! In our opinion, poor Admiral Watkiss is safer in our presence than anywhere else.'

'But – '

'*Safer*, Lord Salisbury.'

'But really ma'am – I have the duty to – '

'And in any case we are not afraid. We, too, have our duty, and our duty is to show steadfastness and courage. And that is the end of the matter, Lord Salisbury.'

Lord Salisbury sighed and admitted defeat. The old Queen was of course splendid, everyone knew that, dedicated to duty and all the peoples of her widespread Empire: she was not

Empress of India for nothing; the Indians adored her as much as anyone else did. She was much loved and admired by the common people of Great Britain despite a somewhat grim expression as she sat in her carriage – for the purpose of being adored, really. But the common people saw her only in carriages, cossetted and surrounded by her horse guards and foot guards and any number of princes, princesses, royal dukes and duchesses. On such occasions she couldn't really be overtly tiresome . . . Lord Salisbury, beating his retreat backwards and bowing as he went, sighed again. Her Majesty's ministers saw her in a different light, that of an autocratic old woman who would never be told anything. As Lord Salisbury reached the door of the chamber the Sealyham emerged and barked at him; it was as though the animal was in league with his mistress and was underlining her victory.

*

Detective Inspector Todhunter, coming along Queen Street towards the main gate, witnessed the chase ahead of him. Initially he had been alerted by the shrilling of police whistles and all his plain-clothes instincts had come instantly to the fore, something that his Chief Super would have much commended: he had withdrawn himself from sight. He had faded so far as was possible into a sleazy doorway next to a public house. From this cover, he observed closely. The whistles were coming from his own Metropolitan police constables.

So something must be up in the dockyard. Mr Todhunter did now recall a person of foreign aspect passing him further back along Queen Street, a male foreign person it had been, with a shifty aspect. He clicked his tongue in annoyance and self-admonition: bother take it, he had been remiss and that would never do, a real black mark. He was considering this matter when the door opened behind him and he found his arm taken in a firm grip. A woman stood there, grinning at him from a toothless mouth, Mr Todhunter's police mind registered the seamed cheeks and the predatory air and the obvious lack of much clothing beneath the dirty outer garments, a skirt and a vest. Clearly a prostitute and somehow or other his rump had agitated the door knocker when he had taken up his cover position. This woman announced her terms.

'One-and-six, dearie, for a short time, all right?'

Mr Todhunter raised his bowler hat. 'Thank you,' he said politely, 'but no.' He turned away; she kept her grip on his arm.

'Bob, then.'

'No – '

'Bloody old skinflint! I ain't ate for a bloody week and I need the money, see.' She became aware of what was rapidly approaching her domain. 'Coppers – see 'em? Gimme a bob or I'll hand you in charge. Say you molested me.'

'Oh, please let go of me, madam,' Mr Todhunter said desperately. With his free hand, his umbrella clasped between his knees, he reached into his pocket for his purse. He brought out a coin and handed it to the woman. Too late he saw that it was a gold sovereign; it vanished like magic and the door was banged shut behind him. Mr Todhunter brought out a handkerchief and mopped at his face. A near thing, and possibly cheap at the price. To have been handed in charge to his own squad would have been most mortifying.

The pounding constables surged past; puffing along behind came Sergeant Sadley, smelling of Brickwood's beer and his brother's fish shop. They failed to spot Mr Todhunter. Behind the chase came Canon Rampling and Mrs Weder-Ublick, who did see him.

'Hurry, Mr Todhunter,' Mrs Weder-Ublick called out. She pointed. 'He went that way.'

'Who did, madam?'

'The Chilean. The assassin! Kindly do your duty, Mr Todhunter. My brother's life depends on you.' She pounded on, her skirts clasped in her hand clear of her feet. Canon Rampling eased his pace thankfully and looked apologetically at the detective inspector.

'My heart, don't you know. I'm terribly sorry but I simply cannot maintain such a pace.'

'Do you know anything about this, sir?' Todhunter asked.

'A suspect, according to Mrs Weder-Ublick. Personally I tend to doubt her diagnosis, but it doesn't do to say so.' Canon Rampling was blowing like a steam engine and looked on the verge of collapse. 'I suppose one ought to lend a hand . . . but I fear the fellow will have made good his escape by now in any event.'

'Possibly, sir, but no stone must be left unturned when it is a matter of life and death. I shall endeavour to pursue the person, sir. Just in case like.'

'Oh, very well. Do you require my assistance, such as my presence?'

'I think I shall move faster on my own, sir, thank you very much.'

Canon Rampling gave a sigh of relief. Detective Inspector Todhunter set off at a fast trot behind the now distant Mrs Weder-Ublick and the Metropolitan Police Force. The whistles receded into the far end of Queen Street and Canon Rampling began limping back the other way. He might just as well stick to his earlier resolve and go aboard the *Taronga Park*. What Mrs Weder-Ublick would have to say about being abandoned he dreaded to think; but it was an ill wind, according to the proverb, and she might prefer to be rid of so pusillanimous a priest. With luck.

*

Sergeant Sadley and his men returned along Queen Street; they were empty-handed and were sweating profusely into their thick uniforms. Sergeant Sadley's helmet was off and he was mopping at his streaming red face: passing a public house he looked with longing at a ready source of Brickwood's beer but of course he couldn't partake, not when on duty. Mrs Weder-Ublick was marching alongside him, angry that the Chilean had been allowed to escape. As for herself, she had done her best by crying out from time to time 'Stop thief' but none of the passers-by had taken any notice preferring, it seemed, to make themselves scarce in advance of the police whistles. She had remarked on this to Sergeant Sadley, saying scornfully that all the citizens of Portsmouth appeared wary of any close association with the police.

'Down this way, madam,' Sergeant Sadley had said, 'they mostly are.'

So Mrs Weder-Ublick's quarry had made good his escape, vanishing without trace. Sergeant Sadley did his best to pacify

Mrs Weder-Ublick, saying that in his opinion it had been a wild goose chase. This was the wrong thing to say. Mrs Weder-Ublick drew her stout body up. 'I call that extremely rude, Sergeant, and I shall have words with Detective Inspector Todhunter.'

'I'm sorry, madam, for 'ow I put it. What I meant was, the person you observed was likely innocent of any ill intent. A mere passer-by 'oo 'appened to 'ave a dark complexion, madam.'

'Stuff and nonsense,' Mrs Weder-Ublick responded briskly. 'I know guilt when I see it, Sergeant, even if you don't.'

As it so happened, she had been right. The observed person was not only a Chilean but as an official of the previous, and now discredited, Chilean administration he had been present in the Ministry of Marine in Santiago at the time Admiral Watkiss had been charged with disloyalty to his adopted country and he had noted Mrs Weder-Ublick, so very like her brother, sitting outside the chamber where the Admiral was being formally charged with his offence. That, of course, had been some while ago but Mrs Weder-Ublick remained unchanged and he had recognized the kinswoman of the intended victim.

Not that the Chilean dreamed for one moment that Mrs Weder-Ublick had in turn recognized him. But police whistles were in the circumstances not to be ignored and the Chilean had made himself scarce by locking himself into a cubicle in the public lavatory in the roadway leading down to the Unicorn Gate into the dockyard. Emerging when the furore had died down, he had made his way to the terraced house near the Crown and Jackstaff public house.

Here he had met other Chileans, including the one who made more or less regular contact with Petty Officer Steward Washbrook and who had supplied the curare. He reported his having seen the sister of Admiral Watkiss and he reported the juxtaposition of the Englishwoman and the police whistles and the subsequent pounding of the constabulary in his general direction.

Two and two were hastily put together.

'There is obviously suspicion,' Washbrook's contact announced. 'And we know that the Admiral Watkiss lives yet.' He shook his head, showing anxiety. 'I am coming to believe that the steward will not after all co-operate. If that proves to be the case, then of course the steward must die. But I believe we must give him just a little longer. As the steward of the Admiral Watkiss, he it is who will know when the Admiral Watkiss is the most curare prone. The customary food of the Admiral Watkiss, you understand.'

There were nods of agreement: the speaker was a diplomat, or had been under the old administration, and he knew everything. But a question was asked nevertheless: 'How much longer is it safe to rely on the steward and the curare?'

The answer was pat. 'If the Admiral Watkiss is known to live until tonight's midnight, then we must adopt the alternative plan of striking during the review of the fleet. This will be of course much more dangerous, but we are all committed men acting for our beloved country or at any rate for our party and we are prepared to sacrifice our lives. Also,' he added, 'to assassinate the Admiral Watkiss so publicly and during the presence of the Queen Victoria will be most impressive.'

*

A little before midnight, a rowing boat stole in through the entry to the harbour, pulled by a man dressed as a fisherman and carrying as a passenger another man similarly dressed. The second man carried a bulky package, something heavy wrapped in an old sack.

The boat was pulled past the South Railway jetty, and was propelled onwards towards where the *Almirante Smith* lay preparatory to moving out the next day to take up, under Captain del Campo's command, her position in the review lines. Notwithstanding certain strictures issued by the Commander-in-Chief designed to ensure the security of his ship and his person against the vile threat posed by the Chilean dissidents, the watch on deck was still pretty useless: it had been impossible to instil any real sense of urgency into either Captain del Campo or Commander Latrinez; and really the whole thing was as much of a shambles as ever. Much had been promised and very little had been done. And the task of the boatmen was eased by the darkness of the night; there was no moon, the sky being heavily overcast. Also, the routine harbour patrol mounted nightly by the guardship had already made its rounds of the ships in the port, answering the challenges from the gangway of each and interrupting a game of cards aboard the *Almirante Smith*, where the quartermaster and corporal of the gangway were closeted with two of the ship's cooks in the quartermaster's lobby; these challenges proving (erroneously in the case of the *Almirante Smith)* that the ship was in watchful hands during the hours of darkness.

The rowing boat pulled unmolested – for cards had been resumed the moment the interfering but now satisfied British had gone – below the Chilean battleship's counter. The oars were rested as the bulk of the Admiral's sternwalk loomed overhead. As stealthily as a cat approaching a mouse, the boat's passenger, sack slung over his shoulders, hauled himself up and over the rail of the sternwalk. As stealthily he approached the door leading from the open sternwalk into the Admiral's day-cabin.

He peered in. He heard a snore. He saw the Admiral Watkiss lying at full length upon a settee, his mouth wide open, and on the deck a Bible that had evidently fallen from hands overtaken by sleep.

So the Admiral Watkiss, as had been suspected, lived; and it was now past midnight. The boat's passenger reflected that the Admiral Watkiss was currently at his mercy. Had he had a gun, or a knife for preference because of the noise of guns, the deed could have been so easily accomplished. But of course the danger would have been immense: the Admiral Watkiss might have retaliated had he woken unexpectedly and the ship's company of the *Almirante Smith* might have woken up also, and the result would have been a harbour filled with boats with British sailors and marines and police constables with inimical intent; and even patriots prepared to sacrifice their lives preferred to give themselves the best possible chance and on this occasion the best possible chance lay in sticking closely to the agreed alternative to the curare.

So the Admiral Watkiss was left to snore above his fallen Bible (and had he been reading the Bible because he had had a premonition of death?) and the watcher drew himself and his burden up once again on to the guardrail of the sternwalk and from there, by making use of handily placed ringbolts and other projections in the ship's plates, to the quarterdeck, where all was quiet. Or quiet anyway in the desired sense. Sounds came from the gangway, where in the quartermaster's lobby cards were leading to bad-tempered disagreement. From the seamen's messdecks for'ard in the ship came singing and laughter, somewhat boozy laughter, for a party with alcoholic drinks was in progress. From a hatch a man emerged, and the intruder froze behind a big bell-mouthed ventilator, but this was not necessary for long: the man, who wore the uniform of a commander in the Chilean Navy, gushed with a bout of sickness and then collapsed to the deck and lay inert in his vomit, and the intruder came out from his cover and continued towards the navigating bridge where tomorrow the Admiral Watkiss would stand in order to steam past the British monarch, hand at the salute. At about that time, the Admiral Watkiss was to be blown into small fragments.

SEVENTEEN

And now, at last, it was the morning of the review.

The day came up fine and clear; just a little wind from the south-west to bring tiny white horses to the waters of Spithead as the ships' companies turned out to the calls of the bugles to give the spotless wooden decks a final scrub before Her Majesty moved past aboard the stately *Victoria and Albert*. Orders were shouted by hard-faced petty officers anxious to earn the approval of their captains for the smart turn-out of their particular parts-of-ship. On the flag decks of the fleet the yeomen of signals sorted through piles of coloured bunting, getting the messages of loyalty ready for bending on to the signal halliards. At the great batteries gunners' mates inspected paintwork and brasswork and made sure the tampions were in place in the mouths of the gun-barrels and that none of the massive weaponry was befouled by seagull shit. Below decks, men under the command of a petty officer known as the captain of the heads, the heads being the seamen's term for lavatories, made sure everything was clean and bright and smelling of carbolic even though Her Majesty was unlikely to get to close quarters with them. Steam picquet-boats were called away in each ship so that the sides and upperworks could be scanned at a distance for faults of paintwork, a kind of Queen's-eye view.

From the harbour the *Taronga Park* emerged with Lieutenant Seaton embarked, for the pretence of Admiral Watkiss being aboard was being maintained, just in case, to help fool the Chileans. Halfhyde's orders were to maintain station astern of the *Victoria and Albert*, acting in place of the customary Admiralty yacht that normally carried the Board of Admiralty at such reviews; this time Their Lordships were to be aboard the royal yacht itself, clustered protectively about Her Majesty.

'What's the bloody point of us being there, mate?' Victoria Penn asked.

Halfhyde grinned. 'Don't you want to see your namesake, Victoria?'

'Don't know that I care all that much. But that's not what I bloody asked, is it?'

'No. And I don't know the answer. It's probably just because we were ordered down to Porstmouth in the first place and they don't want to waste us.'

'Sounds bloody daft to me, mate. I reckon it's to do with that Lieutenant Seaton bloke.'

'Perhaps it is. Perhaps we're extra back-up for Admiral Watkiss, who knows? I don't. And now,' Halfhyde added, 'just leave me to take my ship out through the exit channel and – '

'What do we do then, eh? Hang about for the Queen?'

'More or less. I'm to anchor off Cowes and then follow the royal yacht once Her Majesty's embarked.'

'What a bloody carry-on, eh,' Victoria said. 'Typical pom, I reckon! And if that Seaton bloke tweaks me tits I'm going to yell, Queen or no Queen, right?'

She had made this announcement rather loudly. From the fore well-deck Lieutenant Seaton looked up with a scowling face. His reputation as a gentleman was important to him in any situation where senior officers might be within earshot, and Miss Penn's voice had certain qualities of clarity that could carry across the harbour towards the signal tower where his lord and master the QHM was standing on the open platform to watch the ships proceed outwards.

*

A picquet-boat collected Canon Rampling in his cassock and clerical hat, and attended by Churchwarden Tidy, who had been advised of a possible introduction to Her Majesty and didn't go much on it because as a Yorkshireman he disliked pomp and pageantry and general blooming fuss. The picquet-boat, waiting at the Clarence Pier, also embarked Mrs Weder-

Ublick, honoured as the sister of the inventor of the Salvation Navy and also as a one-time missionary to the African natives in her own right.

She sat close to Canon Rampling for the trip to the royal yacht, scheduled to leave the harbour for Cowes Roads at four bells in the morning watch for the royal pick-up. She remarked on the weather.

'So fortunate for the dear Queen, Osterley.'

'Yes, indeed it is, indeed it is.'

'Doan't see why there's all that much fuss about it,' Churchwarden Tidy said in an aggrieved tone. 'Folks in Yorkshire have to make do with rain and moock and like it. Take the average farmer, like – '

'Yes, yes, Mr Tidy – '

'Doan't you yes yes me, Reverend. You know what it's like in t'dales when t'moock's flying, all them pig-sties an' such, and the clearing out – '

'Oh dear, Mr Tidy, please don't spoil such a splendid occasion by being *difficult*.'

'I'm not being difficult, Reverend. An' I'm not against the Queen, like. Not at all. But I reckon she might be a sight happier for less fooss and a slice o' good honest moock – '

'Oh, really – '

'All reet, all reet, don't go and get in a tizzy, Reverend. I reckon I've had my say.'

Canon Rampling decided that Tidy was getting above himself. The boat proceeded towards the royal yacht, all spit-and-polish with her gleaming buff funnels and sparkling white upper-works.

*

Admiral Watkiss was already aboard the *Victoria and Albert*. He was striding up and down the quarterdeck in his full uniform as Commander-in-Chief of the Chilean Navy. He held a Bible in his hand for ready reference; the Bible was rather a nuisance since it tended to impede his telescope and sword but he knew very well why he had been bidden aboard the royal yacht and he must be prepared for searching questions. There had already been a difficulty, one that had put him in a foul temper:

the boat that had brought him from his flagship had had a patch of spilt tar on the seat and he had sat in it, with sorry results to the seat of his trousers and to the broad band of gold lace that ran down his leg. He had made a fuss about this on boarding the royal yacht and stewards had been sent scurrying for hot water and cleaning materials and irons whilst he had sat trouserless in a cabin lent by the Fleet Paymaster, whose responsibility was trousers, stewards and irons. He had been unable to stand up when a woman, probably a lady-in-waiting or some such, had put her head round the door of the cabin; and he suspected that he had been mistaken for a mannerless Chilean. But his trousers had come back – still smelling of tar which was not the way in which to be presented to Her Majesty – by the time the *Victoria and Albert* was under way and proceeding out for the buoyed channel and its unfortunate associations.

*

Aboard the *Almirante Smith*, also now getting under way to represent the Chilean people before Her Majesty, Petty Officer Steward Washbrook was biting his nails in terror of his life. The buggers were sure to get him now; the curare having failed because it had been withdrawn, the assassins' best chance must surely be gone. Old balls-and-bang-me-arse couldn't be got at during the review and tomorrow the *Almirante Smith* would start on the long voyage back to Valparaiso with the old sod alive still, and where did that get him, Washbrook?

It got him a cut throat, that was where. Death, and a grave.

As he gnawed at his finger nails he remembered his duty. He shouted in his pidgin English for Leading Steward Escobar. 'Up to the bridge, lad. Set up the Admiral's tray, right?' Admiral Watkiss liked to have a tray with coffee at hand, plus other small comforts: extra socks for use inside seaboots when there was any spray coming over the bridge, a box of medicaments, bandages and plaster and so on in case he should be thrown against a steel bulkhead when the wind blew strong – things like that, quite a bloody performance really but always insisted upon because he was the Admiral. . . .

Leading Steward Escobar pointed out that the Admiral was not aboard the flagship.

'*That* don't matter,' Washbrook said irritably.

'But if the Admiral is not – '

'I said, didn't I, that don't bloody matter. We *acts* as though 'e is, right? Matter o' routine, that's what. If the old – if 'e should come back aboard and find things not done, see, 'is orders not obeyed . . . well, you know what 'e's like. So get up there pronto and don't let me 'ave to tell you twice.'

*

The Queen was much looking forward to the day's glorious event. All those ships, so very magnificent, Great Britain's sure shield, filled with men who would never let her down. She would be sorry when they dispersed: it was to be her melancholy task, after she herself had steamed up and down the review lines, to watch them all weigh their anchors and steam past her, out into the vastness of the deep ocean, fading into the twilight past the sea-forts of Spithead to vanish as they went past the easternmost point of land on the Isle of Wight, moving out to great waters where they would be wholly in the hands and care of God.

God.

Yes, she was much looking forward to meeting Admiral Watkiss and hearing him expound his theories. The archbishop had been non-committal when, after she had received Communion at his hands in preparation for her day, she had mentioned the subject. But then the archbishop was rather an old woman, which was all very well in a way but was wrong for a man, and it was of course *she* who was the head of the Church of England. . . .

Her Majesty's carriage bore her to the embarkation jetty at Cowes, together with two duchesses, a countess and two plain women of the bedchamber. On arrival alongside the royal yacht she was with some difficulty assisted up the starboard accommodation ladder and once she was aboard, the vessel got under way followed by the *Taronga Park*. As the ships moved towards the starting point of the Queen's inspection, Her Majesty's Sealyham became something of a nuisance and an embarrassment as well: it cocked its leg against a nearby stanchion close to where the senior officers were lined up in greeting and spray borne along the slight breeze added to the tar on Admiral Watkiss' trousers. Then the dog spotted the ship's cat; at once a chase was started and there was screeching and frenzied barking.

The Queen said, 'Naughty Pitzie.'

No one seemed to know quite what to do. To abuse or chastise the Queen's animal was scarcely the thing to do; it was the sort of occurrence polite persons, loyal persons, passed over with an indulgent smile. But not, however, Admiral Watkiss, tarred and now urinated upon. 'Oh, God damn,' he said loudly. 'Filthy little beast – ' He cut himself off; he had gone too far. The Queen had heard.

'What did that man say?' she demanded. 'And who is he? The uniform is strange to me.'

Admiral Watkiss took a pace forward. 'Ma'am, what I said was, God's hand is stealthily for peace.' He came to a dead stop, his face a deep red.

'What a stupid thing to say. What, pray, does it mean?'

'I don't know, ma'am. I read it somewhere . . . a book written by a bishop. I – I think it means that God will bring peace to all situations. Stealthily. Like the little – like Your Majesty's dog.' The little beast's act had certainly been stealthy, but Watkiss flushed red at his indiscretion even though HM failed to see the point.

'What nonsense. Am I in a madhouse? Who are you, my good man?'

'Ma'am, I am the Commander-in-Chief of the Chilean Navy . . . my name is Watkiss.'

'Admiral Watkiss?' The Queen's face cleared. 'So that is why you referred to God's good offices? How very natural for you, my dear Admiral. So very right and proper, though I confess I fail to see the relevance to Pitzie . . . however, it will no doubt become clear. We shall talk, Admiral. There is much to talk about.'

'I shall be delighted, Your Majesty.' Admiral Watkiss preened and surreptitiously shook his wet leg. The talk was evidently not to take place just yet; the Queen was placed in the bath chair that had been sent aboard ahead of her, and wheeled away. Looking about the decks, Admiral Watkiss caught sight of Canon Rampling, and with the canon his sister. He turned his back and, stepping over a coaming, went through a door into an alleyway with many doors opening off it to one side. From one of these doors an elderly woman wearing a tiara and little else but a vast pair of pink stays stiff with whalebone emerged, saw Admiral Watkiss and screamed. Watkiss turned round hastily and went back to the upper deck. It had possibly been the sight of his blasted Chilean uniform, he thought, making him look like some blasted gigolo or nancy boy.

On deck there was a familiar figure in a blue serge suit and with bowler hat, Gladstone bag and umbrella.

'What the devil are you doing here, Todhunter?' Watkiss demanded. 'And what's that blasted umbrella doing aboard a ship, may I ask?'

'In case there is inclement weather, sir. My Chief Super – '

'Oh, balls to your blasted Chief Super, Todhunter, and I do wish you'd get out of the habit of referring to your Chief Superintendent in such a fashion. It's very common. And whatever he has to say about it, umbrellas are *never* used aboard ships.'

'I do indeed apologize, Admiral Watkiss, sir. But my Chief Super . . . intendent, if I may be allowed to say so, always says that a wet detective is an uncomfortable detective and an uncomfortable detective is – '

'Oh, hold your tongue, Todhunter, do. Just answer my question: what are you doing aboard Her Majesty's yacht?'

'Acting as protection for your good self, sir. Also for Her Majesty. I considered it my duty, sir, as did the naval authorities.'

Watkiss grunted. 'So did your Chief Superintendent, I expect you'll say.'

'He would expect no less, sir.' Detective Inspector Todhunter cluched at his bowler hat as an eddy of wind around the royal yacht's upperworks took it. 'When I was a young rookie on the beat in London, sir, down the East End like – '

'Oh, balls and bang me arse, Todhunter, I don't want to hear your experiences in the middle of Her Majesty's review.'

*

Now the *Victoria and Albert* was steaming down the lines of warships, whose ships' companies were manning the sides and manning the yards as well, standing hand to outstretched hand high above the decks. On those decks officers stood in their full dress uniforms of cocked hat and sword and lightning-conductor trousers, epaulettes and tassels and gilded belts; medals and decorations glittered from their left breasts. As Her Majesty went past each ship the cocked hats came off and were lifted into the air and a stentorian voice bellowed out:

'Three cheers for Her Majesty the Queen. *Hip, hip, hurrah!*'

As one the seamen and stokers and miscellaneous ratings lifted their sennit hats and shouted, '*Hip, hip, hooray,*' hurrah being reserved for the officers. From the main deck of the royal yacht Her Majesty inclined her black bonnet and beamed her acknowledgment of loyalty. 'Such splendid men,' she remarked to Canon Rampling at her side. Rampling, casting a sideways look of triumph at the sub-dean of the Chapels Royal, whom he had displaced at the Queen's command and who was now standing at a distance, said that indeed the men were splendid. 'Very manly, ma'am.'

'Of course they are, Canon. They are our sailors.' She wished the archbishop was more like them. As the approach was made to the end of the main battle line and the royal yacht turned to steam down the next one, a line of heavy cruisers, the Queen said, 'We understand you were responsible for putting forward the *excellent idea* of a Salvation Navy, Canon.'

'Admiral Watkiss' idea, ma'am, yes – '

'Admiral Watkiss, that is his name. We wish to have words with him.'

'Now, ma'am?'

'That is our wish. Be good enough to convey it.'

*

'No doubt you have thought this out very deeply, Admiral?'

'Yes, Your Majesty.' Well, there had been that Bible study.

'Who would you propose should be in charge of it? Naturally, we would consider it should be you. But you have your loyalties to the Chileans to consider, of course, have you not?'

This was a poser. Watkiss had not got around to considering

the question raised by Her Majesty; but he was not going to have it said he was loyal to a bunch of dagoes: the Queen – God bless her of course – had touched a very raw spot. He answered her question. 'My loyalty is to you, Your Majesty. Not to the bl – the Chileans.'

'Oh?' The black bonnet was turned towards him, its peak like a spear aimed at his head. Her Majesty had sounded, in that simple 'Oh,' hostile. 'But we are given to understand that you are their naval Commander-in-Chief?'

'True, ma'am. But – '

'We would consider it unworthy of you to deny your loyalty to your superiors, Admiral.'

'*Superiors!*' Watkiss gave a gasp of astonished anger. How could she? He was very badly shaken. Her Majesty was not, after all, a dago. 'Ma'am, I do not regard the Chileans as my superiors, a bunch of – '

'Really. We are surprised, Admiral. We would consider it unworthy of any Briton to denigrate his employers. We *do not* like to hear this. In our view it is not consistent with Christianity, or with your own concept of a Salvation Navy, which would be founded upon religious principles, naturally. In the eyes of God, Admiral, all men are equal even though we have to confess there are degrees of equality. Certainly all nations are equal in His sight and we have always done our best to impress this upon our ministers and to ensure that our Empire is run upon such lines.' It was almost as though HM believed Chile to be part of her Empire. She paused as the *Victoria and Albert* reached the end of the line of cruisers and, once again turning, began her approach to the foreign war-ships. All at once, as the royal yacht straightened on her review course, the Queen pointed.

'Tell me, Admiral, which is that very dirty-looking battle-ship?'

Admiral Watkiss answered with some relish, though at a later date Captain del Campo would be given a very heavy piece of shot up his backside. 'The *Almirante Smith*, ma'am. The Chilean flagship. *My* flagship.'

'Oh. Yes, I see. Perhaps it makes a difference, Admiral, after all.'

'Yes, ma'am. Degrees, ma'am, of equality.'

'Yes.'

The Queen said nothing further as the Chilean flagship was brought broad on the starboard bow. The ship was indeed filthy, which was the fault of Commander Latrinez. Admiral Watkiss had issued a string of orders about cleanliness but Latrinez was simply not capable of taking charge of a booth in a fairground. As for Watkiss himself he had been too busy with other matters – attending upon the Second Sea Lord to try to get his back pay, and wasting time with the wretched quacks at Haslar Hospital and so on, so *he* couldn't be blamed. No doubt the Queen was realizing all this, realizing that he couldn't possibly have any loyal feelings towards persons who ran a crap-tin flagship.

As the *Victoria and Albert* steamed close to the *Almirante Smith*, slap abeam now, something unexpected happened. Something more or less unexpected, anyway. There was an immense explosion. There was much bright red flame, followed by thickly billowing clouds of black, acrid smoke from the Chilean flagship. There was a gasp of fright from the Queen and as the officers on the royal yacht's bridge reacted there was an urgent ringing of the engine-room telegraph. Astern, Halfhyde increased speed to bring the *Taronga Park* up between the two ships to act as a screen for Her Majesty; and for the bomb's obviously intended victim, Admiral Watkiss. But before Halfhyde could interpose his ship, the blast had taken its effect. From out of the smoke and flame a hail of onions hurtled across from a shattered seaboat, a number of them striking Admiral Watkiss as he rose to his feet in protection of his Queen-Empress, taking him on the head with such force that he was rendered unconscious and, falling across the guardrail, pitched head first into the sea.

*

'Blasted buggers,' Admiral Watkiss spluttered once he was safely aboard the rescuing *Taronga Park*. 'By God, I – I'll have their blasted balls for breakfast, just see if I don't! What blasted use has that fool Todhunter been, I'd like to know!'

There was no answer to that. Watkiss was attended by Miss Penn as to his various bruises and the lumps where Petty Officer Steward Washbrook's onions had hit with all the force of cannonballs such as had been suffered by the wooden walls of old England in Lord Nelson's day. His underwear was removed and dried out and outer clothing was provided by St Vincent Halfhyde.

A signal was made to the royal yacht indicating that Admiral Watkiss was little the worse. A return signal indicated that Her Majesty was unharmed though much shaken and somewhat blackened by the smoke and had onion leaves adhering to her bonnet and person. The very strongest protest would go the Chilean Embassy and the Queen sent her sympathy to Admiral Watkiss on the count not only of being projected into the water but of having been put in jeopardy by his own flagship. No mention was made of the Salvation Navy.

As the *Taronga Park* steamed back into Portsmouth Harbour bearing Admiral Watkiss, another signal was received from the royal yacht, a private one from Canon Rampling: he would be rejoining the *Almirante Smith* the next day for the return voyage to Valparaiso. Alas, Mrs Weder-Ublick, who had been ascending a ladder when the Chilean bomb had gone off, had descended instead and in so doing, somewhat precipitously, had broken a leg. The 'alas' had failed to carry a convincing ring. With this signal, Mr Todhunter sent his best regards and sympathy, adding that after all the threat to Admiral Watkiss had been thwarted and his Chief Super would be very pleased indeed. Arrests were expected to follow later but Todhunter did not go into details about this.

*

'Washbrook, you blasted idiot, what about my onions? And why were they blown up?'

Washbrook did his best to explain why the onions had been in the seaboat. It was to do with the curare, he said, and the fact that he needed to have an excuse tc go ashore and see the reverend in order to confess his crime. 'My very heinous crime, sir. I see that now, sir.'

'I should damn well hope so! You're a blasted rogue, a villain. I hope the buggers do cut your blasted throat when we reach Valparaiso.'

Washbrook had broken out into a sweat. 'Beggin' your pardon, sir, and with respect like, sir. I don't want to go back there, I'd sooner face the – '

'You have no option, you blasted wretch, you're going back with me. Dammit, man, what would you do in Portsmouth other than go to detention quarters for your past blasted crimes? You've no ties in Portsmouth.'

Not since Maisie Mutch had been squashed he hadn't. Watkiss went on venomously, 'Tell me more, Washbrook: why was that bomb planted in the seaboat and not in a more lethal place?'

That, Washbrook said, was Leading Steward Escobar. Finding a package that gave out a tick when obeying the order of his petty officer steward to prepare the bridge for the Admiral, Escobar had removed it for inspection later, but had shoved it into the seaboat when he had become alarmed that he might be accused of stealing a clock. 'Escobar, sir, 'e's like that, sir. Dim-witted like, sir. No savvy.'

Admiral Watkiss grunted. 'Blasted idiot! It so happens I was perfectly safe. Damn thing could have been left on the bridge. If it had been, it would have blown up Captain del Campo and that useless idiot Latrinez – wouldn't it?'